Back to the 80s

S.E. REICHERT
KERRIE FLANAGAN

5 PRINCE PUBLISHING

Published by 5 PRINCE PUBLISHING & BOOKS, LLC

PO Box 865, Arvada, CO 80001

www.5PrinceBooks.com

ISBN digital: 978-1-63112-315-3

ISBN print: 978-1-63112-316-0

Cover Credit: Marianne Nowicki

F07092023

Acknowledgments

I wouldn't have made it this far in my writing career without Kerrie Flanagan. From my first (very) rough drafts, through failures and successes, she has been a constant supporter, friend and writing mentor. This book wouldn't have made it into the world without her. I wouldn't still be a writer, without her. I want to thank my mom for indulging in my 80s cassette tapes and letting me spend summers watching and rewatching John Cusack movies. Thank you to the places that provided inspiration, Totally 80s Pizza, Fifty-Two 80s, and 1UP Arcade in Denver.

~Sarah

It began over dirty martinis at a writer's retreat while tossing *Better Off Dead* quotes back and forth. My thanks goes to Sarah for her friendship, all the laughs and her openness to doing this book together. I admire her creativity, incredible writing skills and love her taste in movies. I'd also like to thank my parents who allowed me to go to my first Journey concert at age 13, my twin brothers who put up with me blasting 80s music every morning while I got ready for school and my husband who has been a huge supporter of my writing career.

~Kerrie

Also by S.E. Reichert

Raising Elle

Granting Katelyn

Composing Laney

Back to the 80s

Back to the 80s

Chapter One

The first thing Blaine Reynolds' mother taught her was that she was named after a main character in an 80s movie. The second thing was that if we don't remember our past, we are doomed to forget the journey of our humanity. Humans were cyclical like that. Advancements and wars, rebuilding and flourishing. Old countries demolished, new ones beginning.

But sometimes you could freeze time and remember when things were simpler. Sometimes you could even find your happiness again, nestled in a shop left to you by your mom that paid homage to the best decade ever—the 80s.

Blaine stared into the eerie eyes of the red-haired Cabbage Patch Kid doll, its chubby cheeks sprinkled with freckles above a freakishly small mouth. This was definitely not part of her happiness. Some of the items from private collectors or donations to the shop were too much, even for her. She shook away the chill that ran up her spine and set down the creepy new tenant before moving on to the next box. How and when her mom had acquired so much, she'd never know. It had been two years since her mother had passed away, and Blaine was finally getting to the last boxes from the old storage unit on the outskirts of town.

She opened each box with a sort of giddy anticipation. Her mother's version of buried treasure. Each box contained remnants from the past: Casio keyboards, Walkman tape players, boxes from cereal no longer made, like Mr. T's Crunchy Corn and Oats. Autographed photos from Don Johnson and movie posters from the Cinema House in Old Town, some of them, like *E.T.*, were tattered around the edges but still sellable.

A lot of the items were still in good shape and could be sold at the store. Blaine couldn't believe she hadn't gone through this stuff sooner, but she never seemed to be at a loss for items. Oddly, for all the items she auctioned, she still managed to find others to buy in the thrift stores around town and bargain sites online to sell in her store. Sometimes people just donated their old toys and tech, because they wanted their childhood treasures to find a home outside of their crawlspace and be loved again. It made the small strip mall store seem crowded with treasures of an era before Blaine was even born. Her mom's favorite decade.

The 80s had become Blaine's favorite too. The music, the movies, the glory days of MTV and music videos. Every day, she went into work surrounded by the neon pink and cool turquoise aura of a time when the world seemed happy. A time when she could imagine her mother in scrunchy socks and big permed hair, dancing to Wham! and Cyndi Lauper Ten years before she'd ever had a child of her own, her mom had been a child of the decade of excess.

Blaine smiled at the photo above the cash register, of her and her mom fifteen years ago at a Mötley Crüe concert, both rocking ripped jeans and Converse. Even though her mom was gone now, being in the shop was like getting to hang out with her every day.

The tinkling of the bells above the door roused her from the memory as she watched JT, purple hair tucked into a Slipknot ball cap, in orange overalls and lime green Converse, scurry in with a blast of the early spring morning air. The way JT came at her with pursed lips could only mean the best gossip had just come from the salon next door.

"You're not going to believe what I just heard," JT said, coming around the back row of mixed cassette tapes and players, some in boxes, some as is.

"Who's sleeping with Deb now?" Blaine laughed and tucked the Cabbage Patch Kid behind the counter. That might be an online special only. She couldn't imagine putting it out on the shelf to stare at her all day.

"No, Blaine, this is bad—"

"Worse than sleeping with Deb?" she asked.

JT shook their head and tried to take a deep gulping breath.

"Oh, God, what is it? Did someone die? Did the sewer back up again?"

JT, in their trademark dramatic fashion, put their hands on the glass counter, leaned into the harrowing news stuck inside, and took a deep breath. Then in a whoosh—

"The Petersons are selling the mall."

Blaine leaned back and shook her head.

"Well, that's not such a big thing. We all knew they were getting ready to retire. I mean, the new people will still have to sign into the rent control addendum, right?"

JT shook their head. "No. Blaine, they didn't sell to another property manager."

"Well? Who did they sell to?"

"Morales Construction."

"Mor—Morales? Like *the* Morales Construction. The ones who've been putting up swanky apartments all over town?" Blaine squeaked. Her heart ticked one beat off. The Morales family weren't landlords. They were demolitionists. Leveling dozens of old buildings in the growing town to make room for larger, more modern amenities.

"That's them—"

"But, they wouldn't. I mean, the mall's been here since, well, forever." Blaine paused, thinking of her mother's shop and how hard she'd worked to build up her clients and establish her business. She thought of JT's salon, The Mane Event, and even Talon Karate; all the little shops and their struggling owners. The Petersons had been kind to let them sign a rent-controlled agreement and keep their costs manageable. The older couple had especially loved Blaine's quirky mother.

Morales Construction only loved neat bottom lines, modern buildings, rising profits, and all things new and shiny.

"I'm sorry Blaine. I think we're all gonna be out of a home in a couple of weeks."

Blaine didn't like getting too emotional, or jumping into drama if it could be avoided. She was level-headed, even if at times a little day-dreamy, so to hear that the foundation of her life was in danger of being pulled out from underneath her brought all her high-flying plans down to the hard ground. Where would she go? She couldn't afford rental space in the booming town of Marshall, Colorado. Rent, mortgage rates, and even just the cost of living had been going up for the last decade.

"I'll figure something out," Blaine said.

"Something?"

"Well, we can't just give up!"

"I'm sorry, maybe you didn't hear me the first time, when I mentioned MORALES CONSTRUCTION," JT enunciated the words slowly.

"I'm sure they can be reasoned with—"

"I heard that John Morales once tore down an orphanage to build a parking garage." JT leaned in for emphasis.

"Well, that's just ridiculous. I'm sure he did not."

"Okay, maybe not, but I could see it happening."

"JT," Blaine sighed, "let's just keep calm."

"Easy for you to say. You have a house and all of this awesome inventory. You'd be fine working out of your home, selling the stuff on eBay. My apartment's sink isn't big enough for half the hair I get!"

"I have no desire to switch to an eBay business and I don't have enough room for all of these things—" she stopped to look out at all the memorabilia. "And Charles Dumar would be traumatized if I moved this next to his cage." She pulled out the creepy Cabbage Patch Kid and its face met JT's. They yelped and jumped back.

"What the hell is that thing?"

"Top selling toy of 1983."

"Unbelievable. Your guinea pig is definitely going to have a heart attack if you show him that. This all makes sense now. I believe that thing is what cursed us for demolition. Or at least caused the downfall of the stock market in '87."

"This?" Blaine looked down at the doll and back to JT's pale face. "Nah, she's sweet."

"In a Chucky had a baby with an actual cabbage kind of way." They both laughed and then fell silent.

"What are we gonna do, JT?" Blaine said and hugged the strange doll to her chest. She looked around the shop that might be gone in a matter of weeks.

"I don't know, Blaine. But if I know you, you'll find some way to make it harder for them to move us."

"I'll try." Blaine sighed, drummed on the top of the doll's plastic head with her fingers and bit her lip. She had to try. They agreed to invite the other shop owners for drinks that Friday, after the Morales' first inspection of the mall. Blaine hoped she'd have something to contribute by that time.

Chapter Two

The first thing that Eric Fonseca Morales was taught was that the family construction business would one day be his to run. The second thing was that the world was always evolving, and if you didn't keep up with it, you were destined to be left behind forever. From the time he was small, he remembered business meetings and site visits with his father. Falling asleep under his mother's desk while she worked tirelessly on spreadsheets and contracts. His older sister, now the Assistant CEO of Morales Construction, Inc., had always been one step ahead of him and pushing him to do better.

He was one project away from his very own corner office. John and Carmen Morales had standards for their children. They weren't going to be some trust fund kids. If they wanted their share in the company, they would work for it. Eric always assumed he had no other choice. This project, the Marshall Mall's acquisition by Snake River Brewing, would be the multi-million-dollar deal that would finally land him a top spot in the company, where his sister Loraine would have a harder time bossing him around.

As he prepared for the first site visit that morning, he straightened his tie and sipped his espresso. He and his sister were supposed to have dinner with their parents that night to discuss the project. Come to think of it, Eric couldn't remember a time when they'd just had dinner, without the details of the business being the main course of the evening. His hand stilled on his tie. He loved his job. He loved his family. But sometimes . . . He looked down at the dying plant beside his kitchen window that he'd forgotten to water because of all his late nights at the office. It felt like he was building his life out of concrete and contracts.

Wasn't there more?

A cackle shouted from his phone. Loraine's personal ringtone. The Wicked Witch of the West. He scowled and tapped the screen.

> Don't be late this time.

> When was I late?

> The last two meetings with Snake River Brewing. Don't you want that office?

> I'm not going to be late.

Eric scowled, dropped the phone, and finished the strong coffee in one gulp before grabbing his jacket and satchel. No time for breakfast, not even time to give the dying pot of dirt and sticks a wave. It was time to work.

Blaine was informed that Loraine Annaliese Fonseca Morales, oldest daughter to John and Carmen Morales, and newly minted Assistant CEO of Morales Construction, Inc. would be coming by to inspect the ground, foundation, building, and utilities of the Marshall Mall before the acquisition was formalized. Loraine wanted the owners of the rental spaces to be out by then, but Blaine found no law that could rightfully remove them until the building had actually been sold. Blaine had done her research on renters' rights and used what little she could to stall. She and the other owners weren't going to make it easy on Morales Construction.

The five shop owners at the Marshall Mall, including JT and the staff of The Mane Event salon, refused to close their businesses for the day. They told Morales Construction's administrative assistant that if the Moraleses were keen on seeing the building, they would have to do so around their clients. None of the business owners were going to let their small but loyal customer base lose one of the few days they had left. And any thorn in the company's side, no matter how small, was worth it. Blaine refused to leave also; not because she had a ton of regular customers or that she wasn't sure she trusted people in her shop without her, but because she wanted to look Loraine Morales in the face. To plead her case. To ask the company to reconsider. She didn't have anywhere else to go.

The small house her mother had left her was cozy and cared for, but it didn't have the space to be her shop, too, and the wifi was always glitching out there. It wouldn't be reliable if she had to move the entire operation online. Though she had very little overhead cost, if she had to find a new, more expensive place, she might have to sell some of her best collector's items just to pay rent. Maybe even to eat.

Unless she could somehow convince Morales Construction that what she had was worth trying to save. That the Marshall Mall still had years left in it to be useful to the community. JT's salon gave deep discounts to seniors and veterans, and helped train new stylists. Sensei Williams's dojo was free to low-income kids in the community, and offered self-defense classes to women free of charge as well. They were all doing good in the community, and she hoped that the Morales family could see that the space was more than just a space. It was a central part of what made Marshall a good place to live.

When Friday arrived, Blaine got up especially early to clean and organize her shop, as much as the old retail space could be cleaned and organized. The ceiling tiles were water stained and sagging in places. The lights, still the long fluorescent bulbs, were prone to flickering. She swept the checkered tile floor she'd put in less than a year ago, and turned on every neon sign she could. She switched the large TV in the corner to her favorite playlist of 80s movies. *Dirty Dancing*, *St. Elmo's Fire*, *The Goonies*, and of course, *Pretty in Pink*.

If the Morales Construction CEO wanted to see what the company was destroying, she would show them the best of all she had. In a brash move, she took the satanic Cabbage Patch Kid from behind the desk and set it up on the shelf by the cash register. Who knew what piece of the era would touch the right nerve? Maybe Loraine had a soft spot for the red-headed daughter of Chucky.

Blaine tapped her fingernails on the clean countertop, rearranged the display of collector's cards, checked the clock on the wall, and took one breath after another, blowing each one out slowly.

Then she waited.

Chapter Three

This was Eric's tenth site visit of the week, and it was only Friday morning. But this one, for Marshall's newest brewery, would be his chance to finally earn his place at the high table of Morales Construction. The old strip mall, once on the outskirts of town, was now surrounded by new buildings, packed together houses, and a road that had expanded from two lanes to four. The Marshall Mall had been there since sometime in the late 70s. In Eric's opinion, fifty years was too old for any building to still be standing, unless it was protected by the historical society. Not only were there safety concerns, but the place was an eyesore, and probably driving down the property values for miles around. Eric shuddered as he parked against the crumbling concrete curb. He hated to think what kind of asbestos, faulty wiring, and horrific plumbing must be living behind the dingy gray stucco walls. Luckily, he wouldn't have to think about it long.

He'd heard some rumors that the tenants of the mall were having a hard time accepting the fate of their little business building. Instead of being gone and letting the contractors and project managers come through for the inspection, they were all continuing business as usual in the face of their certain demise.

This was the worst part of his job, having to meet the people they'd be displacing on the odd site visit. Usually, tenants in this situation were given more time to vacate their spaces. But the brewery was insistent on getting their new facility up and running with some of the summer left to make a profit, and before the cold weather could halt construction, so they gave only the necessary notice stated in the lease. Snake River was the newest, award-winning brewery in a slew of breweries riding the bandwagon of microbrews in Colorado. Eric didn't drink much beer, but he was a fan of the business it was bringing to the city.

As he waited for the other members of the group to arrive, parked in his black sports car at the far end of the mall, he went through his work emails, answered the quick ones, and tagged the more involved ones. He was at the end of the strip mall where Loraine had instructed him to park so they could start with the north-south view of the building, which didn't allow for him to see the businesses fronts.

He pulled the file from his satchel. A karate dojo, a hair salon, a curiosity shop. *What did that mean? Like shrunken heads?* Eric sneered and continued. A fairly new frozen yogurt shop that had already found alternate business space in downtown, and a seam-stress/tailor shop. Did people even get alterations these days? Especially people who lived in this socio-economic area of town?

Guilt hit Eric in the gut. His grandmother had been a seam-stress and had worked hard enough to send his mother to one of the best engineering schools in the state. His hands froze on the paperwork. Each shop was a person trying to make a living. Eric sighed. None of them had been born into an empire like he and Loraine had, but even that was a double-edged sword. He had very little in his life except the work. This seemed to suit his overbearing sister fine. He, however, often wondered what it would be like to have a weekend free. Or to have anything on his mind other than work and their next big project.

The rest of the men pulled up, along with his sister in her large

SUV. Why she needed something that size when she was single, too busy for a family, and still lived with their parents, was a mystery to him. He suspected it was part of the prestige. She didn't even have a dead houseplant to call her own.

Eric joined the rest of the crew on their tour of the outside of the building, foundations, and specs. He preferred to hang out at the back of the group, allowing more time to really study the outlines of the building, envision what would become of it, and imagine what it could be made into. Since it was so old, nothing with this project could be saved, but he liked to think of how the foundation lines could be used to create something new

Loraine snubbed him for his *artistic* eye when it came to the building planning in any of their projects.

"Leave that to the architects and the soft-hearted artists. There's no money in that." The Morales creed was if there wasn't money in it, then it didn't serve a purpose.

First, the group entered the small dojo on the corner of the building. It was bare of unnecessary furnishings. Just an old Formica desk with an ancient Dell laptop sat to the left of the mats as you walked in. A short row of chairs faced the majority of the empty space, which was dominated by a mat-lined floor in front of a wall of mirrors. Bins of equipment and hanging bags lined the opposite wall. The space was unoccupied, and Eric wondered what it would be like to see a class in session. A small part of him always wanted to be the Karate Kid. The walls not covered in mirrors were painted in hard black and red lines. Eric smiled as he looked at the writing on the wall above the mirrors. Talon Karate. Vague memories of Mr. Miyagi made him shake his head. Apparently, someone else also had the same little boy dream.

A tall, blond man came out from the back room, a beer in his hand. Eric checked his watch. It was nine in the morning. The man scowled and belched.

"Great. The doomsday committee," he grumbled.

"You don't have to be rude, Mr. Williams," Loraine shot back. "You're getting plenty of time to move on."

"I just barely got my classes to a decent size. You think they're going to want to move farther out of town? Some of those kids take the bus. But thanks for the sunshiny disposition." He nudged a chair out of his way as he moved to the front desk.

Eric watched the strange and almost predatory way that Loraine studied the lumbering former surfer turned karate sensei. Usually, that kind of guy wouldn't even get the time of day from her.

"Well, that's hardly any of our concern. You're a big boy. I'm sure you'll figure it out." Loraine smiled at him with sharp teeth. "Though I'm not sure I believe you have a base, what with all of these . . . devoted students and your *stunning* intellect." She motioned to the empty floor, and he scowled at her.

"Listen, you heartless, capitalistic—"

"Eric." Eric came forward with his hand outstretched. "Eric Morales." Even he had to admit that his sister didn't always know when to keep her mouth shut. There wasn't any reason to ruffle feathers more than was necessary. Especially the feathers of a guy who might know how to do some damage. "I love this place. I always wanted to take up karate as a kid. I'm sorry we have to move you out, but I know what you do is valuable, and you'll find a way to make your new place even better."

Lawrence Williams's eyes fell away from Loraine and to Eric. He straightened his spine and looked down at Eric's hand. "Yeah, well, you two have probably never been homeless, so I don't expect either of you to understand." He turned away without shaking Eric's hand.

"Two weeks, Mr. Williams." Loraine sang at his back as if she couldn't stand that he hadn't even acknowledged her after Eric had stepped up.

Lawrence turned to her with a cruel smile and held up both of his middle fingers. "Is that this many?"

"*Malparido.*" Loraine seethed and whipped around on her heels, passing the rest of the group to leave. The group stared after her, dumbstruck. Eric nodded to Mr. Williams with a smile he couldn't seem to hold back. Sometimes, his sister deserved the reaction she got.

Next, the group moved into the adjacent rental space; The Mane Event hair salon. Eric jotted down notes about the plumbing lines and took rough estimates of the square footage. Only two stylists were there. One woman with large, feathered bangs in an unnatural shade of blonde, who scowled over her generous bosom and crossed arms. The other stylist wore clothes that defied gender, and had a short, angled haircut colored bright purple that hung in front of their eyes, which were lined in black to magnify the dark glare being shot at him. He looked down at his notes and nodded to himself.

Most were not happy with losing their place of business. Eric was usually confronted with nothing more than a few dirty looks and quiet curses. He avoided the angry emo stylist and kept to the back of the line. When it was time to move on, he hurried behind the rest to the next shop, not missing the fact that the edgy stylist's eyes followed their group all the way out the door.

The last stop, next door to the salon, had bold neon signs reading "Rad" and "MTV". Cardboard cutouts stood in the window. David Hasselhoff and Hulk Hogan guarded over the display tables between them, where the owner had set up a city of Matchbox Cars and Micro Machines. Eric stopped and gawked at the detailed precision used to construct a whole city from a different era. He looked back up to the bright and bold sign above the door: *Back To The 80s.* It was even painted in the same font as the time traveling movie itself.

Next to the shop's name was a picture of a DeLorean, looking like it was bursting through the old stucco exterior. Eric smiled and went in to catch up with the rest of the group, who had gone ahead. He let the door close behind him and stood in sudden and overwhelming awe.

"*Madre de dios*," Loraine said beneath her breath as Eric stepped in and back into a different time. His eyes didn't know where to settle first. The shop was clean, well-lit, and ordered in rows of shelves, pocketed with displays and old arcade games. His heart leaped into his throat as he saw an original *Pac-Man* and *Ms. Pac-Man* against the far wall, lit up and still functioning.

His eyes grew big and his heart hammered as he remembered the flashing high score of his youth, one of the best days of his young life.

"Can you believe all of this shit?" Loraine came to stand beside him and snapped him out of the daze. "What in the hell is all of this?"

Ignoring Loraine, Eric walked slowly down the aisles along with the group. Even the other investors and engineers had stopped talking about the structural aspects of the building to look around. Some of the older men laughed and pointed with joy at the obscure and long forgotten treasures. They stopped to study the different concert posters from Bon Jovi, Aerosmith, Def Leppard, Whitney Houston, Journey, and Wham! A whole back wall was devoted to old and near obsolete types of music including cassette tapes, LPs, old 45s, even a few 8-tracks and a slotted shelf of CDs. Eric's fingers itched to go and see what odd bands and classic artists might be hiding there. On the shelves above the music were different types of players, band posters, signed pictures from Axl Rose, and one from Hall & Oates. He swung his head around to see what other oddities he could find.

Their head architect started chortling over a set of still-in-the-box Transformers. Eric looked across the shelves to the display case at the front, filled with lunchboxes. The Muppets, Knight Rider, MacGyver, Rainbow Brite, and Charlie's Angels.

Eric didn't see the shop owner. He guessed it was probably

some old hippie that had been there from the beginning of the mall.

"This place is going to take forever to clean out," Loraine grumbled with a snort at a Casio keyboard on display next to her.

Eric remembered she had begged their parents for one similar to that when they were children.

"All right, let's get on with it." She broke the spell of nostalgia and the rest of the group snapped to attention. "Where's the tenant?" She checked on her device and scrolled through the previous tenant's information. "Blaine Reynolds? What kind of name is Blaine? He must be a child of the...," she paused to look up at the hodgepodge. "Well, who knows with all of this crap?" She started walking through the checklist. Eric straggled behind, inching closer to the arcade games while pretending to look at the worn ceiling tiles.

Chapter Four

Blaine wasn't ever one to hold back her thoughts, but when the group of sharply dressed contractors and investors walked into her shop, she knew she should try. Rather than the completely closed down and clinical response they'd given the other shop owners (as she'd heard via text from JT), she saw a few of them warm up to the strange sense of wonder and nostalgia that seemed to swirl through them with each new discovery from an era before cell phones and Facebook. More than just objects, her mother's shop was a treasure trove of memory, and transported people back to a simpler time. The only one who didn't seem to care about any of it was the sharp-eyed woman at the front who cast judgmental glances at everything, including Blaine herself when she came out from the back room. Given this woman's sharp commanding tones, and the no nonsense air about her, she was probably Loraine Morales, daughter of the construction megalith, and apparently not one to have an ounce of nostalgia.

Loraine ignored her, probably thinking she was just an employee, not the owner. The group moved on to inspect the back room. A tall, younger man stayed behind. He stared at the *Pac-Man* game with almost childlike wonder in his broad smile and a sparkle in his brown eyes. Her first thought was that he was very handsome for someone intent on ruining her future. That was, if you liked that straight laced, boring type that probably brought his case files to dinner and spent weekends golfing with his future business prospects. Blaine snorted. Still, the joy in his eyes was real, which meant he wasn't all spreadsheets and ugly pressed pants. There was a human in there.

In this guy, she saw an opportunity to sway the hands of fate.

She fluffed her unruly curls, adjusted her neon blue mini-skirt and off the shoulder black sweatshirt bearing the shop's name in blue, which matched her scrunchy socks and black Converse. She even put on the lacy blue gloves that coordinated, to look the part of the invested shop owner. Blaine took a deep breath and followed him. He was tall, and she felt a strange sense of intruding when she tried to sidle up beside him.

"How long have you worked for that soulless harpy?" Blaine said, out of the corner of her mouth. The man's head snapped back to glance at Loraine as if he was afraid she'd heard. Then he looked down at Blaine. His brow furrowed.

"Uh. Excuse me?"

"I mean, I'm sure she's great, real fun at parties and stuff but, can you believe they're about to take down another building? Ruin more livelihoods, when it's already so hard? What kind of people do that? And it's not like Marshall even needs another brewery selling subpar IPAs and driving up the cost of living."

"Do I know you?" he scowled.

Misreading the question as a good sign, Blaine stuck out her hand, fingernails painted with polka dots in bubble gum pink.

"I'm Blaine. Blaine Reynolds. This is my shop. And you? Some poor unlucky intern, huh?"

The man stood straighter, turning his head down as he curled up an intense smile, revealing perfect teeth. "Eric."

"Eric..."

"Eric Morales."

"Eric Morales." Blaine parroted before looking at the severe woman sneering at the screen where Molly Ringwald was sitting atop the hood of Andrew McCarthy's car. She looked back at him. "Eric. Morales?"

"Mmm hmm. And that soulless harpy is my sister, Loraine."

"Uh . . ." Blaine felt her freckled cheeks burn with embarrassment, and the air trap in her lungs. "Well, I couldn't have possibly made that more awkward." She cleared her throat.

Loraine, who seemed to reach her limit of nostalgia, stormed back to Eric and sized up Blaine uncomfortably.

"Hi," Blaine held out her hand, and tried to regain her composure. "You must be Loraine, I'm—"

"I don't really care. And it's Ms. Morales, if you insist on talking to me."

Blaine watched as Eric looked from his sister and back to her. A spark of something flashed in his eyes and he stood up straighter.

"This is Blaine Reynolds, and she owns this shop."

"Well, not for long. Technically, we'll own this shop." Loraine corrected.

"Right," stuttered Blaine, "except, well, I mean I own what's in it."

Loraine sniffed, disinterested. "Well, that'll be your problem to deal with. In two weeks." She moved to leave, but Blaine reached out and took her by the arm.

"Please. I don't have anywhere else to go, and this shop, everything here, it belonged to my mom, and she's—"

"Look, Blaine," Loraine said with some disgust and pulled her arm away. "Maybe you didn't hear me the first time, but it still stands that I *really don't care*. Life is hard, and I'm sorry if this move will upset your little clutter fest but—"

"It's not a clutter fest." Anger built inside Blaine. "These novelties are a historical gold mine. They're important pieces of the era—"

"Junk."

"It's not junk!" Blaine yelled.

Eric's head swung her way.

Blaine clenched her jaw and fought to hold back tears. She looked up at Eric and his gaze softened. He studied her face closer. Blaine felt uncomfortable, and her eyes fell to his lips before shooting back up, embarrassed.

"Two weeks." Eric looked back to Loraine. "Seems like maybe a rush."

"A what?" Loraine said.

"I'll bet you." The words flew out of Blaine's mouth.

They both looked at her.

"What?"

"Let's make a bet. Give me a month and I'll convince you that this shop is worth saving."

"That's not really a bet," Loraine sneered.

"If I can't convince you, then I'll—I'll take my 'clutter' and leave, no hard feelings. If you come to love it as much as I do, then . . ." She paused and looked back to Eric. "Then you find a new place for a brewery."

"Utterly ridiculous, the permitting is already underway," Loraine said, looking at her brother, who seemed to be considering.

"But it's not done yet. The building is still standing, right?" Blaine held her hands out.

"No," Loraine said. "We don't negotiate with hoarders."

"Yes," Eric blurted out. Both women looked at him. "I'll take the bet."

"What? Are you out of your mind?"

"If she loses, and she can't convince me, then we level this place and I get to keep *Pac-Man*. If she somehow convinces me in a month that it's all worth saving, then I'll find a different place for the brewery."

"You are out of your goddamn mind," Loraine seethed. "Mom and Dad are gonna be pissed."

"It's only a month, and the permitting will take that long anyway."

"Eric, I won't allow it."

"Take my hand, Ms. Reynolds." He turned and held his hand out.

Blaine hesitated, then shook his hand. His grip was firm.

"There, a Morales's handshake is as good as his word."

Some inside code of morality must have been thrown down, Blaine thought as she watched Loraine's face light up with anger.

"I can't believe you!" she yelled before storming out.

Blaine watched her as the other men trailed out in her wake. Eric still held her hand, his face turned to where his sister had left. He looked down at Blaine and took his hand away.

"Thank you, I—"

"Don't thank me. That was probably the stupidest thing I've ever done. But sometimes it's hard to not be the bratty brother."

"Like Alex P. Keaton."

"Who?"

"Uh, it's a character in Family Ties?" She shook her head at his blank stare. "It doesn't matter. I'm happy that you stood up to her."

"You don't know me," he said with a scowl. "I'm highly doubtful this is going to change anything, other than give you a couple of extra weeks for you to pack up all of . . . this. And I'll get something I really want out of it." He gestured to the game.

"Well, I still think I can change your mind." She stuck up her chin resolutely at him.

"Oh?" He flashed the hint of a smile. "And how exactly are you going to do that?"

"Just give me your phone number and I'll call you tomorrow," Blaine said, not actually sure how she would change his mind, either. But at least by tomorrow morning, she might have a plan.

Chapter Five

"Are you insane?" JT asked, mirroring what Loraine had accused Eric of.

"Yeah, kinda."

"You can't just stop this from coming, Blaine."

"You don't know that. People like the Morales family are powerful and have money. They can do a lot of things when they set their mind to it."

"People like the Morales family got powerful and have money because they didn't put their minds and their hearts to the same purpose." JT sighed and finished disinfecting the last station in the salon.

"Shoot," Blaine whispered and bit at the nubs of her nails.

"You should stop doing that."

"It's because I'm stressed."

"Because you knowingly and willingly bet one of the most powerful families in the state that you could convince them that some nostalgic bric-a-brac store was more important than a six-million-dollar brewery?"

"S—six—six million?"

"Yeah, didn't you read the article I sent you? This is supposed to be the biggest brewery this side of the Rocky Mountains. A shining beer tap on a hill." JT fanned their hands out dramatically towards the west.

Blaine blanched and attacked another nail. "What am I going to do?"

"You know the best places to find 80s quirk. You know that whole decade like the back of your hand. Hell, I didn't even like the era until I met you, and now look at my damn Flock of Seagulls hair." JT flipped their hair with one hand. "If anyone can convince someone that it matters, it's you."

"Yeah, but you didn't meet him. I mean, JT, the guy is..." she swallowed. What was Eric? Hard, unreachable, stoic? The only emotion he seemed to have was anger at his sister and a strange softness for arcade games. Specifically, *Pac-Man*. And she didn't even know if he had a fond memory of the game or just the desire to own it as a strange status symbol. "He's just kinda—"

"Hot AF?" JT leveled their eyes on Blaine.

"Uh, what? I didn't notice that."

"You're a living human being. A young and healthy female, who hasn't had a date since the Cold War era."

"Stop, I wasn't even born yet—"

"Well, a long time ago."

"Two years," Blaine said, suddenly sad. "Patrick and I, right before my mom died. When I got the shop, I just didn't have the heart or time."

JT stopped sweeping the hair clippings from under Deb's station. Putting the broom against one of the salon chairs, they pulled Blaine in for a hug and held her there until the sniffling stopped.

"If I lose her shop, JT—"

"You won't. Blaine Reynolds is no quitter. You're gonna make that buttoned up, hot hunk of man crazy for you."

"For *me*?"

"For the shop, I mean." JT frowned. "It'll be like Michael J.

Fox in *The Secret of My Success*. A little man taking on big corporate America."

"Yeah, but didn't he have a rich aunt he slept with?"

"Well, we can skip that part. Unless—wait, do you have a rich aunt?"

"No."

"Well, then, let's just take down the man with our wits and charm." JT laughed and finished sweeping. They shut off the lights and locked the doors to the salon.

Blaine checked to make sure she'd closed up everything at Back To The 80s and sighed as she looked through the glass. So many memories of her and her mom in that little space, coming there after school, playing the games, listening to customers talk and reminisce as they traded, sold, or bought little pieces of their childhoods. What would she do? Her whole world was in that shop.

She supposed she could go back to school. Finish her degree in business. Or find a new job, or three, to try to make the rent on the storage unit for all the shop's curiosities, along with all the other expenses living in a growing town brought.

They met the other shop owners at a small, run-down bar two blocks from the Marshall Mall, and crowded into a corner booth. Lawrence Williams brought a round of Coors Banquet to the table while JT and Deb sifted through their phones for any space to rent that might be affordable. Blaine always thought it was strange that those two got along so well. You couldn't have had two more different co-workers. One in her late fifties, the definition of a big-busted, doting female, all pink and fluff and feathered bangs. The other, JT, a quirky, brightly dyed rebel, who defied all gender and societal expectations. But Blaine supposed that's how good relationships were built, finding someone whose excesses filled in your shortages. When Lawrence sat down, he groaned and touched a bruise on the left side of his jaw.

"What happened?" Deb asked, hissing painfully at the purple-turning-green mark.

"Got into a little discussion." He took a long pull from his beer.

"I thought you were only supposed to use your might for right." Blaine smiled over her beer.

"Yeah, well, I was right. And I won."

"You should teach me how to do that sometime," Blaine said sadly. "Win against a bigger guy."

"Yeah, I heard about your bet from JT." Lawrence picked at the beer label. "Kinda ballsy for a little thing like you."

"David and Goliath, right?" JT interjected.

"More like Strawberry Shortcake and Skeletor." He laughed at his own joke. "At least David had a slingshot and a higher power on his side."

Blaine sighed and took a drink, her eyes filled with tears. Lawrence rolled his eyes.

"Don't cry." He leaned back with mock disgust. "Look, kid, I think it's really Suzy Sunshine of you, but I know how these rich guys work."

"They're not all *guys*." JT rolled their eyes.

"'Guys' is a nonbinary, general term."

"No, it's not. Do you even know what nonbinary means—"

"Whatever. The point is that the rich will always just get richer, and they don't give a sh—"

"Care?" Blaine interrupted.

"Right, whatever. They don't care what or who goes down in order to stay that way."

"So then?"

"I hate to say it, kid, but that mall is as good as dust." He took another drink.

Blaine did too. JT followed. Deb ordered another round as she'd finished hers somewhere in between Goliath and dust. Blaine sniffed and wiped a tear on a cheap, crinkled napkin.

Lawrence's features softened. He sighed. "Don't worry. I've been through a lot of sh—stuff in my life. It'll be alright, at least you picked the better sibling to try and reason with. That she-viper probably eats her own young."

"Loraine?" Blaine sniffed. "She is pretty awful."

He squared up to Blaine. "Listen, shit happens. And right now, we're in the thick of it. I appreciate you trying to stall for us, but don't put the weight of our future on your shoulders, okay?" His lower voice caused Blaine to look up.

Big, tough sensei was hiding a soft heart. She smiled at him. "I'll do what I can to buy us time, at least."

"Attagirl. Chin down, eyes up." He raised his beer in a toast and the table joined in. "To the Marshall Mall and whatever the future brings us."

Chapter Six

Eric Morales was in his office after the Marshall Mall site visit, trying to concentrate. But his mind wouldn't buckle down to the various tasks, spreadsheets, and reports in front of him. He wasn't sure if it was Blaine Reynolds's insults about his sister and the stupidest bet he ever made distracting him, or if it was Loraine herself. He could hear her from across the hall in her office. Why did she always have to use the speakerphone? It was like she needed the rest of the office to know how busy and important she was. He stood, closed his door, and sat down with a huff.

A spreadsheet sprung to life when he clicked on his tabs. He looked at the metrics for the Marshall Mall shopping center. The rental contracts had been highlighted, and he opened the downloads to read through the provisions. He scanned the jargon quickly, looking for the one name that stood out. Amanda Louise Reynolds had the longest standing rental agreement with the Petersons, and a strange provision stating that she had to agree to the sale of the mall before it would go through. Eric sat back in his chair, folded his hands into a steeple, and rested his lips against them. Obviously Amanda was Blaine's mother, but he wondered if Blaine knew about the provision or had any control of that decision. Maybe he should have asked to speak to her mother before agreeing to such an asinine bet.

Eric sat back in his chair. This was going to complicate things. It may mean that they would have to buy the Reynolds out, or risk losing the whole contract. Unless he couldn't be convinced the shop was worth saving, then Blaine would leave like she agreed upon. Was she a woman of her word? Would Amanda Reynolds overrule any agreement they made? Why had he agreed to something that would only delay the inevitable? Delays were about the worst thing you could face in construction. He supposed it was good that he'd come across Blaine and the strange rental disclaimer. Now he just had to convince her that a monetary payout was better than anything she could possibly earn from her odd shop. Still, he could have done that without agreeing to whatever strange plan she'd hatched in that pretty head of hers.

Pretty—Eric stopped up short and looked out the window. She was pretty. In a strange, spritely way. A little too eclectic for his tastes, with all the bright colors and the off-kilter shirt exposing her bare shoulder. While he was okay with that and the miniskirt, she was awkward and unprofessional; not like the women he worked with. Certainly not like the ones he dated. Not that he'd been on a date in a long while. Eric shook the train of thought away. Blaine Reynolds was . . . messy. He thought of the wayward curls and upturned nose. The whole thing was messy. Exactly the situation and type of person that his sister hated. Blaine was like a bundle of loose ends, chaos in a strange, pretty and charming package. He heard Loraine cursing someone out across the hall through his closed door. She erupted into Spanish and her pitch rose until she slammed the phone down. He wanted to do something against the tight and perfect grain of his world. For once.

Blaine got home from the bar, one beer down and no viable solutions for their problem. She still didn't know what she'd have to do, or where she could possibly take Eric Morales that would change his mind. Especially with six million dollars involved. She hung up her jacket. The summer heat was right around the corner. College kids would disperse, trails would get busier, and tourists would find their way into her shop.

If she still had a shop by the summer. Summer was also construction time, and she knew that Morales Construction was probably counting on the demolition to be done early, so the new brewery would be up and running with some summer still left to spare. Blaine's gut hurt, the kind of burning pain that erupts when you're about to lose something you love.

"Think, Blaine," she whispered and sagged against the couch. A small squeak, followed by a chatter startled her, and a small, black-and-white-patched guinea pig shuffled out of the couch cushions and wriggled its tiny pink nose at her.

"You look like a fine little helper. What's your name?" She cooed to the guinea pig and picked him up. Nose to wiggling nose, she smiled. "Hello, Charles Dumar."

His warm, small body cuddled into her chest. She'd have to clean out the couch cushions again. Try as she might, she couldn't seem to keep him from escaping his habitat. He had free run again while she was gone, and the mess he left in his wake was not always easy to clean up.

"You know, someday I might get a cat and then you'll be in a world of hurt." She tried to scold him, but he chattered and chuckled and she couldn't keep a straight face. "You're right, I probably won't."

Setting him back into his pen, she went into the kitchen, washed her hands, swept up the floor, and started the oven. She opened the freezer and sighed. She didn't have a plan for dinner. Or for Eric. Grabbing a bag of slightly freezer-burned chicken nuggets, she turned to find a pan and grabbed a can of green beans from the cupboard.

What had her mother done with her to make her love these

things so much? To build the appreciation for something older, that had managed to pass the test of time? Blaine folded her arms over her chest, sat back against the counter and closed her eyes.

Well, for one, Blaine had only been a child. As with any kid, she'd been easily influenced and prone to love whatever made her mother happy. Amanda's laugh could charm the angels down from the sky, Mr. Peterson had often told her. Blaine moved to the fridge, got out carrots, lettuce, and some fading strawberries, cut them up and dropped them into Charles's pen along with some more hay and pellets. Charles grunted happily and feasted.

She and her mom went to concerts, watched old movies, and went to antique shows and pop culture conventions. They'd just hung out. And Amanda's joy had spread like a contagious fever. Blaine sighed. Maybe the best solution was the one that was simplest. She'd take Eric to all of the best and strangest examples of 80s pop culture still operating today, and share her joy with him.

There was the arcade, The Tilted Token, in Downtown Denver, with tons of games to play. She had, of course, her own shop, which she'd seen him admiring before his sister had intervened. He seemed like the kind of guy that might like music. Maybe she could find a cover band to go see. They could have a movie night. Blaine looked at the one cozy couch she had. Would they both have to sit there? Together? Would he even fit on her couch? Heat rose in her cheeks. Blaine shook away the thought as the oven beeped. Everyone was hot in the kitchen.

As Aunt Vera from *The Secret of My Success* would say, "Love is love, but business is business," and she wasn't going to let Eric's square jaw, melty dark eyes, or perfect smile get in the way when it came to saving her shop.

Chapter Seven

Denver was a hot spot for fun and funky businesses, but the short trip to the city always excited Blaine for another reason. Its hidden-away niches of quirk that had sprung up in recent years, as well as the parts that had been there for decades, catered to and existed for anyone nostalgic enough to look. Her constant research into pop culture and events of the era gave Blaine a strange, full-scale picture of what it had meant for human expansion, contraction, and survival. But it was her heart and memories of her mom that brought her back to The Tilted Token, again and again. Getting lost in the lights and noise, the presence of something real to touch and play, had so much more meaning than just tapping against a screen.

She knew that it was not the kind of place someone like Eric Morales went. It was a little shady. A little dank. And more than that, it was cheap entertainment. She was fairly certain the Morales family didn't do anything that was cheap.

She bit her lip and paced on the sidewalk. When she'd called to arrange their first meeting, she wasn't sure she'd even be allowed through the switchboard to his office. Switchboard, as though it was some 1960s Rock Hudson rom com. Blaine rolled her eyes.

But within a few moments, he'd answered, low-voiced and serious. She hadn't known what to say, so she stuttered through her name and a deluge of random thoughts followed.

"M—Mr. Morales? This is Blaine—Blaine Reynolds, from the store," She took a breath. "From Back To The 80s? We spoke during your tour? I'm the one who insulted your—well, we don't need to rehash that. I mean, I *am* sorry about that. I'm sure you get a lot of calls from displaced tenants so you may not remember who I—"

"I remember you, Ms. Reynolds. Having second thoughts about our wager?" he'd said, and she swore she heard a smile behind the words. She hoped he heard her scowl as her brain found its voice and she straightened her spine.

"Absolutely not. As per our agreement, I have scheduled out a series of meetings to plead my case. As you have given your word, I expect that you will find the time to attend them." Then, she promptly gave him the day, time, and the address of their first meeting. There was a slight pause. Whether he was surprised, impressed, or annoyed, she couldn't tell.

All Eric said was, "Fine. I'll see you then."

Then he'd hung up. Not even a goodbye or a "how are things?" He probably knew how things were for her. Desperate.

Now, standing on the streets of Denver, she just hoped that he was a man of his word and that he wouldn't leave her there alone on the sidewalk while he was off making other million-dollar deals.

She sighed and adjusted the light scarf around her neck. It was still cool in the evenings, and even with the heat of the asphalt keeping things warmer than normal, she felt a small chill spread up her back. What if he didn't show? She checked her phone again. He still had three minutes. She watched another couple descend the stairs, laughing, arm in arm.

She hadn't walked arm-in-arm with anyone since Patrick, and even she knew early on that it wasn't going to last. He was an artist and moody. He found her quirk amusing, but didn't stay long when Blaine became consumed with the serious task of burying a parent. She sighed, looked up, and blinked quickly to rid the tears.

The Tilted Token was a restaurant and arcade, and made its home in an underground, abandoned bread factory basement. Almost like some strange "decade of excess" speakeasy. But instead of contraband booze, guests were treated with old arcade games, the best 80s rock, and a collection of memorabilia, similar to hers, but smaller and more dispersed. She often traded with the owners and expanded her own business through their good relationship. If she was going to go through with this bet, she would hit Eric hard, right out of the gate. One thing she knew about Eric Morales was that he was interested in video games. If he didn't at least get a little glassy-eyed over the extensive, working collection of The Tilted Token, then she wasn't as good at reading people as she thought, and the rest of the meetings she'd prearranged wouldn't go very far.

She paced and toyed with the end of her scarf between her fingers while more what-ifs filled her nervous brain. What if her first impression hadn't been right? He'd looked so uncomfortable with the group, so on edge by his sister, she had thought he must have been an intern. He definitely looked too young to be so high up in a company the size of Morales Construction. With his strong jawline, dark eyes, and hair that was a little too long on top for a completely straight-laced guy, he looked a bit more like a telenovela heartthrob than a project manager. She kicked at the sidewalk with her ratty Converse and wondered what madness had possessed her, and how she was going to make it through even one evening with him, let alone a month. Maybe after tonight, he'd call the whole thing off. Maybe after he met her, and saw the odd way she saw the world, he'd completely renegotiate the bet and she'd be out of the mall tomorrow.

It's not like a handshake was a real commitment. She'd known that when she'd taken it. Blaine had a weakness when it came to believing in the goodness of people beyond what they deserved. Her mom had been that way too. She blew out a breath, and a strand of hair danced away from her forehead. A dark, shiny sports car passed by her and splashed water up from the gutter and across her sneakers before moving on and parking down the street.

"Jerk," she grumbled and rolled her eyes. She watched as the car swung into a spot with frightening precision. Eric Morales stepped out with a smug grin, shrugged on his suit coat, and straightened the collar around his thick neck. He walked towards her with a smile that could only be described as a shark honing in on prey.

"Oh, was that you? Sorry." He adjusted his cuffs. "Let's get this done."

Blaine scowled. "Uh, hi? How are you?" She enunciated the phrase.

"What?" Eric said.

"That's how normal people greet each other," she said, perturbed.

He rolled his eyes and checked either side of the street. Probably hoping no one saw them together.

"We're not old friends meeting for a fun night on the town."

"No, I don't suppose we are." She stepped closer to him, and in an odd twist, Eric stepped away as if not certain what her intentions were. "But we could be new friends. Meeting for a fun night."

"I'm not your friend."

She leaned toward him. "Not yet," she said and raised an eyebrow. He leaned away, cleared his throat. His momentary discomfort, opposite of the swagger he'd approached her with, gave her a small light of hope. He wasn't unshakeable.

"Where exactly is this place?" He looked up at the dress shop in front of them and the gallery on the other side. The burger joint across the street flashed signs for vegan options.

"This." She pointed to the dress shop. "Is Milner's Fine Bridal Clothes. But that," she pointed to the dark staircase descending towards the lower level, "Is going to be the trip of your life."

"We'll see about that," he grumbled.

Eric had misgivings when he'd first seen the address. It wasn't the drive. He liked driving, especially his new, jet-black Chevy Camaro that wove in and out of traffic like a dark ghost and felt like the closest thing to flying he'd ever experienced. What made him nervous was meeting her outside of his comfort zone, in a dodgy part of Downtown Denver, without a desk between them or a contract. He wasn't good with human interaction outside of business. He actually couldn't remember his last date with a woman. It was probably set up by his mother in a not-so-subtle attempt for him to start thinking about something other than work. He'd never been interested. They all came with high-profile jobs, life planners, and a schedule of life events. Thankfully, Blaine was not a date, and she certainly didn't seem like she had anything planned for her life. The complete opposite of what his family expected him to settle on. So, this would be safe. Right?

The fact that he'd even agreed to meet her was a huge and uncomfortable step for him. When he'd seen her waiting on the side of the street, just as he'd splashed through the puddle, his heart had done a strange flip. He wasn't sure if he was happy that she'd shown up, or worried. He followed her down the staircase peppered with old oily circles of gum and cigarette butts. He had to duck beneath the wood scaffolding as he followed her into the darkness until they stood at an old wooden door with an iron caged peep hole. She'd jumped up to see inside, and he had to guard against smiling at her cute determination.

"Hey, Ralph." She waved happily at the meaty face that appeared.

"Hey Carrots! Been a long time." The man didn't ask for any identification or fee before he swung the door open and let them in. The warmth on his face faded when he looked up at Eric and nodded.

Blaine slapped the man on the shoulder. "Thanks. It's so good to be back. Oh, this is Eric Morales, and he doesn't like to have fun." She said it with a serious tone. Eric's head swung down to scowl down at her and she smiled back.

"Well, he's in a terrible place." Ralph said and admitted them.

Eric sighed and followed her into a small hall that opened up into the loudest, brightest menagerie of sound and color he'd ever seen. Eric had never been in such a place. From the time he was small, he only remembered eating where people had polite and quiet conversations over clean, white tablecloths. Voices were never raised, music was kept to a respectable volume, and the food was hardly ever fried. Stepping through the heavy door, he was assaulted on all sensory fronts.

The smell of stale beer was the backdrop for the neon lights and flashing displays of pinball machines and arcade games. They lit up the space, and the pinging, ringing sounds of aliens being vanquished, balls getting through bridges of obstacles, and shouts of players invaded his quiet calm. On the walls were old movie and concert posters plastered over one another in an odd historical layering of entertainment from the late 70s up to the end of the 80s. He didn't know where to look first. Every time his eyes landed on one thing, another light or sound stole away his attention and his mouth gaped open.

"I know, right?" Blaine nudged him. "Come on. You gotta make the rounds."

"I don't 'gotta' do anything." He corrected her grammar.

"You made the bet, and I believe a Morales handshake is as good as a contract. Unless you'd like me to call up the Post and send in an editorial?"

"Fine," he seethed between his teeth. Apparently, Blaine wasn't all sweetness and sunshine. She seemed to have a pretty good handle on how to make him squirm, which didn't bode well for the rest of their month.

"Now stop acting like I'm asking you to kill a kitten. This is supposed to be fun."

"This is not my idea of fun," he grumbled as he followed her in a twisting path through the arcade. He resisted the urge to look around to see which games he recognized, or to smile and laugh at the TV-show-themed pinball machines: *MacGyver*, *Addams Family*, and *Miami Vice*. He stopped briefly and studied the picture of Crockett and Tubbs and the shining scoreboard. His dad only watched *Miami Vice* when his mother was away on business, but he remembered loving the suits and the haphazard ease with which the detectives would solve crimes, have luck with women, and look cool doing it all. Something touched his hand, and he pulled away on instinct.

"Ease up, big guy," Blaine said and held up the gold and shiny token. "Give it a go."

"No. Thanks."

"Come on, you came all this way. You might as well *try* to enjoy yourself." She leaned in and whispered, "I won't tell your sister if you do end up having fun."

Eric didn't move. Blaine's hair smelled like something light and floral, and he resisted the urge to lean in a little closer. She pressed the cold metal into his palm, and he looked at her warm fingers before she drew them away. "Go on."

Eric felt strange. The noise of the bar fell away, and her soft smile below twinkling green eyes made him awkwardly compliant.

"Fine—okay," he stuttered and plopped the quarter in. "Why is it only one quarter? Shouldn't they be charging more?"

Blaine shrugged. "How *hardened businessman* of you to worry. I think they make up for it in the food and drinks. Plus, there's something kind of beautiful about getting a whole five minutes of joy out of one quarter."

"No one carries quarters anymore. They should retrofit them with credit card slots and charge three times as much."

"Not everything is about the money, Eric." Blaine whispered.

It caught him up short, and he watched her expression change. The clatter of five shiny balls settling into the holding spot drew him away. He pulled back the lever and launched the first ball. It arched up and over the first set of metal cages, and his heart did a funny dance to watch it light up the board as it passed by. So much so that he failed to react when it bounced off one of the bumpers and sunk down into oblivion.

"Aw...maybe only two minutes for your quarter. But don't worry, I hear that happens to a lot of guys."

Eric straightened up and scowled down at her smile. "Two minutes? I'll show you, Mrs. Reynolds—"

"Miss, but I'd rather you call me Blaine. Especially if you're intending to show me something."

"Blaine of my existence." He retorted and fired the second ball.

"Oh, pretty clever for a buttoned-up suit," she chuckled and leaned against the game, watching him and the play with equal interest. By the third ball he was smiling and laughing and lamenting the loss of points, and he glimpsed the most beautiful genuine smile forming from one corner of her mouth to the other. When he looked up before shooting his last ball, Blaine giggled and blushed. Something felt tender inside his chest.

He didn't want to like her. But she was making it damn hard.

"Well? You gonna finish this thing, or are you scared?" she grinned.

He leaned back, took off his suit coat, and handed it to her. He rolled up his sleeves and loosened the top button of his shirt.

"Uh oh—he's getting serious," she said.

"Hold on to your knick-knacks, lady." Eric shot her a false glower before firing the final ball. Keeping it alive for several passes, his arms were tense on the machine, but his hands remained light to the touch on the controls. Every volley brought an excited rush. He was pulled away from contracts, work, obligations, and requirements. His only concern was keeping the tiny metal ball in play. As it struck a point-scoring bumper, it rebounded quickly to the bottom of the machine, headed straight for the drain.

Blaine emitted a funny little "ooh" and bumped the machine with her hip, sending the ball just far enough that his left paddle sprung it back up and aloft. The ball struck three more obstacles and lit up the board with sounds, and the theme song began to play.

He pumped his hands in the air, adrenaline coursing through him. "Yes! Did you see that? If you hadn't hip tricked it..." he was suddenly breathless and light.

Blaine shrugged. "Even Tubbs had Crockett."

Eric took his jacket back from her and rolled down his sleeves. He had to remember why he was here. Fun though it may be, it wasn't worth the project. "I'm totally Crockett."

"No way! I'm Crockett."

"You're more like Calabrese." He nudged her.

Blaine returned it with mirth. "Oh my God, you remember."

He cleared his throat. "Right, well, that was a long time ago. And they were just reruns."

"Reruns that wouldn't have happened if all we ever did was look forward."

"Looking into the past doesn't do anyone much good. We can't ever go back," he said and pulled his suit coat back on.

She studied him a little too closely, and he walked ahead of her, feigning his disinterest. No matter how much he wanted to enjoy the place and the shielded memories of his own past, he needed to keep his sights on the future.

Blaine sighed and watched him walk away. She nodded to the bartender, who smiled and waved back as she caught up to Eric. He wasn't making this easy, and he sure as hell wasn't going to be bowled over by a couple of pinball machines and her charming personality.

"So, you didn't have fun back there?" she asked.

"I just don't get your fascination with it all." He shook his head and stopped in front of an occupied Atari game, watching the *Pong* ball bounce from paddle to paddle and the older gentlemen laughing over it all.

"Some might ask why you're so fascinated by erasing the past?"

"I don't want to erase the—"

"Why you're so fascinated with making buildings that all look the same, with absolutely no character, where renters end up paying for an excessively high lease?"

"Wow." He stopped to look at her. She wasn't smiling anymore. "Bitter isn't something I've seen on you yet," Eric said.

"I'm not bitt—"

"Miss Reynolds, the world will keep moving, and changing, and progressing. If you can't move and progress with it, you'll get left behind."

"I—argh!" She stamped her foot down and balled up her fists at her sides. "It isn't that I don't like progress. If we didn't have it, I wouldn't be able to vote, and weekends wouldn't exist, and medical advances wouldn't cure . . . cancer." The word stuck in her throat oddly before she continued on. "I'm saying that bigger is not always better. More is not always the epitome of what and who we are."

"You're defending an era that was the epitome of excess."

"The 80s had the biggest recession since the great depression—"

"Yeah, but on Wall Street."

"Yeah. What about Wall Street? Big companies like Morales Construction taking advantage of the everyday man and—"

"Wait a minute. My family worked hard for—"

"I have no doubt that they did. But they never stop working. Even when it hurts other people's livelihood."

"Then you should have picked a better livelihood."

"Do you two want a turn?"

They turned to see the two older men holding out their controllers. At gaining their attention, the men stood up.

Blaine and Eric both stopped and refused to look away from each other. Eric glared at her, and Blaine could feel the heat in her cheeks.

"Here." The man in the *Top Gun* baseball cap handed Blaine his controller. "No sense hollering at each other."

"Yeah." Agreed the second, who handed his controller to Eric. "Settle it the old-fashioned way."

"He probably doesn't even know what this is," Blaine said.

"I do so."

"What are you two, like, five years old?" *Top Gun* chuckled before taking his beer and leaving. Blaine sat down with a huff. Eric did the same, leaning as far away from her as possible. The bartender came over, two cold beers on a tray and a bowl of pretzels.

"Hello, Carrots. On the house."

"Thanks Jerry. We probably won't be here long. My friend here thinks your bar is subpar."

Eric looked at her in shock, and then to Jerry. "I said no such thing! She's just angry because she knows I'm right."

"You are not—"

"I wouldn't argue with her, son." Jerry smiled. "She'd charm a priest right outta his pants." He chuckled before leaving.

"Charm a priest out of his . . ." Eric blushed and refused to look at her.

She took a long drink of her beer, trying to calm the mix of emotions surging through her. She set the glass down louder than she intended.

Eric turned to her. "Why does everyone here keep calling you Carrots?"

Blaine swallowed another gulp of beer and selected a new game on the Atari.

"My mom used to bring me here when I was little, to play."

"Your mom brought you to a bar?"

"It's an arcade, and it's not like she put me up at the bar with a beer in a sippy cup."

"Okay, so? Carrots?"

Blaine sighed and slid the pad of her finger across the cold, wet top of her glass. Sadness took over; sometimes going back to the past wasn't so easy, especially when the little girl who used to stand on a milk crate to reach the game controllers had no idea her life would end up the way it did.

"Every time she'd bring me, I refused to eat anything on the menu. I only wanted carrots . . . and back then my hair was bright red and unruly." She blew a curl off her forehead.

Eric looked at Blaine's hair, picturing a curly strawberry blonde kid skipping along from game to game with a basket full of carrots instead of fries, because who could resist a request from Blaine Reynolds? Hadn't he done just the same thing? Her hair was still a little unruly, and he had the strange urge to brush it away from her cheek, but he resisted.

Eric thought hard. He knew himself. He knew the dangers of a wrongly made bet. He worried that the more time he spent with Blaine, the cloudier his intention and direction would become. He would be wise not to spend another minute with her. What if she was right? Maybe he didn't want to look too deep into the reasons for his family's success, or if there was any worth in holding on to any part of the past. What if the new and confusing things he felt for her muddled his ability to make the right decision for his company? He turned to her while the game loaded at its glacial pace, and narrowed his eyes.

"New proposition."

"What? You want carrots instead of pretzels now?"

"No." Eric shook his head and tried not to smile. "If I win this game, you give up the bet, and the tear-down of the Marshall

Shopping Mall happens as soon as the permits come through. Even if it's before the month is out."

"Are you out of your mind? You want me to give up my one shot to save it, over *one* game of *Pong*?"

"No. I'm not a monster." He took a drink of his beer and stared at the screen before picking up his controller again. "Best two out of three." He settled back and rolled his neck out in preparation.

"You're such a jerk. I think you know you might lose."

"No."

"Then why make a sub bet?"

"I just want to see what you're really made of, Reynolds."

"If I win, the stakes stay the same. If you win, you can have one extra week. That's all."

Eric stared her down before shrugging. "Deal."

"I'm going to enjoy beating your little flat paddle." Blaine shook out her shoulders, and they started the game. Each focused like never before, on the small, pixelated screen between them.

Chapter Eight

Eric threw the embossed invitation on the side table with the rest of his unwanted mail. He had to get through it eventually, but after the evening of light game play and low-key company, he didn't feel the uptight urgency that he came home with most nights. He smiled as he unbuttoned his collar down a few buttons, and thought of the adorable Blaine Reynolds and her lighthearted laughter when he'd let her win. The truth was, after their second round of *Pong*, when she had smoked him in the first, he let the warnings in his business brain get pushed to the side. He became . . . curious. Maybe it was the beer, or the way her nose crinkled up in joy, or being pulled out of his straight-laced world, but he felt good when he was around her.

He looked back at the invitation. The grand opening of the Putnam County Museum of Modern Art. One of the biggest projects Morales Construction had garnered in the last three years. The museum was one of the most beautiful buildings in the state and met impeccable standards for its environmentally responsible specs and clean lines. Its completion had earned Loraine her title as partner and given her the god complex that was driving him nuts. The brewery would be his chance to even the playing field.

But there was a small, curly haired wrench in that process currently.

Maybe he could ask Blaine to go with him. That thought seemed ridiculous, but he stood silent with it for a moment. Going with her to the opening might make the evening a bit more bearable. Then he would at least have a buffer between him and his sister. Maybe when Blaine saw the work Morales Construction was capable of, she'd understand that the Marshall Mall had outlived its purpose. And it was at the end of their agreed upon time, so it would be like getting to have the last word. Final arguments packed the biggest punch, and he hoped by swaying her, it would make the building of the Snake River Brewery a walk in the park. He knew he was meeting her for lunch in a couple of days; maybe he'd propose the idea and try to get an edge on winning her over.

Eric needed to clear his head. Business was still business. He needed her to sign the amendment to the lease so they could complete the project on time. She hadn't mentioned the contract the Petersons had drawn up with her mom. She hadn't really mentioned where her mom was. Retired? Moved? Eric's heart felt tight. Had she passed away? Could that account for the moments of sadness he'd watched pass over her face at odd times during the night?

The next morning, he'd gotten into the office early to finalize two other projects, set up his meeting notes for the day, and arrange for his lunch to be free with Blaine. It was a juggle, and he was sure there would be some protesting from Loraine and the construction manager for the park project across town when he'd shift them to a different day. He didn't really care. He was actually looking forward to visiting the mall again, and more specifically, Blaine. When he typed "Marshall Mall Re-Inspection" in the newly cleared lunch time slot, he wondered if it might arouse suspicion.

Both Loraine and his dad were probably far too busy to read his schedule too carefully, right? He sighed and sipped at his black coffee. Did Blaine drink coffee? Or was she more of a tea drinker? Maybe more like Tab Cola, he snorted, and an easy smile faded from his face. He shouldn't be wondering and thinking about her, yet he couldn't help it. Was she an early riser? Did she get up, groggy and hair a mess, late and rushing around, one leg in her pants while trying to get into work on time? Or was she a quiet self-starter? People who ran their own businesses, and had done so for a while, usually weren't the hopping into one leg of their pants out the door late kind of people. Still, she had that uncanny air about her as someone who slid into life just in time.

Two hours later, the second horseman of the apocalypse entered his office.

"Hola *Pollita*," he said without looking up. Loraine screwed her mouth up into a nasty frown.

"Don't call me that."

"You used to love when I'd call you that," he teased, still not looking up from his spreadsheet.

"What has gotten into you lately? When did you revert back to a *bebé*? You know we have actual work to do in this office, right?"

Eric shrugged and pointed to his screen. "I'm doing it. You're the one standing there with no purpose."

"*Hijos*," came a voice from the hall, and both spines straightened immediately. A strange intensity filled the room as John Morales entered. Like a cloud of expectation paving the way for the carrier of the family torch of success.

"Hola, Papá," Loraine said in a saccharine way that sent annoyance up Eric's throat like bile.

"Hola, Papá," he said and shot his smiling sister a dirty look.

"*Mijo*, I saw you changed your lunch meeting tomorrow? Everything at the Marshall Mall going all right? Have you sent the permitting in yet?"

Eric felt sweat erupt under his shirt, and he looked quickly at his sister, who raised one perfect, dark brow.

"Yes, Eric, tell Papá all about your brilliant work at the mall."

She crossed her hands in front of her chest and leaned back for the show.

Their father, so much like Eric himself—tall, imposing, but with gray patches on either side of his temples—turned his sharpened gaze on his son.

"Is there something I need to know?"

Eric shook his head and tried to put a nonplussed look on his face.

"No. Everything is going along as planned. I've delayed the permitting only by a few days because of an inconsistency in the rental agreement of one of the tenants. Which is why I'm heading there for lunch, to talk to the tenant and see how we can resolve the issue in the quickest way possible," Eric said all in one quick breath. Did it sound like a lie? It wasn't really a lie. Yet, it sort of felt like a lie in the center of his chest, sitting heavy. His eyes never left his father.

John Morales met his son's gaze in that stoic, unemotional way that had managed to cow both of his children for most of their lives. The kind where you never knew if he was judging you, praising you, or ignoring you. He nodded slowly.

"Good, I like that you're taking the initiative yourself. You could call one of the lawyers, but it shows character that you're stepping up to take care of it yourself. That's the mark of a true leader." John nodded and turned to Loraine.

"Aren't you supposed to be managing the museum's final inspections before the opening? It's only a few weeks away, Loraine."

"But, Papá. Eric was—"

"He's trying to work, *mija*, you need to stop bugging him and do the same," John said, and Loraine huffed before leaving Eric's small and cramped office. John turned back to his son. A knowing glint in his eye. "Keep your head on straight, *mijo*. This is your big break. I'm not going to say there's no pressure. There is. Just don't crack under it all, yeah?" John nodded with a wink.

"No, Papá. I won't. I'm . . . focused," he added lamely.

John left the room, and Eric stared at the empty doorway. Was he focused? Absolutely not. Would it only get worse after another afternoon with Blaine? Odds were, yes. Eric sat back, deflated, in his chair and wondered what madness had come over him. He rubbed his eyes with his hands and blew out a hard breath.

Would inviting her to the museum opening be a mistake? He had been so sure that it would be a good way to convince her Morales Construction did beautiful and good work, but also to ease the pressure of the situation. His whole family would be there, and the vision of Blaine in the middle of shark-infested waters, circled, alone and afraid, filled his head. There would be no way to pass her off as an acquaintance or someone of no consequence, since Loraine knew who she was. His father would be livid and may even take away the project from him. Especially after he'd just promised that he was in the game to win.

Eric pressed both fists to his eyes, growled, and spun in his chair. This project shouldn't have been this hard. Why did he take that stupid bet?

"So?" JT held out their hands in question.

"So what?" Blaine grumbled.

"So what happened? Did he fall irrevocably in love with you?"

"What? No! What's wrong with you?"

"You'll have to ask my mom. I'm sure she's got some ideas." JT grinned.

"You? You're perfect as is." Blaine smiled. "No, he didn't fall in love with me. And thank God for that. Who'd want that kind of cold shoulder to lean on? I did almost lose the whole mall though. Over one game of *Pong*."

"What?"

"That guy likes to bet. A lot. He might have a gambling problem." Blaine thought out loud, trying to find some reason to dislike Eric, even though she couldn't help but remember the warm touch of his hand on her lower back as he escorted her back up the stairs. He had been a gracious loser, even smiling as she celebrated with the one quick bounce that sent her ball through his goal on the final, tied round that determined she would still stay in the game. When his hand had touched the small of her back, lightly, on their way up the stairs, she'd pulled away, not wanting to muddle the lines of what they were. But the pressure stayed even as he put his hand back in his pocket. They'd parted at the top of the stairs; him to his fancy car, her to her Ford Escort in the parking garage four blocks away.

It had been so long since she'd been on a date, or even been kissed. Since her mom had passed, she struggled to keep the shop alive and manage the online trading of the inventory. For all the love she had of 1980s romantic comedies, she sure didn't have much romance in her own life.

"So, it didn't end in some heated love-making?"

"Ugh, no." Blaine helped JT pack up some of the older supplies in the back of their salon. She had a half an hour until opening and was trying to keep herself busy. JT and Deb had found a small salon to open together, and had high hopes that their clients would follow them across town to where the rent was cheaper. Blaine wasn't ready to pack up her own shop yet. She wanted to believe she wouldn't have to.

"You are going to see him again, right?" JT lifted one brow curiously.

"Supposedly, he's coming to the shop tomorrow on his lunch break to see what exactly I do."

"Ooh . . . what are you going to do? Give him a *personal* tour?"

"Why are you like this?" Blaine laughed and threw a hair net at them.

"I know when my friend hasn't been laid in a while." JT shrugged. "And, you have to admit, Eric Morales is a hot piece of man."

Blaine felt heat rise from her t-shirt collar upwards. "He's not. I mean, he's okay, if you like that tall, muscular, uptight, dark-haired, eyes like deep pools of unspent emotion kinda guy," Blaine stuttered and turned away quickly.

"Holy shit. You do like him." JT stopped packing and looked at Blaine.

"I do not. He's about to take away my whole life."

"Love comes in strange forms."

"I'm leaving." Blaine scowled, closed the full box, and walked out of the storage room. JT's laugh followed her.

"See you soon. Have a good 'lunch' tomorrow."

Blaine ignored them and went to open her own shop. It was quiet inside. And cold. She wondered if the Petersons were still heating the units or if they had decided to start shutting it all down. Blaine blew into her hands and circled the room to turn on all the lights, signs, televisions, and display cases. The room, dark and sullen in the morning, came alive with color and bright images. Blaine flipped the sign to open and went to her laptop to check for any orders. There were the typical fifty spam messages, and a few for select items that she might have in her inventory.

There was also a message from Morales Construction. Her hand hovered over the email before clicking. Why did her heart feel like it was about to pound right out of her chest? Why were her palms sweating? It was probably just some generalized email that all the tenants were getting, covering all the details of the eviction and unavoidable destruction of the property. She took a deep breath and clicked on it, protecting her heart against the warm memory of Eric's smile, and the warmer memory of his hand on her back.

Ms. Reynolds,

I wanted to confirm our meeting for tomorrow and offer a new proposal to our wager.

"Are you kidding me?" she whispered under her breath.

It's come to my attention that in our bet, you are hell-bent on convincing me of the worth of your shop and its contents. I would like the opportunity to counter your evidence with a meeting of my own. I will provide the details tomorrow over lunch if you are willing to listen.

Sincerely,
Eric H. Morales,
Morales Construction, Inc.

"This is ridiculous." She scowled. She wasn't going to be convinced, and he was just trying to waste her time. Why should he get a say in it? Why did he need to convince her of anything? Was he trying to break her concentration and keep her from throwing anything else at him that might shake him? Which means he must have been shaken. She lifted her eyebrow and read the message again.

She was more stubborn than him. Her shop wasn't just some fly-by-night venture. He was messing with her whole livelihood, her identity. Maybe she should let him think he was getting ahead. Play it all innocent at tomorrow's lunch, but understand that her enemy thought her quirkiness was her weakness. She wasn't backing down, no matter what he was planning. She sent him a quick response.

Mr. Morales,

I am amiable to your request, but will need all the details before I can provide an answer. I will see you tomorrow, here at my shop at 12:30 sharp.

Sincerely,
Blaine T. Reynolds,
Back To The 80s

After checking to see what inventory she had, she sent out responses to the requests for a set of Burger King *Star Wars* glasses, and a signed *The Goonies* movie poster (it would be sad to see it go, but she needed the money). When she'd finished, she breathed a sigh of relief that she at least had what the customers were looking for, and it would mean one more day of paying the rent. Eric

Morales probably never had to worry about the rent in his whole life. He probably never worried about losing anything he loved. She wondered if he truly loved anything. Money. Prestige. Hopefully, at least, his family.

From the way he reacted to his sister, she wondered if there was any love there. There were some deep animosities that seemed to go beyond sibling rivalry. It was the reason he agreed to the bet in the first place. Maybe he secretly hoped Blaine would be able to convince him, and that would piss off Loraine? Blaine wasn't sure she liked being a pawn in two sharks' game of who-does-daddy-love-more. But if it could save her shop, she had no problem pitting them against each other.

Her phone pinged.

> What are you feeding the hulk tomorrow?

JT texted.
Panic rose in Blaine's chest as she responded.

> I haven't thought about it.

> OMG, Really?

> Ok, so I've thought about it a lot. But there is so much riding on this, it's overwhelming and I can't come up with anything.

> I figured. Don't worry, I got you covered.

> You don't have to do that, I will come up with something.

> You're not feeding him peanut butter and jelly on Wonder Bread with a side of Lays.

Blaine smirked.

What's wrong with PB and J?

Trust me. I've got this handled. It'll be my contribution to the cause,

was all JT responded.

The rest of the day dragged by. The normal midweek crowd was never really big, but it seemed even smaller than usual. She wondered if word was spreading that their days were numbered at the mall, and people were already making other appointments at hair salons or signing up at different karate schools. What she had, though, she knew didn't exist anywhere else in Marshall. People would have to drive to Denver or search online sites. She bit her lip and did what she could to stay busy.

By the time she closed up shop, she'd made one hundred dollars less than a normal weekday and left with a heavy heart. She didn't know what she'd do tomorrow at lunch with Eric, but whatever it was, she'd hit him with her Jedi-level quirk.

Chapter Nine

The next day, Eric began his morning early with a run. Hard and fast, driving out the demons of the last two weeks. The stress of work, the expectation of his family, the other projects that had begun to pile up behind the brewery, and the approaching museum opening—each seemed to be in a pressure cooker on a crowded stove, and one of them could blow at any second.

Today he'd have lunch with Blaine.

Today he'd ask her to the opening.

Today he'd get to see her again and have to put the heavy wall of the project around his heart. This was his opportunity to ask about the amended contract. To see if she'd waive her right to refute the sale. Or just agree to it. He leaped over a curb and sped down another empty street in the predawn light. But if she did agree, he wouldn't get to have any more meetings with her. She wouldn't go to the museum opening. Their time would be over. He stopped at a light and his lungs burned with the increased effort. He didn't want their time to be over.

What was one more week?

Wiping his brow on his shirt, he checked for traffic and ran through the intersection and down the road, leaving all his demons still gnashing at his heels.

Blaine woke up with a start as her alarm blurted out Wham!'s "Wake Me Up Before You Go Go". Her hand fumbled for the phone and knocked down a stack of books, her reading glasses, and a box of Kleenex. Finally, sitting up, she realized that the phone was actually in the bedsheets with her. She'd fallen asleep last night while looking up his LinkedIn page. He didn't seem to have any other social profile. He probably felt other social sites were too frivolous. Plus, maybe he didn't want weirdos stalking him. She just wanted to know a little more about him besides what she already knew. He'd been working for his parents' company from the time he was fifteen. From errands, to office admin, to junior partner, and all the way through college, where he had gone through the exact same program as his father, then graduated with honors. His whole life planned out on a one-way track. Blaine had fallen asleep, sad for him. Did he even want to work there? Had he ever thought of being an astronaut, or a cowboy, or a ballerina?

Blaine closed her eyes again and thought of tall, imposing Eric in a leotard and stiff tutu, and giggled into her covers. She had been looking for a weakness. But the only weakness she found was written in between the lines of his tremendous success. That kind of power came at a cost, and it made sense that he'd almost seemed uncomfortable having fun at the arcade. She rolled over, tossed back the covers, and made her way to the bathroom.

Brain groggy before her first cup of coffee, she didn't want to make any assumptions or plans about lunch until she could think clearly. She fed Charles Dumar, who must have had a late night himself, as he was still asleep and snoring when she put food and fresh water out for him.

The coffee pot made its odd, strangled beep and Blaine sighed. With her cup full, she shuffled to the bathroom for a shower and a good bout of overthinking under the warm spray. She'd already been scoping out the shop for what she thought he might like best. Obviously the *Pac-Man* game, but beyond that, she wanted to start with the toys he may or may not remember (he couldn't be more than 37) and move into the music. Did he ever get to go to a concert or was he always too chained to the late nights of the family business? Then there were the games, the odd tech . . . lunch . . . charming conversation? Blaine sighed and sipped her coffee while she undressed, then stepped in the shower.

She sang to herself and soaped up, trying not to think about the four short hours before they'd see each other again. Eric, no doubt in a suit, pressed and clean, neat. A big contrast to her high-waisted denim and 80s hair-band t-shirts. Maybe she could step it up today and channel her inner Madonna with a black tank top and a net overshirt. She closed her eyes, massaged her fingers through her soapy hair, and thought about what might be beneath his buttoned-up exterior. He was fit, broad in the chest, and tall. His forearms were tight. His backside was too. Soap ran into her eye and she yelped from the burn, trying madly to rinse it out.

"Head in the game, Reynolds!" she yelled as the burning abated. "You can't be thinking about his hot ass and take down his multi-million-dollar plans. Business." She pep-talked herself all the way through her morning routine and on her way to the shop.

Her only fear was that JT would show up with some romantic, candlelit lunch that would confuse the lines and give Eric the wrong impression. The morning went by without too much fanfare. She was busy emailing a group of collectors from Tokyo about a set of Transformers that she'd acquired last fall when she glanced up to see Eric standing at her counter in his nicely pressed suit, tapping on the glass, grinning at her.

Her stomach flipped, and she blurted out, "Konnichiwa."

"Well, same to you," he chuckled.

"Thanks." Her heart was now racing. She really had to pull

herself together. "I was just finishing up an email." She closed her old laptop. "Are you ready for lunch?"

"Are you?" he asked and glanced around.

"Yes. Of course. Why wouldn't I be? I thought we'd start with a little tour first." Blaine said and looked towards the door. JT had remembered, right? Blaine would buy them time.

"Remember, I've seen this place before? I'm pretty sure you were here the first time I was."

"But did you really soak it in?" She held up a finger and shook it. "I think not."

She bounced off her stool and came around the corner of the counter. When he gave her an appreciative once over, she was glad she'd chosen the capri leggings, black half bra, and net top. Madonna was rarely wrong when it came to fashion. Except maybe the pointy cone bra. Blaine cleared her throat. "I've made special concessions just for you."

"Oh? Well, that sounds like you're trying to bribe me. Seems like shady business dealings." He smiled at her.

She stepped closer and looked up at him. "I'm not above playing a little dirty if I need to."

"Are you sure you're ready to play dirty with the big guys, little shop owner?" he said softly.

"I guess we'll find out, won't we?" She tried to not let her eyes settle on his smile.

"De-liv-er-y." JT swung through the door and they both leaped apart from one another. Blaine took in a shaky breath. All of her "business" pep talking fell down the drain when she imagined his lips against hers. JT came around the aisle and stopped to look at them both. "Did I just interrupt something scandalous?" they asked, arching a pierced brow.

"No," Blaine and Eric both responded in unison.

"Huh—really? Because you're both protesting it pretty hard." JT continued down the aisle with two heavy bags and a drink carrier with two large Styrofoam cups. "Never you mind, your awkward little heads. I picked up your order, Blaine," they said with an inconspicuous wink. "Where do you want it? In the back, perhaps? Little privacy?"

"No. No privacy needed," Blaine said quickly and took the bags from them. As she tried to balance the drink carrier, it tipped dangerously, and Eric caught it with quick reflexes, righting it before the drinks spilled. "Thanks JT. We'll just . . ." Blaine looked around and spotted the perfect place, "get set up over there." She nodded at Eric to follow her.

JT waved at him. "Enjoy your time in the magical little world of Blaine Reynolds," they sang and wriggled their fingers goodbye.

Blaine headed to the back wall near the music section. There, she pulled an old sheet off a four-person *Pac-Man* arcade game with a glass tabletop. She put the bag of food down and pulled up two retro red vinyl chairs.

"Uh, are you sure we should eat on that?" he asked, his mind obviously scrolling through the cost of the table and what kind of damage it could sustain.

She quirked up her smile at him and shook her head. "Are you a five-year-old with poor hand-eye coordination who has trouble getting food to his mouth?"

Eric scowled. "Of course not."

"Well, then, just be careful. Or you can pay me the $3,000 it's worth."

"Is it worth that much?" His skin blanched, and he held the drinks with both hands.

"What? I thought you were convinced old stuff was worthless."

"I never said that."

"It doesn't matter," she said. "I trust you."

The words were small, but they seemed to make an impact. His shoulders dropped. She'd never really seen him relaxed, except at the pinball machine, and even then, there was still an air of having to keep it together.

"Okay," he brought the drinks over and she unpacked the simple paper boxes.

The most amazing smells of spice and heat wafted up, and she watched as his eyes lit up.

"Wait a minute. Did you—" He opened the carton, sat back and groaned, his eyes rolled back in his head and he chuckled. "Is this Abuelita's?" Childlike enthusiasm lit up his face, but before she could check the receipt to confirm, he was digging in the bag for the plastic utensils. "Oh man. You did!"

"Of course." She put on a knowing look, like it was silly to order from anywhere else, especially when he seemed to light up like a Christmas tree as he unpackaged the food. She took her horchata out of the carrier and passed him his.

"Oh man, the best horchata too." He slurped it and took a huge sauce-and-cheese bite of his enchilada, like he hadn't eaten in weeks.

"I didn't know if you'd like it. I mean, it's kind of a hole in the wall, and I know you probably—"

He grunted happily and wiped his mouth before waving away her insecurity.

"I haven't eaten there in . . ." he paused to think, "maybe like a year?" His fork paused, and he stared at her with a sudden sadness.

"You okay? Is it alright?"

"My grandmother used to take me there after school when my parents were too busy. And you know if Abuela is taking you somewhere for Mexican, it's probably gonna be good." He smiled at the warm memory. "She knew my mom and dad didn't like it there, but—" he took another bite. "She knew I loved it and that was all that mattered."

Blaine was so enamored with his story, his joy, his ravenous eating, that she hadn't even touched her food. Just watching him, listening to him, made the world sit still.

"What? Do I have something on my face?" He wiped at his mouth in an exaggerated way.

"No," she smiled. "It's nothing." Her eyes felt moist, and she felt like an idiot, on the verge of tears. "I just think that's really sweet that your grandmother took you there." She opened her meal and started in. "My mom used to take me there after school plays for their fried ice cream."

"Yes." He pointed his fork at her, a small bit of cheese hanging off, before digging out another bite. "I can't tell you how many stomach aches I suffered gladly, over and over again, inhaling one by myself."

"By yourself? They're like," she held up her hands in the size of a small watermelon, "this big."

"I was a growing boy." He chuckled and then continued to eat.

She loved seeing the joy on his face. She ate her saucy and beautiful mess of food until she was full, still half of the generous portion there.

He wiped the container clean with his fork and licked the back of it with a satisfied grunt. Blaine watched his mouth, his tongue, the sensual way he approached his food. Her eyes fell to his hands, and her brain fell into thoughts about how sensual he probably was elsewhere.

"*Dios*, Blaine. I could eat you every day."

"I'm—I'm sorry what?" she squeaked, and heat rushed through her cheeks.

"I could eat that every day, I said. Thank you." He put his empty container back in the bag and looked at her strangely. "You okay? You look flushed? Too spicy?"

"No. I like it spicy." Her voice trembled, and she put her box back in the bag to save for later. They cleaned up so she could throw the cover back on the game.

"Well, I have about half an hour to be wowed."

Blaine felt weak in the knees. *All I need is fifteen minutes,* her sex-starved brain shouted. She sighed, trying to keep her mouth closed so none of those horrifying thoughts came out.

"Well, then, follow me." She began with the record, tape,

and early CD collection that had been her favorite to maintain. Most of the materials were in good condition, even if their packaging was a bit worn. Blaine imagined some were worth a lot of money, but she didn't have the time to research it in depth. She wasn't in it for the money. Like any good foster mom, she wanted to see the things she carried, from the smallest toy to the most expensive concert ticket stub and corresponding t-shirt, go to someone who found worth and joy in the memories they made.

When they got to the boxes of framed ticket stubs and signed pictures from various musical artists, he bent low over the crate to gently flip through.

"Is your security okay here?" he asked suddenly.

"Why?" she responded, surprised by his question.

"You have some valuable items in here."

"Oh. Well, I've got an alarm and I think the mall has cameras. Plus, I have Lawrence. He's a big guy."

Eric looked up at this, a strange look on his face. "Lawrence? The karate guy?"

"Yeah. I mean, he's a jerk, but he knows what he's doing if I need him."

Eric leaned back. "So, are you two dating?"

"What?" she said a little too loudly. "No!" She outright laughed. "I mean, I have him for security. You know . . ." She held up her hands and waved them around. "The whole karate thing he does."

"Oh. That makes sense." Eric sighed and then laughed. "I mean, not that I care who you date. He just doesn't seem like your kind of guy."

"I agree. He's too foul-mouthed and abrasive for me." Blaine smiled. "He does seem to be taken with your sister though, if I can let a small cat out of the bag."

A slow, mischievous smile spread across Eric's face, lighting up his eyes. "Really?"

"I mean in that 'god-I-hate-that-woman' but he really wants to kiss her silly way."

Eric didn't respond, but his eyes fell to Blaine's lips. She took a long sip of her horchata, and his eyes never left her mouth.

"That's interesting." He cleared his throat and went back to the frames. "I mean, that you should mention it. I think she might kind of like him, too. Which I'm sure horrifies her."

"I bet it would." Blaine laughed.

"This." He held up the frame with Gloria Estefan's picture, a ticket and a small bangle bracelet, shadow boxed inside. "How much is this?"

"That? I'd have to look it up. My mom got to see her in Boston in 1987 on the Primitive Love Tour. She ended up in the front row, and Gloria threw out some of her 'bling.' I haven't looked at this one in a while. I think I remember trying to sing along to Conga and totally massacring the words."

"Ha, gringa," he teased and nudged her hip with his.

"True, my Spanish is subpar. I should really brush up on it." She smiled.

"Best thing for that is to get a tutor," he said.

"Hmm . . . do you have any spare time?" she said out loud before she could stop herself.

He looked at her and smiled. Heat blossomed between them.

"Normally I would say yes, but I'm busy with this bet I made, and winning it so I can build a brewery."

Blaine shook her head, and all of her heated thoughts fell away. "Ugh." She whispered and stepped away. "I'm an—" she stopped shy of saying idiot.

"What?" He turned, picture still in his hands.

"Nothing. We should get on to it. You only have ten more minutes." Shoulders set and jaw square, she tossed the rest of her horchata in the large trash can beside the desk.

He seemed to settle on the same thoughts, and reluctantly put the picture back in the unassuming crate with the others. For the rest of the tour, she kept her voice even and serious, and stopped only to show him the best and brightest of her collection, as well as anything that had a good story attached to it. Like Marvin Rasley, who was a long-time customer and often brought in toys his family had left him, as well as the collector's editions of Matchbox cars still in their packaging. He never wanted much money for them; his only insistence was that they went to someone who "lit up" when they found them on the shelves among the other treasures.

"Why does he want to sell them, then? Don't they make him 'light up'?" Eric asked.

Blaine felt a lump rise in her throat, and she put the package of Trans Am collector cars gently down. "Marvin is a terminal cancer patient. He used to know my mom." Her voice rose on the last word, too much emotion behind the idea to hold a straight face. "He doesn't have a lot of time left, and just wants to make sure that the things that mattered to him will matter to someone else someday, too. He doesn't have kids. I think he's just looking to make a connection to the future somehow." Her voice trailed off, and she sniffed.

"Blaine, I'm sorry." He touched her arm. "Your mom . . . is she—"

"Oh my God, it's past time." Blaine choked back the tears fighting their way up. She didn't want him to see her like this. "I'm sure you have lots of important work things to do."

Eric took her hand so he could look at her watch. "Shit. I mean, sorry. Yeah, I gotta go." He stepped away, and she was sure he was going to rush out to his fancy car, back to his big fancy job. But he turned toward her, took a slow step and leaned down. His lips pressed softly to her forehead, and his voice was just as gentle. "Thank you. Thank you for lunch and for showing me your shop." He sighed, stepped away, and turned towards the door.

Blaine's neurons were too confused for her to make a coherent response, so she said nothing. He turned at the door and snapped his fingers. "I almost forgot. Are you free the night of the 28th?"

"Friday? The 28th?" It was two and a half weeks away. At the end of the deadline for the bet to end. She knew because she'd made a big red circle around that date on her calendar. Her heart leaped.

"Yeah. Seven o'clock?"

"Sure. I think so."

"Great. You have a formal dress, right? Something kinda sparkly or whatever? I'll pick you up."

Before she could respond, he was gone; out the door, getting in his car, and blasting away from the curb. Back to his busy life, in his busy business. The business of destroying her shop. What did he mean "something formal"? Sparkly?

"Great," she squeaked, and her hand touched the spot he'd kissed. The emotions about her mom, the flurry of him leaving, and the hurried invitation were lost as the warmth of his lips on her skin lingered. It was a strange kiss, and as far as she could remember, no man had ever kissed her there. It felt almost nurturing.

Chapter Ten

The music collection alone was enough for her to make a whole new start without her shop, Eric thought as he drove away. And he found it was easier to think along those lines than to remember the sad way she'd spoken about her mother, and the broken look she'd tried so hard to hide. He could feel that her mother was no longer around. Had she passed away? He should have asked. All he knew was her downcast eyes and fallen smile had turned his world upside down.

Had he kissed her? He couldn't really remember the rationalization that led his lips to her forehead, but it felt right, and it felt like she needed it . . . and he did too. His belly was full, and he wanted to go home and watch a rerun of one of his abuela's telenovelas and fall asleep on the couch next to her while she did her sewing or one of her puzzle books.

Going back in time, to things he'd forgotten over the course of his life, had made something soft and tender open in his chest. When he got back to the office, he didn't feel he belonged; his family's hard-earned successes scattered down the hallway in the form of plaques, accolades, and pictures of grand openings.

He was taking Blaine to the grand opening. Suddenly, his

throat felt tight. What seemed like a good idea yesterday, a ploy to bring her over to his side, now felt a little shady and underhanded, as though he was preparing to throw her into a den of lions. Head down, his rambling thoughts were interrupted when his father called out his name.

"Eric!"

Eric's head snapped up and he back-tracked three paces to his father's open office door. Everyone knew he liked to keep an eye on things going on in the office, and rarely closed himself off. The curse of being a micromanager. It probably wasn't good for his dad's heart, but you couldn't tell John Morales anything he didn't already know.

"Papá, hola—"

"How did things go with the contract at the mall?"

"Good." The word stuck in Eric's throat as he sipped his horchata absentmindedly. John turned his head as he studied his son.

"Just good? And?"

"And not much to worry about. The original signee of that contract is . . ." Eric paused, and the lump in his throat threatened to grow. He cleared it down. "She's deceased, so I'll have the lawyers look through the paperwork to make sure the exemption ended when she passed away." He slurped the horchata until the sad and empty rattle of the straw drawing air resonated in the office.

"Good. Is that Horchata? From Abuelita's?" John's voice was low, and Eric wasn't sure if that meant he was about to get a stern talking to or if his father was jealous.

"Uh, yeah. The shop owner brought lunch—"

"You actually ate lunch with her?" Loraine's angry voice startled them both into jumping.

"Don't you knock?" Eric responded. Loraine stood behind him in her high-priced business suit, arms crossed and glowering.

"I thought this was business?" she led with a glint in her eye.

"It was. Yes, I had lunch. The meeting was over the lunch hour. She bought me lunch."

Loraine lowered her eyes and a shark-like smile spread on her mouth. "Are you fraternizing with the enemy?"

"Members of our community are not our enemies," he growled back.

Their father cleared his throat.

"That's true, there's nothing wrong with lunch and who could resist Abuelita's?" John said. He turned to Eric and fell into a mischievous smile. "What did you have?"

"Enchiladas Ramone. *Dios.* the sauce was just as good as I remember—"

"You two are obviously missing the point here." Loraine's voice cut through.

"Which is?" Eric turned angrily towards her.

"That you made a be—"

"Bed." Eric interrupted. "I made my bed by taking on this project, and I accept that. I'll lay in it however it turns out." He rushed over her words and tossed his horchata cup in the trash. "And speaking of fraternizing, I hear that Lawrence Williams from Talon Karate has been asking about you."

"Wha . . . who? What are you talking about?" she stammered and uncrossed her arms. Her cheeks went red.

"Talon? That martial arts school in the Marshall Mall?" John asked. "*Mija*, you aren't thinking of dating some starving martial artist, are you?"

"No! Papá, that's not at all true. I hate that man. He's an idiot and a brute, and I wouldn't be caught dead in the same room with him," she protested and, in her anger, forgot about Blaine and Eric's ill-made bet and stormed from the office. Still, Eric had seen her blush. Any bit of dirt he could use to toss at her and distract her about his own affairs outside of the office was worth using. It was also kind of nice to see her have a human emotion for once. It made him feel better about his reaction to Blaine.

"We shouldn't laugh at her," their father chuckled. "But it's kind of funny. She must really like him if he makes her that crazy."

"Is that the true sign that a woman likes you?" Eric asked with a quirk of his eyebrow, then regretted the question.

John sighed and sat down at his desk, and motioned for Eric to take a seat. "I know you are busy here at the office and with the new contract. I don't want you to lose sight of that."

"Of course, Papá, I know." Eric hung his head. His father was right. This wasn't the time to be entertaining ideas of romance. He had a big deal to close and couldn't afford to let Blaine Reynolds take up his brain space.

"Someday, *mijo*, the right one will come along. At the right time. But not today, I hope." John lowered his gaze in the serious scowl that told Eric that love would have to wait. Which was fine; he wasn't planning to fall in love with Blaine Reynolds anyway.

"Of course." He shrugged. "I don't have that kind of time right now."

"Good. Speaking of that, what are you doing sitting here? Go work." His father chuckled and sent him on his way.

Eric left, went to his small office, and closed the door behind him. He'd already invited Blaine to the opening. What would his parents say? Especially after the comments his father just made, and especially when his father found out who his date was. Eric groaned and put his head down on his desk. This whole day had been a complicated dance of what he wanted and what was expected of him, and he was tired of the way the two sides pulled at him.

"What do you mean, he kissed you?" JT dropped their shears on the floor mid-trim and had to rush to sanitize them. "Sorry, Shelly. Hang on."

"Tell us, Blaine. Tell us about the kiss." Shelly, JT's oldest and longest returning customer, leaned forward, one side of her graying bangs much longer than the other.

Blaine sighed and buried her head in her hands. "I got a little emotional, just talking about Marvin and his collection, which turned into talking about his cancer and then . . . then I started thinking about Mom." She sighed and shook her head, refusing to cry. "And I freaked out because he got all soft-eyed, and I didn't want that pity, but he looked so kind and handsome and I told him he should go, and he did have to go, but before he could rush out, he just stopped and turned back around and . . ."

"Aaaaand?" JT led.

"And kissed me on the forehead. Then he left."

"What the? On the forehead? What in the hell? I buy the man horchata and the best damn Enchiladas Ramone this side of the Rockies and he wastes a kiss on your forehead?" JT waved their newly sanitized shears angrily above Shelly's head, who ducked and covered her eyes.

"It was sweet."

"You aren't twelve and playing spin the bottle at Bucky Weinstein's birthday party, Blaine."

JT stopped their Edward Scissorhands impression, so Shelly, feeling safe again, sat up. "I think it's sweet. It shows he cares, and that it's not just hot enchilada desire."

JT rolled their eyes. Blaine came out of her hands and started to mope.

"Wait, am I not attractive enough for hot enchilada desire? Have I passed my prime?"

"Shit." JT shook their head, placed the shears down, and came over, urging Blaine up by the shoulders and out of the empty chair. "You are hot. You are desirable. I'm sure macho guys like Eric Morales totally go for"—they looked Blaine up and down—"this frumpy, bed hair don't care, Colorado chic thing."

"What? I'm not frumpy."

"Well," Shelly shrugged her shoulders through her still uneven hair. "I mean, you do like leggings and slouchy sweatshirts a little too much. You kind of look like you're always ready for any random *Fame* audition that might spring up."

"Oh, God! What am I gonna do?" Blaine's sadness was suddenly replaced by panic.

"Girl, you don't have to do anything. If a man doesn't like you for who you are—"

"I mean about the fancy thing he asked me to. I have to wear something formal, fancy, and sparkly?" Her brain suddenly dredged up his last words.

"What in the hell are you talking about?"

"He asked me to some swanky event two weeks from this Friday. Someplace he said I needed to have a formal dress for. I don't own a dress. I mean, not really."

JT looked at her for a moment, mouth twisted up in concentration. "So, he kissed you on the forehead and asked you out on a date?"

"Yeah?"

"And you didn't think to mention the date?" JT asked.

"I—I don't know if it's a date. He said now that he's seen some of my life, I should see something about his life." She said it so resolutely that she'd almost convinced herself. She did not, however, convince JT.

"A formal dress is a date. Nighttime is a date. Friday? Definitely a date."

"What am I going to do?" Blaine asked.

"Something fancy. Eric Morales. Friday the 28th." JT went back to Shelly's hair, and approximately three snips in, gasped and nearly took off the top of Shelly's ear.

"Holy shit."

"Oh, God, not again, JT! It took me two years to grow out the last bald spot you gave me." Shelly moved to stand.

"Your hair is fine. I'm talking about the grand opening of The

Putnam County Museum of Modern Art. A Morales Construction crown jewel and it's happening in two weeks."

Blaine stared at her blankly. "Are you serious?"

"I have friends who have been trying to get tickets for months, Blaine. The museum is supposed to be a modern marvel."

"Modern marvel?" She sat back down, bit her nails. "He's trying to prove me wrong." She said, and her face turned down into a scowl. "That sneaky, white-collar Rico Suave—"

"Who?"

"He's trying to throw in a counter to my bet."

"So don't go." JT shrugged. "But it would be a shame to miss it."

"Oh, I'm going," Blaine said, resolutely. "I'm going and I'm going to sparkle the hell out of a dress. I'm gonna show him he can't charm and woo me out of believing I'm right."

"Uh, okay. But what if he just wants to be around you?"

"Don't be ridiculous. A man like Eric Morales isn't attracted to me."

"But he kissed you."

"Probably just slipped and his lips fell into my forehead." Blaine reasoned.

"You're so weird."

"Maybe you're both wrong. Maybe he's already in love with you and he's taking you to meet his family." Shelly giggled.

"What? No way. That's not funny. Stop laughing, JT."

"Well, you're going to need to go shopping, and I feel like a makeover montage is about to go down." JT laughed. "First is that hair."

"What's wrong with my hair?"

"Nothing, Desperately Seeking Susan. It just might be time for a little trip into this century. And we definitely need to talk about that blue eye shadow."

"But I like the—"

"I know you do. I know it brings you comfort. But I think that in times of war, one must make sacrifices, and I think Aquanet and Cyndi Lauper will understand."

"Why are you so mean?" Blaine couldn't help but laugh.

"I love everything about you. But, girl, this is not the time for plastic bangles and scrunchies."

"Scrunchies are making a comeback."

"You can show Eric Morales that a woman can have a healthy love of the past and still be a part of the future of things." JT interrupted her reasoning.

"Just not his future."

JT paused to raise their eyebrow. "His future?"

"I mean, with the tearing down of the mall and—"

"Don't try to get past that Freudian slip. It's too late. We'll start making a plan as soon as I'm finished with Shelly."

"Which would happen a lot faster if you'd both stop talking," Shelly said with a laugh, and they all started planning how Blaine would go about ruining Eric's plans to sway her onto his side.

Chapter Eleven

Two weeks wasn't a lot of time, and Blaine still had things to do. Her goal now was to convince Eric, even before the museum's grand opening, that Back To The 80s deserved to be saved. And that meant she had to get serious. No more passive strolls through the store, hoping he'd find enough nostalgia to see her side. No. She needed an interactive experience. As many as she could fit in before their "date."

She made some calls to old friends and acquaintances of her mother's. She told herself the other "meetings" weren't excuses to see him again. Not reasons to get close or share space or dark venues with him. But she knew, deep down, that she was just lying to herself. She liked him. She wanted to spend the time with him, and she worried that even if she didn't win the bet, she'd still feel this way about him. And that made it hard to be the tough businesswoman she needed to be to fight the destruction of her shop.

Once she'd called the local indie theater and set up a private screening, she looked online at the local music venues in town and wrote down some dates. She spoke to the ticket sales office, and they had two available tickets, but the price was a little higher than Blaine expected. She looked at the signed concert poster from The

Pointer Sisters. A collector had asked about it last week. They were willing to pay a good price for it. Especially since the lead singer had just passed away. Blaine sighed. One picture to save the shop seemed a small price to pay. She gave the sales agent her credit card number and then sent an email to the collector to arrange for a payment transfer for the poster.

After she packaged it up carefully, in acid-free wrapping and in a secure shipping tube, she called Eric. Expecting a secretary to answer and relay her message to him, it took her brain time to adjust when his deep voice answered, setting off little shivers down her neck.

"Eric Morales, Morales Construction." He sounded hurried, as though he was sorting through the exact details of which brewing vat would be taking over the space where her register now sat.

"Uh . . ." she stuttered and coughed, choking on her spit, and feeling heat rise in her cheeks.

"Hello? Who's this?"

"Yep, I," she coughed again into the crook of her arm and recovered. "Sorry, I was just so surprised you didn't have Loraine vetting your calls, that you startled me."

"Oh, it's you," he said, and she swore she heard his smile break through. The creak of his chair in the background made her picture him leaning back, relaxing now that she was on the phone. She wanted him to lean back when he talked to her. She wanted him to find a reprieve in her voice, just like she found excitement in his. "What can I help you with, Ms. Reynolds?"

"Right, you have to use the full name because you're at the office and they're probably standing over you right now, huh?"

"No."

"No?"

"What is it, *Blaine*," he said her name with a soft rumble that made her toes curl, and she took a moment to reset her brain.

"I have new meeting dates for you, as your super busy developer schedule allows."

"Okay." She heard him clicking on keys, probably opening his schedule. "What did you have in mind?"

"This Sunday at eight a.m."

"8 a.m.? On a Sunday?"

"Yes."

"You're not taking me to church, are you?" She felt the smile in his voice.

"No Hozier—"

"I'm surprised you know any musicians after 1989."

"I'm full of surprises. We're not going to church. While I should probably be praying for a miracle, I don't think I qualify to sit in a pew. You're going to want to wear something comfortable to that meeting."

"Like no tie?"

"Like pajamas."

Silence as he cleared his throat and lowered his voice. "I'm not meeting you in my pajamas."

"Why? Are they Transformer footie pajamas?" she asked.

"I don't own pajamas."

"Wait, you sleep in your suit?"

"I don't sleep in *anything*, Ms. Reynolds." Voice deep and sexy, resonating in her brain. Blaine stammered as the thought played through her brain. Her shop felt somehow too warm, and air seemed too hard to find.

"Oh, I—I see. Um . . . I'm sorry."

"Why? Because now you're thinking about me naked?"

"I am not. Well, now I am." Blaine put the phone to her chest, took a deep breath, and when she came back to the conversation, he was chuckling. "Sunday," she said crisply. "Eight. 1647 Laurel Street."

"Yes, fine. I'll be there."

"With clothes."

"It's your meeting." He chuckled again.

Blaine nearly reconsidered. Would he actually not wear them if she asked? She rolled her eyes and tried to refocus. She cleared her throat and went on.

"Then the following Wednesday night, seven thirty."

"Sure. What's the address?"

Not thinking, she stuttered. "You're—um, picking me up for that one."

"Okay. So what's the address?"

"Right—my home address?"

"Unless I'm picking you up at the shop?"

"Oh, uh, no, my place." Blaine stuttered through her address, and she heard him click a few more buttons.

"Done. Was that all, Ms. Reynolds?"

No. That wasn't all. She didn't want to get off the phone with him. She didn't want to go back to her lonely shop. She wanted to hear him laugh again.

"Unless you have anything else you want to talk to me about?"

He paused. Like maybe there was something. Something he wanted to talk to her about, but he seemed to talk himself out of it and sighed.

"No, I can't think of anything." The tension in his voice said he was lying.

"Are you having a good day?" she said, not knowing why she asked. Except she wondered. He sighed. The chair creaked again, sitting back or forward, she wasn't sure. He made a small grunt, and she pictured him running his hands through his hair, massaging the building tension headache.

"It's been . . . busy and stressful."

"I'm sorry to hear that," she said. "I guess I'm keeping you from it."

"You're giving me a break from it, and I . . ." He paused, dropping his voice. "I like hearing your voice, Blaine. It's like a little island of calm."

She couldn't speak for a moment, and he didn't either.

"I like talking to you, too. I like your laugh," she whispered. "It

makes me smile. Makes me wish I could make you laugh more."
The vulnerability between them was tender and mutual, and
through the silence, she heard him laugh softly.

"Well, knowing you feel happy when I laugh? That's a nice
thought to help me through the rest of this day."

Blaine felt her heart flutter in her chest. "I'm glad it wasn't
Loraine that answered." she smiled.

"I am, too."

She felt it in his words. "I'll see you Sunday." She hung up
before she could tell him any more of the stupid romantic
thoughts that started to fill her head. She wasn't doing a very good
job at separating her feelings. But it sounded like he wasn't, either.

Eric was supposed to work late, going over the specs for the
construction, the scheduling of subcontractors, and writing up a
cost analysis of using a new bidder they were considering. But as he
sat at his desk, staring at the work in neat little to-do tabs in front
of him, all he could think about was her voice, and the way she'd
stumbled over the thought of him naked. She was, he thought with
a small amount of fascination, kind of too sweet to believe. Too
smart and playful and interesting to believe. But he wanted to
believe it. Sunday was only a few days away and already he couldn't
wait. Suddenly, just as he'd told her, she had become a calm place
for him to rest his thoughts.

He looked up from his desk and saw that only his dad and
Loraine's office still had life inside them. Was this their life? All of
it? Didn't Loraine ever want something more? A karate instructor
to come home to? A life outside of the spreadsheets and projects
and meetings? He rubbed his eyes and sighed, leaned back, and
heard a soft knock.

When he opened his eyes, he saw his mother swing into his
office, carrying takeout bags and smiling at him.

"*Buenas noches, mijo,*" she said softly and crossed the room.

She was a small woman, but proud, with beautiful cheekbones and laughing eyes. If Loraine had been quicker to smile, and softer in countenance, they would have looked alike. She brought him a bag. "Your father said you've all worked through dinner. I had a late meeting near Mad Greens so, I hope that's okay. How are you?"

"Too busy. Too much to do. So, same as always, I guess." He stood up to stretch, came around the desk, and planted a kiss on her forehead. It reminded him of the kiss he'd given Blaine, and his features softened.

"You work too hard."

"Not hard enough, according to some." He nodded his head to Loraine's voice filtering through the hallway, on the phone again, even at this hour. His mother waved her hand dismissively.

"That girl forgot how to have fun." Carmen smiled. "Have you, too?"

"I'm—" Eric paused. He thought of the night at the arcade, and the lunch in her shop, and the Sunday morning meeting in pajamas. "I'm finding a little." His mother's face lit up.

"I'm so happy to hear this."

"It's complicating my work schedule, though. I'm sure Papá wishes I'd keep my head in the game."

Carmen grunted and rolled her eyes.

"*Dios mio*. No. This life is so short. Your father works too hard. So hard." Her voice and her eyes turned sad, almost to the point of tears. "He doesn't dance anymore." She shook her head, and Eric leaned against his desk.

"What do you mean by dance?"

"We used to go out dancing," she whispered softly before shaking her head. She planted a kiss on Eric's cheek. "Speaking of, I should go take these to the bulls. They won't remember to eat on their own."

"*Te quiero, Mamá*," he said and kissed her again before she left.

"*Te quiero, hijo*. Find time to dance, okay? For me?"

"Sí, I will." He nodded and took his salad and chicken back around his desk to finish the reports. It made him sad to see his mother cry. She had always been so tough and down to earth that to see her looking back instead of towards the future made him pause. Was she thinking of the trajectory of all their lives, and how they were missing something bigger? He sat down and leaned back. That action alone reminded him of the 80s shopkeeper that had once been a thorn in his side, but who has since turned to something much more.

Did Blaine dance? Of course she did. Probably in her pajamas in the kitchen every morning. Probably in her shop at random intervals when the right song came on. Maybe in a dress, with the right guy. He sighed and looked at his phone. Willing her to call him, just because she wanted to hear his voice. He wanted to hear hers. Sunday was going to take forever to get here.

Chapter Twelve

Blaine arrived early, still a little bleary-eyed, but she wanted to be there to meet him. She hoped he wasn't late. Then again, Eric was a man never late. She sighed and looked down at her pink bunny slippers. They may have been over the top, but she figured a little extra cuteness might go a long way. The front of the theater was quiet, with few souls up this early on a Sunday to go anywhere that didn't have pews. The cool morning air breezed through her pj's and ruffled her ponytail as she looked for his car.

She didn't know where he lived, but it probably wasn't near the older part of town. She was sure he had a swanky loft apartment. Probably with some cold, black-and-white photo art and definitely no color. If anyone needed more color in their life, it was Eric. She watched the light from the sun creep across the red roof of the building and heard the loud purr of his engine a few blocks away and coming closer.

Her heart rate sped up with the anticipation of the morning ahead as she watched him park his car. He got out of his car and smiled at her. At least he wasn't wearing a suit, but he wasn't in his pajamas either. Even his casual clothes, pressed pants, and Morales Construction polo shirt looked businesslike to her. She sighed.

"What is it this time?" Eric said as he approached. "A Van Halen look-alike contest? Tour of the DeLorean? Maybe an 80s karaoke brunch?"

"Wouldn't that be awesome?" She bounced on her feet.

She felt light, and the sunshine on his face made her heart do a strange little flip in her chest. He smiled.

"Sorry, nothing so exciting. You said you have a few hours, right?"

"Yeah, contrary to what you might think about the hard-ass businessman I am, I do actually take Sundays off."

"Good Catholic?"

"Not according to my mother." He shrugged. She smiled up at him.

"Well, I hope I'm not stealing you away from saving your soul."

When he came closer, she didn't back away, and he looked down at her, a mischievous glint in his eyes. "I thought I was a soulless capitalist."

Blaine felt heat rush into her cheeks, and she looked down.

Eric lifted her chin with his thumb and finger to meet his gaze. "Sorry, I know you don't think that."

"I know you're not. I think you have a beautiful soul," she whispered and looked at his lips. "Wrapped in a soulless capitalist suit." The heat dissipated, and he pulled away.

"So? What's today's 80s adventure?"

"Movies."

"Movies?"

"Yeah, I actually pulled a few strings—"

"You pulled strings?"

"I know people too, Morales," she said over her shoulder as she led him to the entrance of the tin-sided movie theater; a relatively new construction from an old venue. The Nabes had been a part of the town for decades, but even it had gotten a facelift. "How much time do you have?"

"All morning? How long will this take?"

"Well, back in the day, my young man, movies were about 90 minutes and there won't be three hours of previews beforehand so, you'll get to see the best selection I can give you."

"I remember movies."

"Yeah, but do you remember the heyday of teen romance?"

"I don't think I was allowed to watch any teen romances," he said.

She turned back to him with a look of shock.

"That's a damn shame, Eric Morales. Come, let me lighten your heart." Blaine reached out and took his hand.

Blaine liked the feeling of his hand in hers, even when he pulled it back to his side as he opened the door for her. The front was uncrowded, and only one attendant was at the ticket counter, which also served as the concession stand.

"Not a very big crowd for the 'best era in cinema'," he noted as she walked past him.

"I told you I called in a few favors. We will have the place to ourselves." She smiled and nodded at the older woman behind the counter.

"Blaine, it's so good to see you. I was happy you called." They gave each other a quick hug over the counter.

"Marylou, this is Eric Morales." Blaine stepped back.

Marylou squinted her eyes up at him. "Ah, yes, I remember your parents back when. They used to be one of my regular Thursday night couples."

"Wait, you know my parents?" Eric's eyebrows shot up.

"Sure. Or I used to. Sounds like they're too busy to go out much these days."

"They do have a lot to do," Eric agreed.

"Self-imposed." Marylou waved him off. "What good is a heap of money if you never have the time to spend it?"

Eric scowled even as she winked at him. Blaine watched the interplay and stepped up between them.

Marylou shrugged her shoulders. "Oh well, you're here now and I'm so glad. What can I get you? A Sunday Special?" Marylou asked Blaine more than him.

"Yes, I was hoping you still did that," Blaine said.

"What's a Sunday Special?" Eric asked.

"You're going to love it."

"How, if I don't know what it is?" he argued.

"Yeesh, have I ever led you astray?"

"Every damn time I'm with you." He shook his head, and both Blaine and Marylou laughed.

"You two go get settled and I'll bring them to you," Marylou said, and Blaine took Eric's hand again to pull him through the swinging door and into the dark and cozy room.

At the front was a large screen, but instead of rows of neat and orderly seats, this one held cozy couches, bean bags, recliners, and even pillows on the floor. If a seven-year-old had invented a movie room, this would no doubt be what it would look like. Eric's grip on Blaine's hand tightened.

"Okay, just follow me," she whispered.

"Why are you whispering, there's no one else here," he whispered back.

"Why are you whispering then?"

"I—" He stopped, and she was pulled back into him, against his chest, and a short, surprised gasp sprung from her throat. Eric smiled, and he pulled her even closer with his other hand. The warmth of his body against the length of hers caused parts of Blaine to melt. She hadn't been this close to someone in a long time.

"What are you doing?" she said and looked up at him.

"Maybe I'm scared of the dark."

She shot him a seductive smile. "Then stay close to me. I'll protect you."

Eric leaned down, but just as their lips were about to meet, Marylou burst into the room.

"Hell-oo! And here we are." They jumped apart and watched as the older woman balanced a tray onto a large ottoman in front of a cozy couch. On the tray were an array of tiny, boxed cereals, a carafe of milk and two bowls with spoons. A bowl of fruit, a plate of donuts, and a couple of coffees completed the breakfast, and she turned back to them.

"Show time in a few minutes. Get settled."

"Thanks Marylou." Blaine looked up at Eric. He looked back at her, and the idea of his warm lips against hers still ran rampant circles in her brain. She took a big breath and sighed it out. She hadn't expected their near-kiss. She hadn't expected wanting it as much as she did. She hadn't expected him. She jumped into the couch with exuberance and patted the seat cushion next to her.

"Come on, I'll even let you pick your cereal first," Blaine said, trying to lighten the mood to be playful in an effort to stop thinking about his lips.

Eric settled into the cushions with a small groan.

"Are you okay?"

"Yeah, I just should have listened better and invested in more comfortable clothes." His eyes scanned her stretchy pants and sweatshirt, and she thought she saw some envy as he did it.

"I told you." She shook her head. "You *should* really start listening to me."

Eric cleared his throat and leaned forward to look at his breakfast options.

"I don't think I've eaten any of this since I stayed at my abuela's house as a kid. She would spoil us by letting us have the stuff Mom wouldn't."

"Sounds like a good grandma."

"She was." His voice turned low, and Blaine watched a sad expression pass over his face. His hands tightened on his knees, his dress pants seemed too confining. His everything seemed too confining to Blaine, and she wished she could loosen him up.

"It's okay to remember things, Eric. It's okay to miss people."

Eric shook his head and glared over his shoulder at her before turning back to the boxes.

"This is all nothing but sugar and carbs." He scrunched his face like he just smelled something awful.

"Right? That's what makes it so good." Blaine smiled and leaned forward to pass him a bowl.

He chose Trix. She let him have it, even though it was her favorite, and settled on Fruity Pebbles herself. The technicolor sea of puffed rice brought her back to Saturday mornings, before she ever knew what her life would be like. When she was going to be an adventurer, a dancer, a pop star—all the things too big to ever reach for. Blaine fought with the small plastic bag and nearly burst it open into a colorful spray of sugar.

"What did you want to be when you were a kid?" She picked a stray pebble off her sweatshirt and popped it into her mouth.

"What? Like what did I think I'd be?"

"No, like what did you *want* to be? Before you were in school or really knew anything about anything," she said.

Blaine sat back and looked at Eric as he poured the milk on his cereal and handed her the carafe. Bowl cradled in his other hand, he cocked his head in thought.

"I can't remember that far back."

Blaine's face turned sad, and the carafe was forgotten in her other hand.

"Come on. I'm sure you can remember at least one thing you wanted to do as a kid." The quiet sound of her pebbles crackling filled the space between them.

He looked down at his bowl, sighed, and sat back. "I used to want to be an architect. To design and build entire spaces. To test the limits of what was already being done, and create something new. I—" he stopped himself and shook his head. "I guess what I do is close enough."

"Close enough? If it's close enough, then maybe you can just start doing what you always dreamed of doing," she said.

Eric stared at her as though she'd lost her mind. The lights dimmed and Blaine cleared her throat.

"Shhh, it's starting." She retreated back into the couch cushions with her bowl. He settled back too as the grainy film began to play and a line of stars swirled around the Paramount mountain. The first spoonful of cereal exploded in sweetness against her tongue, and he grunted next to her. A small drip of milk fell over his bottom lip, and he caught it with the back of his hand.

"See, sugar is good," Blaine whispered as she took another drippy bite of sweet rainbow colors. As the credits began and the synthesizer-heavy rock blared from the theater's new sound system, Blaine shivered with childlike excitement. They finished their cereal, transfixed, and he sat forward to pour them both a cup of coffee.

"How do you want it?" He held up the coffee, voice soft and low, looking back at her. His face was lit by the screen in striking undertones of blue and shadow, and her toes curled into the soft cushions. All the words that came to mind felt dangerous to say. Hot. Dark. Slightly Bitter. Was it coffee or him she was thinking about?

"Blaine?" he asked again.

"Uh, just milk please." He put milk in hers but kept his black.

He barely looked back as he handed her the mug; but she watched him. Of course he would take it black; serious and no frills. Tough and to the point. But she was now seeing the sugary sweet side of him too, showing there wasn't just business in his brain.

Drawn in by the wild clothing and hairstyles, he retreated to his side of the couch. Laughing over arcade games and trying to not glow at his fascination with her 80s music collection was one thing. Being on a cozy couch in the dark, mere feet away from a man whose lips had been warm and soft on her forehead, a man who would cause enormous problems for her future, was a whole different thing. So Blaine pulled her feet in beneath her and decided to focus so intently on the movie that there wasn't room for Eric Morales's lips in her brain.

"What movie is this?" he asked.

"*Sixteen Candles*. Quintessential 80s teen romance."

"If it's quintessential, how is it I've never seen it?"

"I'm sure your mom probably saw it at some point."

"Great, it will give us something to talk about." Eric set his coffee down and threw one arm over the back of the couch, his hand near her shoulder. Blaine bit her lip. She wanted to inch closer, her body interested in making even an innocent touch seem accidental. She kept her hands around the coffee mug and stared into the screen. She could hear him breathing beside her, deep. Even. Relaxed.

"Something strange happens when you watch a movie as an adult that you'd only seen as a kid," she whispered. "Don't you think?"

"What do you mean?" he said and poured another cup of coffee for himself. He turned to offer her more, but she shook her head as she covered the half-empty cup with her hand. Eric snagged a donut and passed her the plate. She took a powdered one.

"Like when you're a kid, you remember the clothing, or the music, or a certain character. You don't really understand most of what's going on. Right?"

"Uh, I guess."

"Take *Grease*, for example."

"*Grease*? The one with John Travolta?"

"Um, is there another *Grease*?" she asked, assured that it was the only one worth seeing. "Yes. As a kid I knew all the words, and loved the clothing, and the music, and characters but when I look back now after watching it and I realize they're talking about sex, and pregnancy, and smoking, and all this stuff that my six-year-old self had no idea about. I even taught myself how to flip a toothpick into my mouth like one of the T-Birds did to hide his cigarette from the principal."

"Now that you mention it, I think I may have gotten slapped by my grandma once for saying 'a hickie from Kenickie is like a Hallmark card'," Eric said. His low chuckle became a full laugh.

"Right, that's why I love watching these movies again. They meant something. You think about *The Breakfast Club,* and the themes of cliques, and rich vs. poor, and nerds vs. jocks. I mean, Anthony Michael Hall was in detention because—"

"Because he brought a gun to school to shoot himself."

They were both quiet. Blaine set her coffee down and watched the screen even as she spoke. "I think they were good commentaries on what was going on. We just don't often see it when it's covered up in so much—"

"Hairspray and taffeta?" Eric nodded towards Molly Ringwald's over-the-top dress. When he looked back at her, his eyes held something deeper. As though he was studying her, seeing her in a new light.

"You're much more complex than I imagined."

"Complex? Don't you mean difficult?"

"No." He shook his head and turned his body towards hers and away from the movie screen. "You're thoughtful and intelligent, and . . ."

"And?" Blaine's heart beat in her chest so loudly she was afraid he could hear it.

"Kissable."

Blaine hugged her knees and bit her lip, unable to answer for a full breath. "Uh, kissable?"

"Yeah." Eric's voice low, his eyes fell to her nose. Then to her lips. He put his coffee cup down and moved one inch closer.

"What exactly do you mean by that?"

"What do you mean, what do I mean by that?" Eric laughed. "Hasn't anyone ever told you that you were kissable?" Even in the low light, his eyes seemed to sparkle when he smiled, and she couldn't look away.

"No."

"Well, then the men of this world are a bunch of liars, Blaine." He slung his arm over the back of the couch again, centimeters from her. Blaine's eyebrows rose and her heart pounded in her chest.

"But surely you don't think that," she whispered.

"I wouldn't have said it if I didn't think so."

"Do you mean you want to kiss me?"

"Maybe I do."

"Maybe?"

"Definitely."

"Oh." She sat back and put her coffee cup down. Eric watched her and sat back, too.

"But, I wouldn't, unless you wanted me to; and maybe you don't."

"Of course I do." The words burst out and she covered her mouth with her hands.

"Oh yeah?"

"I wouldn't have said it if I didn't mean it," she reiterated back to him.

Eric smiled an assured smile and sat back, farther from her. "Well, then I guess that's agreed upon. You're kissable, and I want to kiss you. And you want me to."

"So?"

"So what?"

"So, why aren't you kissing me?"

"Oh, you mean right now?" he teased. Blaine picked up a pillow, hitting him squarely in the side of the head as he laughed.

"You're such a jerk sometimes," she said, unable to not laugh herself as she moved to hit him again. This time, Eric caught her wrist, tugged her gently closer to him, and took her cheek in his other hand.

He leaned down and kissed the top of her nose. "You had powdered sugar on your nose." His hand moved up to gently caress the outside of her thigh, and he pulled her even closer to him on the couch. Blaine's hands found his shoulders, and she clung to his shirt. Warmth and need ran through her body at his sudden closeness.

"I think I got it."

"Is that what constitutes kissing in your world?" She gave him the perfect pout.

"No, Blaine. That was merely a courtesy."

"Could you not be so courteous?" she grumbled. He smiled at her, and Blaine's heart leaped into his hands.

"I can check to see if you have any more on your face."

"I think that's a good idea." Blaine whispered, and her eyes fell to his lips as her hands wound around the back of his neck. Eric's sultry smile and downcast eyes made her whole body feel warm and shaky. She pressed against his hard chest.

"Let me see," he whispered, then placed gentle kisses on the apples of her cheeks and the corners of her mouth. "Hmm, there might be some here." His lips gently pressed against her bottom lip. "So sweet," he whispered.

Before he could pull away, Blaine pulled him in and pressed her lips to his. Her fingers threaded into his hair, and Eric moaned. His hands caressed up her back, and he held her close. He tasted like coffee, and she gasped as their lips parted.

"Eric," she whispered, her voice a breath, a prayer, in the dark theater. He nudged her nose with his and kissed her slower, softer. His warm and strong hand moved up the outside of her thigh, gently up her torso, and cupped her cheek as he continued to kiss her. She made a small, needful noise and shifted closer. His other hand wound around her back and moved up to the soft bun of hair. She felt him loosen it and let his fingers sink into her mess of curls.

The comfort and dark, the quiet of being a world away from

their responsibilities, and her worry made the silence swell with their breath and heat. Just as his hand traced beneath her soft sweatshirt to graze the skin of her low back, the credits began to roll. Eric looked up, his eyes deep and unfocused, his normally perfect hair mussed by her fingers. She nudged his chin with her nose, took a deep breath, and cleared her throat.

"I can't remember the last time I made out on a couch." She smiled. He smiled back.

"Me neither. I'm pretty sure my mom caught me once in my junior year of high school, and I had to go to an extra mass that week." His words were interrupted while trying to catch his breath.

"You *are* a bad Catholic," she laughed.

"Another one?" Marylou's voice cut in from the back of the theater, and Eric jumped. Blaine scooted back to her side of the couch, and she shook her head to clear it.

"Sure, thanks Marylou," Blaine said to the lighted box on the wall behind them. She fixed her hair, bit her lip, and tried to not give into the excited way her body asked for more. More of his hands, his body, his lips. She watched him try to straighten his hair, even though he left his shirt button undone, and he smiled like a naughty schoolboy with her cherry Chapstick on his lips.

She was falling.

No. That wasn't right. It was far too late for that. She had fallen.

"Oh no," she said softly and shook her head.

"What?" he whispered back as Marylou took their tray and left to start another movie.

"I was just thinking . . ."

Eric folded his hands in his lap and looked down at them. He blew out a big breath.

"I know," he said, and she believed he knew exactly what she meant. A small sadness settled between them. As the next movie, *Better Off Dead*, started, he turned to her.

"Can I propose something?" he asked.

"Not another bet," she groaned.

"No." He shook his head and intertwined his fingers. "Can we just . . ."

"What?"

"Can we just take this morning off? From the bet, and the construction, and contracts, and shops, and customers, and parents?" He said it so softly, so sadly, that she stopped trying to build up the wall against how much she cared about him. "Can we just be us?" he asked again.

Blaine looked at him, nervous and fighting his own battles with who knew what kind of expectations. Asking to just be himself with her. Her heart fell even further.

"Absolutely yes." She pulled him close to her.

Snuggling into the couch next to him, she curled her legs up close to his and leaned her head on his shoulder. He sighed contentedly and kissed her forehead before his whole body sank into the couch. Blaine wondered when Eric had last truly relaxed.

"This is nice," he whispered as they watched Lane Myer drying his socks with a hair dryer to the catchy opening credit music.

"Yes it is." She reached up to run her hands through his hair, messing it up for good. They watched the first half this way, and every time he would laugh, it would radiate through her back and up into her throat, and the sound of it made her whole world feel right and full again. When she shifted, he slipped a hand around her waist and leaned in closer to her. He kissed her temple, behind her ear, and her neck. Blaine's fingernails dug into his shoulder and she gasped.

"Do you think Marylou is in the booth?" he asked quietly.

"It's possible."

"Probably not the best time for me to lay you down, then."

"Probably not. I'd hate to lose my Sunday Special privileges." She smiled into his lips.

Eric chuckled and pulled her to the couch to spoon her from

behind as they resumed watching the movie. They stayed silent, though his hand gently traced up and down her leg meditatively. The length of his hard body pressed against her soft curves made her wish Marylou was not in the booth. That they were some place private. She snuggled closer into him and felt his similar desire against the curve of her bottom. He grunted with a laugh.

"Keep that up and we'll both lose our Sunday Special privileges. And I'll have to go to a lot of masses."

Blaine laughed and pulled his arm around her shoulders. They settled in and watched poor Lane's attempts at killing himself over his terrible ex-girlfriend.

"Ever love someone that much?" Blaine asked.

"No, I haven't had a lot of time for girlfriends. You?"

"No. I haven't had a lot of girlfriends either," she giggled. "Or boyfriends. It was me and my mom for so long. Then when she passed away, I just got busy with the shop and there's not a lot of people who—"

"Can stand so much 80s?" He kissed her cheek sympathetically.

"Can *appreciate* the nature of my work," she corrected and pinched his thigh. They were quiet for a moment, and he pressed a warm kiss to her neck, sending a wave of shivers through her body.

"I appreciate it, Blaine," he whispered before nuzzling her neck and causing her to wriggle closer to him. He inhaled sharply as they both felt his body react to her soft backside pressing up against him. "I appreciate all of you a little too much." He sighed. "I don't know how much of this torture I can stand."

"Stand it just a little longer," she whispered back and stilled her body. She wrapped his arm close across her chest and let her eyes close to the warmth and safety. When was the last time she'd just been held?

Her eyes fluttered open when his deep laugh shook through her back as they watched Lane dressed in sheets, looking for a match to light himself on fire. Shortly after, they were both chuckling as Ricky's mom accidentally drank turpentine, thinking it was booze, and chased it with a cigarette.

They didn't say much else, focusing on the movie and trying to not get too excited in public; the comfort of each other's company helped to temper their self-control. When the final credits rolled and the story's two lovers sat on the hood of the "tasty" Camaro in the middle of what used to be Dodger Stadium, he sighed and kissed her.

"Did you fall asleep?" he asked.

"Almost. I'm just so warm." She paused and kissed his forearm still across her chest. "I can't remember when I felt so . . ." Words failed her, and she shook her head.

Eric sat up and tried to fix his hair. She sat up too. Both of them were a snuggly mess.

"Felt so what?" he asked. "Happy?" Eric leaned over, kissed her, and gently smoothed her hair from her face. "Me too, Blaine."

"Okay, I have one or two more in the can if you want." Marylou's voice came from somewhere in the magical booth above.

Blaine and Eric looked at one another. His eyes fell, and she looked away. She wasn't sure if he was battling the urge to stay or the guilt to go. She didn't want to be the reason he felt bad.

"Maybe we should call it a morning?" she said.

"Yeah, you're probably right." Eric nodded, and they both stood up and stretched

Blaine looked back at the booth. "I think we'll call it a day! Thank you, Marylou!"

They both slipped their shoes back on, and when they turned to leave, Eric stopped. He looked like he wanted to pull her in and make the moment last just a little while longer. She wished he would.

"What am I going to do for the rest of this day?" he said and shook his head.

She smiled up at him and thought the same thing. Everything

without them together, warm and close, seemed like an empty and pointless endeavor.

"I have some ideas, but it would only make you have to go to confession later." She lifted her eyebrows, and he laughed, pulling her into his arms, and held her for a moment.

"So, what's the next great adventure up Blaine Reynolds's sleeve?" He pulled away, and his hands traced down her arms to find her hands. Their fingers interlaced.

"Well, next Wednesday, I guess. But it's a surprise and I won't ruin it. Do you still want to go?"

"Absolutely, I'll be there."

"But what if some big meeting comes up or you get called away?"

"I'll be there." He lowered his head to hers and kissed her sweetly.

"Eric, what's going to happen?" Blaine's heart felt like it was in her throat as he pulled away.

"Let's not worry about it now. Please." His eyes were deep, and his mouth fell into a frown.

"I can't help it, I—"

"I know." He squeezed her hand. "I'll see you next Wednesday. I'm picking you up, right?"

She'd forgotten that she'd given him her address. The thought of him coming to her house, after the intimacy they'd just shared, made her conjure up all kinds of different scenarios than a concert.

"You don't mind picking me up?" she asked.

He smiled and a mischievous look lit his face.

"Not at all." He wrapped his arms around her waist. He lifted her off the floor, and she laughed.

"No, next Wednesday."

"Of course," he said and kissed her quickly, deeply, and pulled away. "Wednesday. Seems a long time from now."

"Yeah, it does," she whispered.

"What happens if I run into an 80s emergency before then?

Like, what if I'm working through some engineering specs and I need to know how many gigawatts the DeLorean needs to—"

"1.21, obviously." She cut him off and a strange, sweet smile spread across his face. He kissed her again. "You can call or text me anytime. I'll be your go-to expert."

"Thanks for today, Blaine. I wish I didn't have to go, but I have lunch with my family."

"Oh. Of course, you should go. I…" The heavy weight of loneliness settled in her belly. She had a guinea pig at home. But not much else. No family left. "Thank you for coming. For the morning off."

He kissed her cheek, squeezed her hands, and nodded.

"The pleasure was mine." He let go of her hand, then left through the large swinging door before Marylou could even light up the theater. Blaine's heart felt heavy and confused. She stood still in the empty theater and thought of the morning spent in his arms and how it had changed everything. And yet, maybe not enough. She only had a short amount of time to make him see the value of her life's work. He said he appreciated it. But would that be enough to save the shop? What would they do with this new and tender attraction once it was all over? How could she have let herself muddy the waters of their arrangement?

She touched her lips, still warm and sensitive. Her body felt like it had awoken from a long and lonely sleep. The way his laughter still rumbled through her body. The way his eyes turned sad as he'd asked to just be himself today. She wished she'd never made that bet. She wished they'd met under different circumstances. She wished he was just a man she could spend her Sundays with and bring joy to his over-hectic life. And he could bring her laughter and kisses, and the grounding presence of someone who knew about love, and loyalty, and hard work.

Her eyes teared up at the unfortunate moment that Marylou came back in.

"Oh dear. What happened?"

"Nothing. And everything. I don't know."

"I've never seen you so upset, Blaine. Are you okay?"

"I'm just so . . ."

"Troubled?" Marylou asked.

"Yeah, I am." Blaine sniffed, and she thought she heard the retreating sound of his car's engine as he sped away, back across town to his family's expensive home. She needed to either get her head in the game or get out of the bet. Living in between was going to kill her.

Chapter Thirteen

Eric drove away reluctantly, hoping that she'd come through the swinging doors of the theater to look for his retreating car. He'd stop. For her, he'd stop and go back. God, her lips, he thought, and almost hit the curb. The sweet, supple warmth of her snuggled on that couch next to him. He'd had girlfriends before, but never ones that made him feel all at once at ease and on fire. He closed his eyes as he pulled up to the stoplight; the way she'd pulled him into the kiss, the unreserved way she offered those delicious lips of hers. Someone honked behind him, and he bolted back to reality. He wished she'd come out of the theater. He would have gone back.

But she didn't, and he had places to go. He was supposed to be at his parents' house twenty minutes ago, and he knew Loraine would have words for him for being late. He felt his shoulders creep up to his ears and his hands clench around the wheel. He'd never been tense around his family before. Or maybe it was that he hadn't noticed, because he'd never had anything else to compare it to. Before he could get to his side of town, he decided that he had to tell Blaine about the amendment in the contract if they were ever going to be intimate. It wouldn't be fair or right otherwise.

When Eric drove the ten minutes to the other side of town,

and the gated community where the expensive family home sat, he thought about all the ways she'd changed his life and his way of thinking in the short time they had known each other. Not so much the 80s, though the era had grown on him, but the way she lit up a room and made him unwind, just by being herself. There were so many expectations put on him from his family, the business, the community. Morales Construction wasn't just a successful company, it was a company that was expected to keep up with the breakneck pace of always being on top in terms of the expansion of the town and innovative projects. With Blaine, he could just be Eric. He could laugh and let go. But as with anything in his life, business got in the way. Those stolen moments of just letting go and being himself weren't going to last long. His family was going to come in with all its power and money and kick her to the curb.

As he pulled into the cobbled circular drive and shut off the engine in front of his family home, he was overcome with the feeling that it was less like a home these days. That, coupled with the worry of what would happen between him and Blaine, and the encroaching destruction of the Marshall Mall, put him in a foul mood even before he reached the front door.

The house was quiet inside. The grand formal entry, marble floors, and sweeping staircase was meant to impress from the moment guests walked in—but it was also cold, and his footsteps echoed as he walked past the flower graced side tables. In the back, near the kitchen and dining room, he could hear Loraine's voice and his mother's. Eric took a deep breath and closed his eyes. For a brief moment, he could feel Blaine's arms around him and his heart rate slowed. How'd he get so caught up so fast? He was almost afraid to walk into the kitchen, as though it might break the spell he'd been under all morning. The sparkly, happy, Blaine bubble.

"*Mijo*? Is that you?" His mother called out, and he had no other choice but to join the party. "We were worried."

"Where have you been? Did you sleep in?" Loraine said, and despite her harsh tone, she immediately began serving him a plate. Their father sat at the table, going over contracts on his iPad.

"I thought we weren't allowed to work on Sundays," Eric chided him as he took the plate from Loraine.

"Well, you weren't here, so I figured I could get something done while we waited," John's eyebrow lifted in a subtle reprimand and Eric looked down.

"Sorry. I got caught up."

"Doing what on a Sunday morning?" Loraine asked, as though she already had an idea.

"I was watching a movie."

"A movie?" she responded, crossed her arms over her chest, and leaned back. "What movie?"

"What does it matter?"

"It must have been very good to have forgotten you had your family waiting for you."

"Loraine. Give the man a break. I'm sure he just needed some downtime." Their mother came around, poured their dad another cup of coffee, and sat down with the rest of the family over the meal.

"What movie?" she asked again, ignoring her mother.

"*Sixteen Candles.*"

Silence descended over the table, and they all looked at Eric with brows drawn in.

"*Sixteen* what?" Loraine stuttered. "I know I didn't hear that right."

"And then *Better Off Dead* afterwards. I think I was more partial to that one."

"Ay." John sat back and smiled. "The Camaro is so . . ."

"Tasty?" Eric smiled over his first bite. Loraine looked between them and rolled her eyes. Carmen smiled.

"I didn't think you'd remember that movie," she said to John, and a small, warm moment passed between them. John put down his iPad, took Carmen's hand in his, kissed the back of it, and Eric's world paused.

"I remember, *Cariña*. You made me go watch it with you, and I remember thinking I'd never be able to woo you until I learned to play the saxophone." He smiled, and Carmen giggled, and the mood of the table lifted to something strange and sweet. Eric sat back, unable to help smiling himself. Loraine glared at him over her plate.

"Well, I'm glad you have free time," she grumbled. "You'll be working extra hard this next week if you plan to get all the contracts finalized."

"It's Sunday morning. I have free time on a Sunday, the same as you, Loraine. You should try to take up a hobby outside of work, you know?"

"Oh, is that so? You know so much about me?"

"Yeah, something to work out your aggression. Like, maybe take up karate." Eric shrugged and shot her a crooked grin as he chewed his first few bites. Sunday brunch tasted better today.

Loraine's face erupted in a blush, and she picked up her fork to attack the plate.

"You're an idiot," she grumbled.

"I know a guy, if you want a recommendation." Eric pressed, and Loraine nearly dropped her fork. Or threw it at him.

John grinned. "Do you two have your clothes for the museum opening?"

Eric was reluctant to think about it. No one knew who he'd be bringing. He kept his mouth shut and listened as Loraine talked about her dress and possibly taking some guy from Accounting. He mused what it would look like if she showed up with Sensei Williams on her arm instead. Wouldn't that make his date seem tame?

· · ·

Blaine didn't want to go back to her shop, so she went home. She called JT and asked them to come over. While she waited, she cleaned out Charles Dumar's pen, fed him, and pet him while she relived the moments alone with Eric in the dark theater. JT showed up an hour later, a six-pack of beer in one hand and a bucket of KFC in the other.

"I figured it's been a while since we slummed it. Perfect for a Sunday afternoon," they said with a smile and pushed past Blaine on their way to eat in the kitchen. "So? How did the movies go?"

Blaine stared at them, shrugged nonchalantly, and tried to decide how much to say.

"It was . . . good?"

"Just good? Did he swoon with the romance? Fall to your knees and beg for forgiveness for his folly? Ask you to marry him?"

"No. God, you're awful. When did you become the hopeless romantic?"

"When I saw the way he was looking at you over your horchata," JT said and doled out a beer and a paper plate full of chicken, biscuits, and mashed potatoes.

"Really? You saw it then?"

"Yeah. His eyes just got sort of dreamy, and he fidgeted with his hands. You don't remember that? The only reason I think you have a chance is that the guy has been head over heels for you before he even knew it. So, tell me, for reals, what happened this morning?"

Blaine recounted the morning, in breathless detail, to the point that JT began fanning themselves with a napkin and took an extra-long swig of the cheap Coors.

"Girl! Are you serious?" They laughed. "So what? The bet is off? Obviously, you can't keep up with it after this line has been crossed. When do you see him again? Why aren't you two shacking up right now?" The playful questions came rapid fire, and Blaine was lost to the confusion and hope in her heart.

"The bet is still on. I have until the end of the month and I'm trying not to get my hopes up too high. Whether he likes me or not, six million dollars is a lot of money and he has a lot at stake in the project when it comes to his career. I just don't know what to do. He had to go to lunch with his parents. God, what if," she paused, picked at her chicken and sighed, "what if he's using me? What if he's just seducing me so that I'll give up?"

JT took a moment, studied Blaine's downcast eyes, and cleared their throat. "I don't think so. I think, if anything, he's probably just as confused and worried as you are. I don't get the vibe from him that he's some cold, heartless guy looking to take advantage wherever he can to get ahead. I don't think he expected you."

"I didn't expect him either." Blaine sniffed.

"The beginning of every great love story." JT clutched at their chest dramatically, and Blaine threw a piece of biscuit at them.

"Stop! You're incorrigible."

"One of us has to be. Like good cop/bad cop, only flighty romantic/stern pessimist." JT smiled back. "It's going to work out, Blaine. In the end. Everything always does."

Blaine smiled and nodded, though she really wasn't so sure this time.

Chapter Fourteen

"What do you mean, you're going out? Going out where? We can order food in." Loraine stood at his office door with a scowl on her face. "It's a Wednesday. No one goes out on a Wednesday."

"I wasn't aware there was a law against leaving the office after work to go out. I'll have to look into that later. For now, I'm going out. Maybe for dinner, not just takeout behind my desk, and then who knows?" Eric enjoyed how Loraine seemed to get angrier the more he explained the perks of being an adult.

"With a client?" she asked, still confused.

Eric wondered how careful he should be about his next words. Blaine wasn't a client, not really, not anymore. But she wasn't his girlfriend. Not exactly. What were they? Friends? Not-yet lovers? His neck felt hot, and he thought of her body pressed against his in the dark of the theater, soft, warm curves, smelling of sugar and coffee. He cleared his throat. Certainly not lovers. That would muddy their bet, wouldn't it? Especially since he hadn't told her about the amendment in the contract yet.

"No, not with a client. Just a friend."

"Since when do you have time for friends? What friend?" Loraine leaned against his doorjamb and crossed her arms in front of her, a model of tension and suspicion. She tapped a heeled foot on the floor.

"Not every dinner needs to end in a contract or a deal."

"Oh, I see. So, it's ending in sex then?"

"Loraine! *Dios*, you don't need to talk like that," he reprimanded, but she only glared in response.

"Well, Mom and Dad will be happy if one of us is looking at giving them grandchildren," she scoffed and looked at her nails. "I'm glad you have so much time on your hands." The dig, looking down her nose yet again at his work ethic, riled him enough to stand and tap his files against the desk into a neat line.

"It's not like that. It's just a night. And I don't have any more time on my hands than you do. I just choose to spend it differently."

"What is with you lately? Lunch in the poor part of town, complete with Styrofoam cups? Rolling in late for Sunday lunch last week? Looking, if I may say, bed messy. Ever since this strip mall project and that asinine bet you made with that crazy girl, you've been unfocused and—"

"And what?"

"Well, I don't know. It's like you're too . . . happy." The word died off on her lips as if she just realized what she'd said.

"I'm too happy?"

"You know what I mean."

"I'm not sure I do, Loraine. Are you saying you don't want me to be happy?"

She rolled her eyes. "Of course I want you to be happy. I just don't want you tanking a six-million-dollar project over some dime-store shop owner. I'm not an idiot, and neither is Papa, Eric. He will find out."

Eric huffed. "She's not just some—"

"You know that shop has no future, right? There's no hope for it ever making a decent profit. She'd be better off taking her stuff to an auction. I'm sure there's plenty of people around the country looking for weird-ass pieces of 80s pop culture. It could make her a nice little new start if she just sold it all."

"It's not always about the money!" Eric yelled and they both stopped to stare at one another.

"Are you insane? This is your chance to finally make partner. So you won't have to bust your ass on site every week. So you can settle down. Go on dates. Start a life."

"I don't need to make partner to do those things."

"A wife wants stability and income."

"We don't live in the fifties, Loraine. Who says I want a wife? And if I did, it's none of your business what she'd want."

Loraine looked at him sideways. "You're going on an actual date with her, aren't you? I heard Carlos telling Janice in Accounting that he saw you at some pinball arcade? Unless you're planning on investing in it. Was that another 'friend' meeting or was it a date too?" Her anger rose.

"Loraine, this is ridiculous. People go on dates."

"People do. We don't. Get your head in the game." She turned and left. Eric watched her go and turned back to his window.

He adjusted his tie in the reflection before shifting his focus to look across the city. Not many tall buildings existed in Marshall. Morales Construction owned the tallest one. A view of their town, the domain of their enterprise. The future of their family.

But what kind of future would there be for their family if the only thing any one of them ever did was work? He thought back to the conversation he had with his mother Sunday afternoon after his movie date with Blaine. She'd spoken of how his father used to be different. The small sadness in his mother's eyes when she'd whispered, "It wasn't always this way."

When Eric had asked, "You mean you and Dad used to be poor?" She shook her head and touched his cheek.

"No, *mijo*, we used to work to live, not the other way around. We even used to have time to go see movies, and go on hikes and out dancing." Carmen's eyes had turned far away.

"Dad dances?"

"He used to. We used to."

Eric tightened his tie. His dad used to dance. They used to go out and live. And have children and raise a family. Now they had the business, and the projects, and the work. He paused and watched the city start to light up in the early dusk. He wondered if some of his sister's drive and hard-lining everything had anything to do with the fear of being poor, or was it that she didn't know anything else but work? Didn't Loraine ever get lonely? He had a passing thought of Sensei Williams, and what would happen if Loraine wasn't so busy all the time. Could she find joy in something more than work?

He turned south and searched out the main road that led to the Marshall Mall, where a quirky little shop owner was probably just flipping over her sign, happy from a day of exciting new finds and selling joy to people in the form of their childhood memories. Maybe she was smiling as she drove in her beat-up Ford Escort the two miles to her home to get ready. Maybe she was excited to see him. Maybe it *was* a date.

Or maybe this whole thing was just a huge, fantastical mistake. He couldn't turn the course of the company's plans. He couldn't stop this thing from coming, but he'd promised he'd try if she convinced him. And she was slowly, in charming and laughing ways, gaining ground. Eric's stomach fell and tumbled.

When he left the office, he didn't stop to say good night to Loraine, or his dad, who was still on the phone. He took his jacket and satchel and decided on the stairs instead of the elevator. He hoped Blaine had something distracting in mind. He could use the levity. The museum night was quickly approaching, and he wanted her to feel comfortable with him in the middle of his family. The undercurrent of hope ran through his skin that maybe tonight they could pick up where they had left off Sunday morning. With no sweet old ladies in booths above them, or time constraints, or sisters shouting warnings to not chase after your heart. Eric sighed . . . his heart. He was reluctant to admit that Blaine Reynolds had taken up a space there, and he had no desire to evict her.

Blaine teetered on one high heel, like a flamingo in front of her mirror. Not sure about that shoe choice, she switched legs, where the only other pair of high heels she owned got its chance to convince her. She switched again.

"Ugh. Why don't I have more shoes?" she yelled. JT's voice came from where they were sprawled across Blaine's bed with an old copy of Mad Magazine in hand.

"Because you don't believe in that capitalist machine bullshit?"

"Because I'm too poor to afford more than two pairs of high heels, and too practical to make high heels a priority in my budget when I never wear them."

"Well, there's that too. Practically poor. Let me see what you've got." JT groaned as they fumbled off the bed and straightened their bright purple hair to sling it to the other side of the mohawk. They leaned against the bathroom door, arms crossed, and biting their lip at the sight.

"Uh, where's he taking you? The Putnam County Fair?"

"What's that supposed to mean? You know where I'm taking him."

"It's just a little . . . small house on the prairie."

"That's Little House on the Prairie, and it's not."

"Then what's up with that dowdy collar and the print? Are you a schoolmarm?"

"You are absolutely no help at all."

"I disagree."

JT, whipping a pair of small scissors out from their belt,

snipped them twice in the air menacingly and wiggled their eyebrows.

"What are you doing?"

"Just trust me. It will only make things better."

They raised the hem above her knees by about a foot, and took off the collar and nearly puffed sleeves with deft precision. JT made quick work of the extra material to fashion a waist cinch from a few safety pins in the bathroom drawer. Then, looking not quite pleased with the ensemble yet, they took off the black leather vest they wore, and put it over the dress, buttoning it tight below the plunging neckline. Blaine gasped when she looked down at her own cleavage.

"Honey, you've got them. You need to embrace them."

"But I don't want to be just eye candy."

"To Eric? Yeah, you do. Besides, he's so taken with the good girl persona, this will rock his contracts off."

"I don't know."

"Is this a date?"

"We haven't really talked about it like that. It's just part of the thing, I guess."

"Part of 'the thing'? Didn't he get all snuggly at the movies with you?"

"Yes."

"And by 'snuggly' I mean, hot and bothered and nearly taking you all the way right there with Marylou in the next room?"

"JT!" Blaine blushed.

"And now, less than a week away from the end of 'this thing,' he's going out with you to a pre-agreed upon venue for food and music?"

"Yeah?"

"Um, that sounds like a date."

"He could just be planning to change the terms again," she said and adjusted her collar to try to pull it up.

"Then you should definitely put that back," JT pulled the neckline back down again.

"What about the shoes?" She faced JT, who studied the plain and practical choices and screwed up their mouth in disgust.

"Absolutely not. Neither. Wear your Chucks."

"With a dress?"

"Yes, and put your hair up."

"But why?"

"Because your neck."

"What about my neck?" Blaine touched it self-consciously.

"Jesus, have you ever been on a date?" JT sighed, turned Blaine to face the mirror, and gathered up her hair. They twisted it into a messy bun and secured it with a tie and a few pins. Some of the curls fell romantically around her face.

"Wow, how did you do that?"

"Kinda my job, girl." JT smiled over Blaine's shoulder in the reflection. "Go get him, tiger. And by 'get him,' I mean get laid. Eric Morales's ass shouldn't be wasted on meetings."

"JT." Blaine laughed and bumped them with her hip. She would be lying if she said she hadn't been thinking about it, and wondered if this night would end in something more. It probably wouldn't be a wise choice, given the nature of their relationship. But sometimes the heart and body don't always make wise choices. It doesn't necessarily mean they're wrong ones.

At exactly seven thirty and not a minute before or after, Eric knocked on her door, and she stood with her hand on the lock for a brief second. Her heart raced and her skin felt warm. She let out a deep breath and opened the door. He stood there in a suit, smiling. His tie was loosened, as if he'd just come from the office. Why'd he have to still smell so good after a long day? She wanted to press her nose into his chest like they had on the couch.

"Good evening," he nodded.

"Hey," she said. Why did her voice sound husky? What in the

hell was wrong with her? Wasn't he still the enemy? No, she thought. Not anymore.

"You okay?" His concerned eyes left her face and fell to the bodice of her dress. "You look," he swallowed and took in a breath, "um, good. Pretty. Pretty good." He looked down the street, away from her breasts.

"Pretty good? What happened to your stunning vocabulary?" she leaned forward, making it even harder for him to ignore them, and whispered, "Was it lost in my boobs?"

"What? No." Eric blushed, put his hand to his mouth, turned away, then turned back, composed. "I'm fine. You look fine," he stuttered and looked down again.

"Fine?"

"Can we just go?"

"Uh, I dunno, do you have room in that fancy little sports car for me and the twins?" Blaine laughed.

"The who? *Dios*, you're awful." He shook his head. "I'm sure we'll find a way to make sure no one is left behind."

Blaine laughed full and sweet, and he seemed to relax.

"Let me just get my purse, and then I'll give you directions as we go."

"Where are you taking me this time? Please say it has something to do with you pretending you're Tawny Kitaen on the hood of my car."

She looked at him sideways. "Why, Eric Morales, are you a secret fan of Whitesnake?"

"I certainly remember that video playing once or twice before MTV stopped playing it. It was influential to a young man." His voice was low as he leaned closer. Blaine's cheeks felt hot, and she smiled as she looked at his lips.

"Sounds like you might be ready to be on my side," she said softly.

He moved in closer. "Let's not pick sides tonight," he whispered and kissed her.

Blaine pressed into the warmth of his lips as his hands fell to her small, leather-bound waist and held on tightly. She felt his broad chest against her, and her hands wove around his neck. She sighed and trembled when his hand fell below her waist to caress her backside, pulling her tighter against him.

"Blaine," he whispered against her cheek.

"Hmm?" She nuzzled under his chin and kissed his jawline.

"*Cariña*, we'll never make it anywhere if you don't behave." His voice was low beneath her ear.

Blaine shivered and bit his jaw lightly. The word *carina* was a loving nickname. Someone he cared for. Wanted. Desired. Her hands threaded into his hair, and she bit his lip before kissing him.

"Last time I checked, it takes two to misbehave properly." She smiled. They both came out of it, breathless, and the heat of their skin blossoming between them. Her hand fell to his chest, and she felt the beating of his heart. She wanted to pull him into her bed by his loosened tie and slam the door on the world outside.

"Suddenly I don't remember where we were going," she said and her fingers toyed with his tie, still entertaining the idea.

"We could stay." He kissed her again, nearly lifting her off her feet.

Blaine felt his need press against her hip and nearly lost all sense of reason.

"But I have tickets and it took selling one of my favorite pieces to pay for them," she whispered between his kisses.

Eric pulled back to look at her. Something in his features changed. As if the thought of spending that kind of percentage of your paycheck, giving up something meaningful for time with him, meant it was a big deal.

"Okay, Blaine." He swallowed, set her back down, and fixed his messed-up hair. "I promise I'll try to keep my hands to myself." He held them up in a show of faith.

She stuck her lip out in a pout.

"Well, you don't have to do that all night. Just until we get there safely." She kissed his cheek and sprung away to go find her purse.

Purse in hand, she bounced back through the door. "Let's go."

She gave him a gentle shove so she could lock it. Then he led her to the car and opened her door. She raised an eyebrow at the clean and sleek lines of the jet-black Camaro. "I hope you don't miss the irony that this is the same car Lane Myer drives in *Better Off Dead*."

"Well," Eric shrugged. "It is the newer version. But, yeah, I did notice that, in between kissing you on the couch."

"That's a pretty fancy car."

"Success has afforded me some perks."

Blaine's smile faded a little. What would it cost his family's business to not be able to build the brewery? They'd certainly survive it financially, but would he survive the consequences? She hesitated at the door, unsure.

"Hey. Don't look like that. It's actually quite comfortable, despite being small."

She ducked to crawl in, and swung her feet in.

He smiled. "Nice Chucks."

Blaine looked at him and down to where his expensive shoes must be mocking her, but instead she saw red high top Converse beneath his suit pants.

"Those don't seem dress-code appropriate for an office." She smiled.

"My sister hates them, and my dad really doesn't care." He shrugged. "We have to keep some sense of rebellion, right?"

She smiled up at him and wished she wasn't stuck in the ground-level seat so she could jump up and kiss him.

"How very Twisted Sister of you." She reached for her seat belt, and he closed the door.

Running around to the other side, he opened his door, slung off his jacket, and dumped it into the back seat before getting in. When he slid into the driver's side, it seemed to fit him like a glove, and she wondered how a guy his size could be comfortable in such a small space. But his eyes lit up when he started the engine, and Blaine's picture of Eric filled out even more. A rebellious streak mixed with a secret sense of playfulness. A man who liked to go fast and be in control of power. As the car sped down her street, she gave him simple directions, but not the destination. She still wanted to give him somewhat of a surprise. He shifted smoothly as the car sped up down the short streets, and his hand found her bare knee in between, as if it was a comfortable place to land. His fingers were warm as they caressed her leg distractedly.

"One more right up here." Her body melted into his touch before he moved his hand to downshift into the turn. "Then park to the left if you can find anything."

She felt breathless from the speed and the way his fingers had gradually moved up to her inner thigh. Eric's hands left her to parallel park in front of a meter. How he always found parking was beyond her. Maybe he had the touch. He certainly had some kind of touch, she thought, as his hand returned to her thigh while he looked out the windows to see where they were. She looked down at his roving fingers and smiled. He turned back, then looked at them too.

"Sorry. I didn't even realize I was—" He pulled his hand away, but she put it back.

"I don't mind. I would have said so."

"I would have stopped," he said quietly. "Blaine, this thing between us." He paused to breathe. "After Sunday, I can't stop thinking about you and I and . . ."

"And?" she led, her hand gently guiding his up the inside of her thigh. He closed his eyes and leaned closer.

"And all the things I'd like to—" He kissed her cheek, her chin, the corner of her mouth. His foot slipped off the brake, and the car lurched forward. He quickly returned his hands to the wheel and recovered before bumping the car in front of them. Blaine's heart rate shot up, and she chuckled. It was comforting to know he could be just as riled up and confused as she was.

"Do to me?" she finished.

Eric put the car in park, pulled the brake for good measure, and rested his forehead on the steering wheel for a moment, taking a deep breath.

"Not *to* you, Blaine." He shook his head against the wheel. "*With* you."

"It's complicated. I know," she said. "I wish it weren't so..." she took her own deep breath and looked out onto the city street, lit up and bustling with people. "So complicated."

"I just want to enjoy being with you and whatever it is you're dragging me into, without feeling so torn," he sighed.

Blaine reached out to smooth his hair away, a comforting gesture her mother had done many times. He pressed into her hand, as if he didn't get touched nearly enough.

"I don't want you to feel torn," she whispered. "Let's not think about the bet tonight. Let's just be us," she said, reiterating the morning of the movies.

"Like a date?" He looked over at her.

"Yeah, like a date."

"Deal." He smiled and took his keys before getting out. Blaine extracted herself with some effort, and probably inadvertently flashed her panties to the public trying to get out before Eric could come around to help.

"So?" he gestured around to the charming downtown.

At that moment, they heard the low beat of music coming from up the block. Blaine pointed both fingers in the same direction.

"You actually get credit for the idea. The other day you'd said something about an 80s cover band, and it just so happens there's a great one from Marshall and they play almost every week."

"Every week?" Eric seemed shocked.

"Don't underestimate the power of 80s music to bring people out."

He took her hand as they walked down the sidewalk. The music got louder, and the crowd grew in size on the less-busy side street of the old downtown. Sandwiched between buildings, the unassuming red brick building was plain except for an outdated marquee advertising the local and indie bands for that week. Eric kept his hand around hers, and his broad body maneuvered easily up through the line. The ticket person smiled, said hello to Blaine, and waved them in.

"It's like you know everyone." He grinned at her.

"Maybe I do." She raised an eyebrow at him.

He brought her fingers up to his lips and kissed them.

As they walked down the dark hallway to the back of the building, the music became loud and bright. The hall opened up to a small venue, and three sections of seats spread up from a small stage where the members of a brightly dressed band were deep into a cover of, "Anyway You Want It".

Eric rolled his eyes and groaned. "Journey? Really?"

"Come on! The quintessential pop band of the 80s."

"What about Wham!?" he teased.

She glanced up at him, heart in her eyes. "What about Wham!, indeed," she said to herself.

"I'm going to need a drink if this is going to go on all night." He led her to the bar, where they ordered from the limited menu. She had a rum and Coke, he took a Jack and Coke, and they moved through the crowd to get a little closer. The Journey song ended and a Bon Jovi song started up.

Eric nodded his head. "Now this, I can stand."

"You know, Bon Jovi had some of the sappiest love ballads in the 80s, right?" she sipped her Coke with a smile.

He smiled down at her. "*Always*." He nodded, and she laughed, nearly spitting out her drink.

"You're a closet fan of the 80s and you can't hide that from me now."

"You got me." He shrugged. "I used to raid my mom's tape collection. Bon Jovi, Def Leppard, The Jets, Alice Cooper—"

"Your mom listened to Alice Cooper?" Blaine interrupted, shocked.

Eric laughed at her expression and nodded. "He seems all hard core, but if you listen to the lyrics of some of his songs, they're really kind of romantic. Her favorite, by far, though, was Gloria Estefan."

Blaine remembered his fascination with the photo, ticket stub, and bracelet. He hadn't just been reliving his own memories, but remembering how much the music had meant to his mother. She suddenly wanted to meet the woman who had raised Eric. She had a suspicion that he was a lot like her. She watched him settle in, standing along with the rest of the crowd, swaying to the beat, and even singing softly to the refrain.

"They do take requests," she said in a lull between sets and nudged him.

His free hand went around her waist. A comforting warmth filled her body, and she leaned against him.

"I have no desire to ask for 'Careless Whisper'." He shook his head, and she broke out in a laugh.

"Fair, but I have one." She reached up on tiptoes, kissed his cheek, and ran to the stage, garnering the attention of the bassist, who talked with her, his wild, dark locks bobbing as he nodded. He stepped away, conferred with the band, and within a couple of minutes, the beginning beat struck up, slow with a certain sad intensity. As soon as he recognized it, Eric smiled down at her, boyish and sweet for a moment, a person apart from the pressures of his day-to-day life. He put his drink down on a nearby table and took her hand. Standing in the middle of the aisle, while other people swayed around them, he put his forehead down to hers and nudged her nose. The singer began in low and melodic tones.

Who's gonna tell you when, it's too late?
Who's gonna tell you things, aren't so great?

"I love this one," she whispered and put her ear to his chest.

His hands went around her waist, and they danced in slow circles, bodies pressed together, and the world was locked outside, far away from the beating of their hearts. He pulled away, tipped her chin up, and kissed her, lips warm and seeking. Blaine felt the whole world stand still. She hadn't expected this. Any of this. She'd never expected Eric to come into her life. Hadn't expected to be knocked off her feet by someone like him. Hadn't expected the stirrings of love to invade her heart and plant seeds there.

She'd been so content in her bubble, alone but never lonely. Her work, her shop, and her memories were the only company she needed. But as Eric's hands moved against her skin, his fingers gently pulling her closer into his body as they kissed, she couldn't imagine going back to the way she was. She deepened the kiss, pulling him closer, until they were both gasping. His hands slid up her spine to her neck to hold her into his kiss.

"Blaine," he whispered, the word lost to the beat and the music and the crowd. "We should . . . can we go?" His eyes were deep and searching hers.

She nodded, breathless, and kissed him once more.

"Yes." She nodded again, and he took her by the hand, just as the band finished and started up a rousing version of, "Come on Eileen". They wove their way through the crowd, and though she loved the music and could have stayed until closing, all she wanted was to leave the crowd behind and have him to herself.

He didn't say anything, but he held her hand tightly and there was an urgency to his pace. As they walked back through the entrance and down the street. She scrambled on shorter legs behind him and was thankful she had Chucks on instead of high heels. Her heart beat, both nervous and excited. When they reached the car, he paused and took a moment to bend low and kiss her. The cool metal of the car pressed against her back.

"Blaine." He paused to take a shaky breath. "I want you, but I don't want to complicate your life any more than I already have. I wish we could've met under different circumstances; I wish—" She stopped him with a kiss.

"Then let's pretend."

"Pretend?" he asked, breathless and in a daze.

"Hi," she whispered against his lips. "You don't know me, but my name is Blaine Reynolds, and I'd really like to get to know you better." She bit his bottom lip, and he groaned. Her hands slipped under his shirt and up his chest.

"Hi, Blaine, I'm Eric and I—" He took in a sharp breath when she bit his neck and her nails lightly caressed his stomach. "*Dios*, I want to get to know you too," He broke off in a breathy laugh and pressed his body against hers, hard muscle to soft curves, and he nearly lifted her off her feet onto the hood of the car.

"We should do it, I mean, get to know each other someplace more private," he gasped, before kissing her again and nodding. He pulled away, cleared his throat, dark eyes like night skies as they bored into hers. "Your place is closer."

"I don't want to wait any longer than necessary. Are you okay to drive?" She leveled her eyes on him.

He smiled and held her against him once more, as if he couldn't bear to have space between them.

"Only if you can keep your hands to yourself while I'm driving."

Blaine bit her lip and looked up at him mischievously. "I can try, but I'm not making any promises, Mr. Morales."

The drive back to her place seemed to take forever. He kept his hand around hers, interlocking fingers. She squirmed in the seat as they sped through downtown, older neighborhoods blurring by, until finally turning onto her street. When he parked, he accidently bumped the curb.

"Oops." She giggled. "I think you found it."

"I'm a little distracted," he grumbled as he put the car in park and turned to her. "Blaine, at any point, if you don't want to, know that you can say something."

"Are you backing out on me now? Getting me all worked up and then leaving me? Is Eric Morales nothing but a tease?" She winked and shook her head. "I appreciate you saying that, but there's nothing else I want at this moment but you." She looked down to their hands, interlaced, and lifted his to her lips. A soft sense of familiarity settled in his eyes. "But it's okay if you change your mind, too. I won't like you any less," she said.

"Why would I change my mind? I've wanted you since I watched you and that horchata straw." He flashed her an evil smile, and she laughed.

"Well, I've wanted you since you licked enchilada sauce off the back of your fork, so I guess we both have weird food fetishes."

Eric chuckled and caressed her chin, bringing her in for another kiss. "Let's get out of this car and find someplace with more room to maneuver."

He let her go, and they both got out of the car, knees shaking and pulses racing. Blaine searched her purse for the keys, finally finding them on the very bottom. He stood behind her as she unlocked the door with trembling hands. When she pushed it open and put her purse down on a small table, he followed her inside and kicked the door closed behind him. Just as she turned around, Eric took her in his arms with a pleased grunt.

"Blaine." He gasped and kissed her as she backed him up towards the bedroom.

The sudden and petrifying squeal caused them both to jump apart and look for the source. Eric's eyes fell to the carpet where a potato shaped ball of black and white fur with a twitching nose and buck teeth grunted angrily up at him.

"What in the hell is that?" He pointed, as if there could be anything else in the room so frightening.

"Charles."

"Charles?"

"Well, Charles Dumar the First, King of Kale, and Guinea Pig Master of the Universe. But I usually just call him Charles."

"Is it a rat?" Eric scrunched his face and looked down at the squeaking Charles, who still sat there looking up at them.

Blaine wondered if Eric's family was unaccustomed to pets. Probably too messy. Too unrefined. Too much work for a busy family with real jobs. She sighed and picked Charles up.

"He's a guinea pig." Charles chirped happily in her arms and stared up at Eric with curious deep eyes. "Want to hold him?" Blaine held her companion out.

Eric backed away with his hands up.

"No, thanks."

"You don't like animals?"

"I don't like rodents."

"Oh, come on."

"I'm not sure what's worse, the fact that he's out loose, or that he has a last name." Eric stared at the creature, then moved closer. He reached out and touched the soft fur. Blaine watched how gentle his large hands could be and how he wasn't shying away.

"He also has a top hat if that isn't enough 'worse' for you. But he only wears it on special occasions."

Eric lifted one dark eyebrow at her. "You're so weird."

"Excuse me, I'm quirky." She smiled, then frowned. "Hopefully not so quirky that you don't want to stay anymore?"

He shook his head.

"Not a chance, Reynolds. You can't get a guy all wound up on Journey and then leave him hanging." He pointed at the guinea pig. "But Charles Dumar needs to be contained. I'm not into guinea pig voyeurism."

"Fair." She nodded and put him back in his pen with a scoop of food. "Sorry he startled you."

She turned, but Eric interrupted her apology by lifting her up into his arms. Her legs wound around his waist, and she smiled, kissing him. The warmth of his body against hers sent shivers through her and she clung to his neck.

"Down this hall?" he asked, breathless, as he walked, still kissing her.

"Yes..." She got distracted when he moved his lips along her neck. "Just, down to the end of the hall, there."

They came to the end of the hall and into her bedroom. Eric set her down and paused. He stared into her eyes, smoothed a loose curl from her forehead, and kissed her softly.

"Still okay?"

"Yes." She started to undo the buttons on his shirt. "You?"

"I don't think I've ever been better." He took off his shirt to reveal his bare, hard chest. Blaine sighed in approval and kissed it lovingly.

"I'll see about making you feel even better than you are now," she whispered and undid the buttons on her vest.

Chapter Fifteen

Eric went back to his downtown condo early the next morning. He would have rather stayed in bed with Blaine. Even in her small bedroom. Even though his feet hung off her queen-sized bed. Even with Charles Dumar snoring in the pen down the hall. The quiet comfort, the smell of coffee and her laundry soap, her curls across his chest, her sighing giggle radiating through his heart. She'd made him breakfast, coffee with eggs and toast. Sat across the small kitchen table in nothing but a Van Halen t-shirt and her boy shorts. They'd laughed and talked about the weird things they remembered from being kids, and what their parents used to obsess over. Before work and family businesses. Before cancer diagnosis. Before the world made them grow up and shed the veil of that sweeter time. His heart wanted to burst. It also felt the sting of guilt, knowing that he hadn't told her about the contract. He told himself, after the movies, that if it were going to go any further, he should tell her. But the night and the magic of her had swept him away. When she'd reintroduced herself so they could start over and not talk about the bet that was sure to ruin one of their lives, he lost his nerve.

He walked through the door of his apartment and felt the

absence of her. His loft was a modern one bedroom, sparsely furnished, with few personal touches. A place that was, by all measures, one step up from a hotel room. Very different from Blaine's. Her apartment wasn't like her shop. It was modern, eclectic, more like she'd built it up from pieces she loved rather than a calculated interior design. It was cozy and comfortable, without feeling slouchy. Pictures of her and her mom, JT, and groups of smiling people in the shop were all over her walls and her bookcases, telling a story of her life by the people she loved.

He only had a couple of pictures of his family, ones from a long time ago when he was a kid, when they'd had time for vacations. One from when they'd gone to Spain. One from skiing trips up in Breckenridge. Did Blaine ski? Did she like to travel? His phone chimed angrily from his pocket. Loraine texting.

She'd taken the initiative to check with the lawyers if the amendment to the mall's ownership passed down to Blaine or if it had ended with her mother. He scrolled down.

Loraine claimed that it did not, and Blaine did not have the final say on the sale of her space. But he also knew his sister to be the sort of person who might say anything to get a deal to go through. She asked if he'd known that Blaine didn't have any rights in the matter all along, and had he been stalling?

He knew about the amendment, but hadn't checked to see if it passed down to Blaine, and he hadn't asked her about it. Whether he'd forgotten or purposefully put it out of his mind, Eric wasn't sure; it was probably a little of both. But it didn't seem to matter now. He didn't respond. He didn't know how to, or what to say. If he claimed he didn't know, Loraine would think he was incompetent. If he did know, then he was sabotaging his own project and their family's reputation.

It didn't matter if Blaine used to ski or liked to travel. It didn't matter that her shop was a beautiful and diverse mix of nostalgia and history that made so many people happy. It didn't matter that the last three weeks were the best in his recent life, or that she made him feel human and valued again. It didn't matter that he was head over heels in love with her. None of it really mattered because, bet or not, the mall would be under their ownership soon enough. Every shop in it would be closed down, and the mall leveled to the dirt. Nothing would be left but a plot of land, fresh for building. Her shop would be destroyed and, he imagined, it would destroy her as well. There wasn't anything he could do to stop the process. No matter how much he wanted to. He'd lied to her. The small amendment hadn't mattered in the grand scheme of things.

But, he thought, with his heart clenching in his chest, she mattered, and he didn't know how he'd ever go about telling her the truth. But if he didn't do it, Loraine would, and he couldn't decide who it would be worse to hear it from. He at least wanted to spend the last remaining "meeting" with her at the museum opening before telling her. Maybe in the span of those hours, he could convince her that it didn't have to mean the end to her way of life or the things she loved. That she could rebuild, move on. Make a new life of her own.

Maybe he could even be a part of it.

Blaine sat on her couch with her coffee, and Charles Dumar curled up in her lap. She knew it would be hard to focus on much of anything except Eric today. She knew there were bigger problems outside of her bedroom. She knew her whole world was about to change in a matter of days. But her heart was content with the ways her world had already changed with him being a part of it.

She ran her fingers down Charles' back. He purred at her while she looked over to the bookcase near the TV, where pictures of her and her mom were scattered on each shelf. Graduations, birthdays, trips to concerts and conventions. Lazy Sundays at the theater, or outside in the mountains. Did Eric like the mountains? Did he ski? Did he have time to be outside or do anything not on a spreadsheet?

She wished she could be the one to help him find more happiness. He seemed happy last night, her eyebrow raised remembering. They'd both been happy. Very happy, a few times over. She bit her lip and looked at the clock. The shop was supposed to open in an hour. She should shower and get her life together, but all she wanted to do was crawl back into the sheets that still smelled like him and pretend that things were different.

"That's not how the world works, is it Charles?" Her furry friend stared up at her and squeaked.

"That's what I thought." She put him on the floor, then went to take a shower.

The mall felt like a graveyard, with JT's salon already empty and the old storage space completely barren. Even Talon Karate had been stripped bare. Gone were the lime green mats, bins of gear, and motivational posters. All that remained were bare walls and the cheap front desk where Lawrence sat on a corded phone trying to make arrangements for a new space for his students. Blaine waved sadly as she passed, and felt the sting of being a traitor to all of them in some small way.

It wasn't her fault this was happening, and maybe after last night, Eric wouldn't have the heart to go through with it. She wouldn't let it happen if she were in his shoes. Then again, she thought of his Chucks, she wasn't in his shoes.

She unlocked the door and stared at the still full shelves, like a beacon of naïve hope. Was she just being stupid? The idea that her heart and body had betrayed her ability to keep a clear head sunk her into sadness. What would happen if Eric Morales marched in here today and told her to get out? Her heart fell to her feet. Her phone pinged.

> I don't want to go to work. Want to play hookie?

Blaine's heart leaped, and she turned on the lights and perched on the chair behind the counter. She stared at his words. How could she not want to be with him? If it was all just a ruse, he was far too good an actor. Plus, she wanted to believe.

> Yeah, I do. But I'd have disappointed customers and you'd have to answer to Loraine.

> Dios...

> I miss you.

The words were out before she could think of not sending them. But to be honest, there was much more she wanted to say. Just not via text.

> Miss you too, Cariña, so much that I'm thinking I might have to put on some Journey while I work.

Blaine laughed out loud.

> A sure sign of a desperate man

The three little dots rolled over and over before disappearing, and she wondered what he had not said.

> I can't wait to see you tomorrow night. Am I picking you up, since you're nearly out of gas?

> Sure, if you think you can handle Charles Dumar in a top hat.

> He's not coming is he? LOL

She crinkled her nose and typed.

> Don't pretend that you don't love him.

> He is . . . bearable.

> You'll come around.

> I always do with you.

Blaine's breath caught in her throat. She wasn't sure if he meant it sexually, or in a deeper emotional way. Did he mean he was coming around to agreeing she was right? And that he was working on a solution? She told her brain to not hope, but Blaine's brain was hardwired for hope. She typed slowly, checking the front door as if someone might magically come in and offer to buy her store and relocate it to a safe location, and she could be free of the worry. No one came. The parking lot was still empty when she looked back down to her unfinished thought.

> Get back to work, before Loraine catches you slacking on the job. We'll get to talk tomorrow.

> I hope that's not all we'll get to do . . .

> Naughty man. Don't let those thoughts distract you or you might forget to put a wall somewhere.

She hoped he was laughing. She hoped her words gave him a little peace to start his day with. She looked back out to the parking lot. She hoped the universe would send her a solution, and fast.

Chapter Sixteen

That evening, with the approaching museum opening with Eric less than a day away, a nervous flurry of worry wound itself through Blaine's belly. Not counting the concert they hadn't seen much of, it wasn't so much that she hadn't been on a date in over two years. It wasn't that she hadn't met someone's family in years. It wasn't even that she hadn't had a boyfriend who was probably going to destroy her livelihood in . . . well, ever. It was the conflict of what she wanted in her heart to happen, and the reality of what probably would.

He hadn't talked much about his family except that they worked a lot, and that most of his warm memories came from his grandmother. And that his sister was an absolute ice queen.

What was she even going to say to them? Did his family even know about the ridiculous bet he'd made? Would they be angry with Eric? Or her?

Going through her closet had been a sad affair. Blaine sighed. JT was right. She owned an awful lot of off-the-shoulder sweatshirts, jeans, leggings, slouch socks, and a few crop tops with vintage logos. Like MTV, and Whitney Houston—but dresses? They were all pretty informal, flowery, flowy ones that JT referred to as *Little House on The Prairie meets boho 90s chic,* whatever that meant. Not anything formal. Certainly not anything sparkly. Not anything one could wear to the opening of Marshall's fanciest new building, amidst hundreds of other posher people than her.

Some of her mother's old clothes hung behind her own collection, which only stood to make her feel worse about where she was. On her way to enter the den of an affluent family that threatened to destroy her shop. She slid another hanger over. Even her mom didn't have a lot of clothes to choose from. Blaine came across one old black dress that was more appropriate for a funeral, a couple of leather skirts, and a plain blue shift dress. She ran the cloth between her fingers and remembered the feel of it from when she was little, clinging to the skirt as her mother had walked through the shop with Mr. Peterson for the first time.

Strange why and how memories sneak up, but this one made Blaine sink down to the floor of her closet and take the dress with her. She held it up close to her nose and inhaled. There wasn't much left of her mother's smell. There wasn't much of her mom left here. Just the shop. And her memories. Pictures of them and things that had been loved by her. She ached to have her mom here with her. To talk to and give her advice on what to do.

"Mom, why did you have to leave me?" she choked out, tears now streaming down her cheeks. "I need you."

Helplessness crept through her, and she realized there was no way she could go through with this. She wiped her tears and got up to find her phone so she could tell Eric she wouldn't be able to make it.

The doorbell rang before she could find her phone. Nearly running over Charles Dumar in her hurry to answer, she tripped over the edge of the couch and stumbled into the doorframe before opening it, bruising her shoulder.

She opened it to see JT holding a garment bag and a pleased smile.

"Please tell me you have a miracle," Blaine begged

"Well, it's not exactly a miracle, but it's no Laura Ingalls either."

JT rushed inside, hopped over Charles, and hung up the garment on a knob in Blaine's kitchen. "Now, I wasn't sure of the size, so I guessed, but I think it should work."

Blaine held her breath as JT unzipped the black cloth bag and the shimmering rose gold material seemed to light up the drab little kitchen.

"What in the name of all that's holy . . ." Blaine gasped. It was tight fitted, long and, she noted with dismay, strapless. "JT."

"Right? It's so chic. I found it at the thrift store, but it can use a few alterations."

"Please say you mean straps."

"What? No. Why? You don't need straps. It'll highlight your decolletage."

"My what? Is that some kind of kindergarten art project?"

JT rolled their eyes. "That's a decoupage. I'm talking about your neck and chest."

"The chest is the problem JT. What am I going to hold it up with? My imagination?"

JT looked from the dress down to the slouchy, off-shoulder sweatshirt Blaine wore. Sans a bra, because, well, she didn't have much to worry about there, and she was no longer at work. JT's eyes stopped at Blaine's neck, and they quirked their head to the side.

"That's an interesting mark."

"What?" Blaine put her hand to her neck before the realization dawned on her what JT was talking about. "Uh . . . curling iron burn?"

"Does your curling iron have teeth?"

"Maybe."

"Don't explain. I think I understand," JT laughed and knocked her on the shoulder. "I'm glad you finally loosened that boy's tie."

"He's not a boy." Blaine tried not to giggle.

"Oh, I'm sure he's every inch a man." JT's eyebrows rose suggestively.

Blaine broke into a heated blush. "Let's get back to why this dress will not work."

"It'll be fine."

"What if it's not? What if I show to the biggest event of the year with Marshall's elite and Denver's social royalty, and my damn dress rolls off my flat chest and becomes a skirt?"

JT stared at her, expression of a tired parent on their face. "Look, I get that you're nervous, and you're not really sure you want to do this. But don't blame the dress. Now, go get some decent undergarments on and we'll see how far up I need to hem this thing."

JT was nothing if not a miracle worker with both thread and hair. Within a short hour, they had secured the dress with a tighter waist stitch to accommodate Blaine's small stature, and hemmed it to graze the tops of her high-heeled feet. JT stepped back with an appreciative nod.

"Kid, it's sad to think you've been hiding all that under mom jeans for years."

"What?" Blaine giggled.

"Seriously, I know he's already seen you naked but this . . ." they waved their arms around like Vanna White. "This is gonna melt his little construction brain."

"Really? Just his brain?"

"I think his heart is already there," JT said.

Blaine looked in the full-length mirror and couldn't believe it. She had to admit the dress looked pretty amazing, and it made her feel like a movie star. Not like Marilyn Monroe, but more like Molly Ringwald in *Pretty in Pink* when she finished creating her dress. The bottom line was she felt beautiful. She just hoped that was enough.

JT put their sewing and pins away in the case. "You only have a day. How are you feeling?"

"Nervous. Ready to call him and say I can't make it."

"Don't you dare do that. I'm sure you're nervous, but you'll get over it. You have the heels I sent with Deb?"

Blaine looked around the small bathroom and felt the weighted fabric swish against her skin. She felt like she could melt a man's brain in this dress. There was a slightly dented box by the sink. "Those?"

"Have you been practicing in them?" JT reprimanded, acting the part of surrogate parent on Blaine's own adult prom night.

Blaine bit her lip. The truth was, she hadn't even looked in the box.

"Sort of?"

"Sort of and close enough don't count in heels. Walk around your house in them as much as possible between tonight and tomorrow. Just remember to keep your weight on your toes."

"I'm already going to be on my toes." Blaine smoothed the front of the sparkly rose gown, and the fitted waist. "Oh, god, can I really do this, JT?"

"Yes." Not a shade of doubt in their face or voice. "You're going to charm them with your pluck, and wow them with your smarts."

"Pluck?"

"Sure, your whole 'sun'll come out,' Pollyanna thing."

"You have your plucky girls mixed up."

"Potato, potahto," JT said. "I'll be over tomorrow night to help you with your hair, okay? Just don't eat in the dress. In fact, take it off right now before you get something on it."

"Right now?"

"Yes. I mean, let me leave first, but then, hang it back up under its protective barrier and don't let Charles near it, under any circumstances."

"Yeesh, okay."

Blaine did as she was told and hung the dress safely in her closet. When she retrieved the shoe box from her bathroom, she opened the lid. Expecting Deb to have gotten her some gawdy pure white church heels, Blaine winced away as she pulled back the tissue paper. Inside was a post-it. "Because you deserve a Cinderella story—love Deb."

Blaine felt tears sting her eyes as she pulled the shoes out. They were high-heeled pumps, clear with a spray of rhinestones across the open toes and heels. They were all at once magical and classy, and Blaine held them to her chest. She did feel like Cinderella. Except that it wasn't the prince's heart she had to win. It was his family's.

Chapter Seventeen

Eric picked up his tux from the dry cleaners for the big event that night. He hated wearing one. They always seemed too tight in the shoulders, and definitely too hot. Truth be told, he wished he could be in his jeans, picking Blaine up for a night of Abuelita's and dancing afterwards. On his way to his parent's house to drop by some contracts for his dad to sign, he wondered if the old salsa club his parents used to go to was still open.

He walked through the front door and yelled his hello. The sound echoed in the house, and he heard Loraine from upstairs yell his name back.

"Do you have the Drew contracts?"

"Yeah, where's Papá?"

"He's not home from the office yet." She stuck her head out into the hallway upstairs as he ascended.

"Should I take them to the office?"

"No, he said he'd be home soon."

His mother came out of the master bath in a slip and her hair up in curlers. He hadn't seen her in the process of getting ready, and it turned him into a fascinated little boy. Was she always so small? He turned away out of respect and looked at Loraine.

"Why aren't you ready yet?" Loraine glared at him.

"I needed to drop the contracts off and pick up my tux."

"Well, go get ready. We can't be late. Any of us." She turned in her own robe and hair up in hot curlers and slammed the door to her room.

Eric's eyebrows rose. "Do you think she's nervous?" he asked his mom over his shoulder. His mother slipped on a robe and came to kiss him on the cheek.

"Oh, sí. She's miserable."

"I'm fine!" came Loraine's frustrated voice through the door.

"I think she asked a young man to the opening," his mother whispered. Eric looked down at her, surprised.

"Really? Loraine knows a young man? I mean, socially? Is that possible?"

His mother's eyes twinkled, and she smiled at the closed door where Loraine's music got louder, as did the bumps and curses of a woman in a state of frenzy.

"Sí, but I think he might have said no."

"Oof, that's too bad." Eric meant it.

Had all his talk about trying to find happiness outside of the office switched something on inside of his normally stoic sister? Had she put her heart out there and some guy had dashed it? His jaw popped when he clenched it, and he wondered if he needed to get an address. He hadn't felt protective over his sister since they were kids.

"We'll see. I'm not sure who it is, or if he comes, but we'll know it's him if her mood improves." His mother turned to him and ruffled his hair as though he was seven. "And you? Are you bringing someone?"

"Sí, Mamá," he said softly and felt a lump in his throat.

"Oh, she must be important to see your face like that. Why are you afraid? Don't you like her?"

"I do like her, Mamá, very much. She's not like anyone I know. She . . ." He paused.

"Does she make you want to dance?" Carmen asked with eyes twinkling.

"Sí, Mamá, every day, every minute I'm with her. She makes me feel it," he touched his chest absentmindedly, "here."

Carmen's face lit up with joy, and she took his arm in both her bird-like hands.

"Oh, *mijo*. I can't wait to meet her."

"She may just be a friend. I'm not sure what it is yet."

Carmen leaned in closer, kissed his cheek, smoothed away her lipstick, and gave his cheek a gentle pat. "*Mijo*, when you feel the happiness, the dancing in your heart? You don't have to be sure. Just hold on to it."

JT pulled bobby pins from their teeth as they affixed Blaine's updo, a tumble of curls on top of her head. They stepped back every so often, sprayed the whole thing down, and flipped the teaser comb around in their palm as they planned out the exact shape. Blaine was quiet. She didn't want to mess with the process. Leave the transforming to the professionals. She had enough on her mind. JT pulled a few strategic strands free to cascade just in front of her ears, and they bounced lightly on her shoulders. Then JT went to work on the makeup.

"I suppose it would be too much to ask for blue eyeshadow?"

"It would be. Way too much. Nope, not tonight, kid. Tonight, you're going for smoldering and determined businesswoman." JT worked their magic on Blaine's eyelids. "Don't smear it. Don't touch it. Don't cry."

"Can I breathe?" Blaine grouched.

"Hmm . . . I dunno. Lightly. And only if you don't blink while you do it."

"Ugh, this is dumb."

JT stepped back after the flurry of powders, potions, liners, lotions, and sparkles had settled. "Lord, that man is going to fall to his knees."

"Really?" Blaine squeaked.

"His mom might get a shotgun to keep her baby boy safe from the marauding, sexy shop owner."

"Oh, stop. But I'm glad you reminded me, I have to get that package out of the garage."

"You are going nowhere near the garage!" JT yelled and put their hands out. "Stay here and stay clean. I'll go get it. In your car?"

"Yes. Thank you."

When JT had gone, Blaine faced the mirror and barely recognized herself. Had she always looked so glowing? She couldn't remember a time when she'd felt so grown up, or so nervous. She wasn't sure if this was a new her, or just a part of her that had always been there, covered in the comfort of the world she knew.

JT came back in with the package, wrapped in plain white paper and a card taped to the front.

"What is this?" JT asked.

"Something for his mom. Something I think she might like."

"Already bribing the parents? Is this to grease the wheels for when you ask for his hand in marriage?" they asked.

"What? No. I'm just trying to emphasize the importance of what I do."

"Uh huh," they said, with a sideways glance and arms crossed.

"Maybe partly a bribe." She shrugged and felt secure that the dress didn't immediately fall down. The sound of a powerful engine pulling up made them both look towards the front. Eric was here, right on time. Her stomach flipped. She wasn't sure she was ready for this.

"Okay, little shop girl. This is your big moment. Be cool. Don't freak out."

"Too late, but I'll try to fake it."

"Best we can hope for." JT gave her a kiss on the cheek and

squeezed her arms. "I'll go get the door, you take a few breaths. You look like you might faint. You got this, girl. They're going to love you, and if they don't, then they don't deserve you."

JT left, and Blaine heard them opening the door with a mock serious tone. "Well, well, well. If it isn't the destroyer of dreams."

Blaine rolled her eyes and imagined Eric blushing and looking down in embarrassment. She didn't want him to squirm . . . too much. She took a deep breath, nodded to herself in the mirror, and grabbed her small clutch along with the gift. She went down the hallway carefully, as if she might tumble forward and have to spend the rest of the night in the ER. As she felt the butterflies growing in her belly from the anticipation of the evening ahead, she wondered if that might not be the better option. Lifting the drapey fabric from her line of steps, she took a deep breath as she rounded the corner of the hall and saw him. In the dark fabric of the tuxedo, his broad shoulders seemed like a wall. His hair had been combed over and probably felt like her own in its concrete perfection. She preferred it messy and sweet over cereal bowls.

His mouth fell open as he looked at her from the tips of her jeweled shoes to the crown of curls on her head. Her smoky eyes lowered, and she pursed her lips, moist with some gloss JT had said was called *Kissable*. She hoped he thought it was.

"*Dios*, Blaine," Eric whispered, and his hand went to his heart as if trying to protect it from falling irrevocably in love.

JT rolled their eyes.

"Look at you two dumb-struck kids. This isn't exactly the senior prom, you know. Still, it is kinda cute, but it makes me want to gag. Get out of here and bring her back by midnight or I'm going to have to take Charles Dumar to the police station and file a report." JT shoved Eric towards Blaine.

She held her clutch and the present close to her side. His white and pressed shirt, the smooth and well-fitting tux, and shiny black shoes, every part of him, spoke of wealth and he looked like an out-of-place stranger in the middle of her small living room. He stumbled towards her and offered his hand. She shifted the package to her other hand and took his. He gave it a gentle squeeze and pulled her towards the door.

"You look amazing," he whispered as JT opened the door for them.

"You do too," she whispered back.

"Ugh, you two are killing me. Get out of here." JT gave Eric another shove out the door after Blaine.

"Goodnight JT. Thanks for your help."

Eric smiled back to where JT was waving and shaking their head at the two of them. Weren't they just two idiots in love and the whole world could see it? Blaine wondered if he was as worried as she was about that, given that they'd be spending most of the night with his family, colleagues, and business partners. Her body started to tremble.

Eric looked at her. "Are you okay?"

"I don't know. I'm really nervous."

"Why?" Eric's brow rose. "Just because my parents and judgmental sister will be there, and a whole bunch of rich strangers who you don't know will be talking about all the ways they burn through money?"

Blaine's stomach turned, and she held the package against it.

"Wow, thanks for putting that into words. Didn't really help." She shook her head and hoped she wouldn't throw up on her dress.

Eric smiled and shook his head. "You're going to be fine. They will love you."

"Not Loraine."

"Well, she doesn't love anyone." Eric shrugged before pulling Blaine close. The corner of the package poked him in the sternum and he pulled away. "Ouch. What is that?"

Blaine looked down at it as though she'd forgotten it was in her hand. "Oh, it's just . . . something for your mom."

"You got my mom a gift?" he smiled.

"Well, I mean, I figured she needed some compensation for having you and Loraine for kids." Blaine rolled her eyes, and he laughed, moved the package to the side, and closed the space between them.

He kissed her as though he'd been waiting all day for it. Blaine melted into him and the warmth of his lips against hers. He pulled away, breathless.

"I think I'd rather take you back inside," he whispered.

"No way. I didn't put on this and the undergarments to support it all for nothing." Blaine gave him a mock scowl.

"Mmm . . . undergarments?" He smiled wolfishly and kissed down her neck to her exposed collarbone.

"Not super sexy when their sole purpose is to hold everything up and in."

"Everything you wear is sexy." He pulled her close, and she pressed her body into his. "Because it doesn't matter what you put on, the woman I want is still inside." He pecked her on the cheek and stepped away. "We'd better go, before I convince you we need to have a 'unwind session' before the big event."

"Well, that does sound like a nice distraction. But I think JT might protest." She followed him to the car.

He opened her door for her, and she quirked her lips up, noticing that some of her *Kissable* lip gloss had transferred to his mouth. She wiped it away with the pad of her thumb. "Should get rid of the evidence before I meet your parents."

Eric's face fell into something between worry and sadness. "Blaine, you really didn't have to do all of this."

"I wanted to. You put up with me running you around, looking at old relics, kicking your ass in *Pong*, and watching old movies. You let me show you my world."

"I like your world."

"Now it's your turn." She finished with a sigh and got in the car.

They pulled away from the safety of her home, to go throw themselves into his world.

Eric tried to keep the heat from rising in his chest as she sat next to him. She was so beautiful. So nervous and still so determined. She carried in her the bravery to face an entire room of his family and coworkers; the ones who wanted to take everything away from her. A process he still wasn't sure he could stop. But he knew, this night, no matter how it turned out with his family and Blaine, that he was determined to try.

Chapter Eighteen

They arrived at the packed parking lot and drove through the front, circular covered drive where valet parking was waiting. Eric got out, and Blaine followed, not wanting him to help her, even though she stalled out on the heels, and had to grunt and tug at her dress to get off the low seat. She checked to make sure every round and pink part was still beneath the cover of the dress before looking at him, hand held out.

"I could have helped you."

"I know." She adjusted the bodice self-consciously. "We ready?"

"No, but let's do it anyway." He smiled down at her and offered his elbow. Blaine took it with her free hand and held the gift in the other. "What's in the box for my mom?"

"I can't tell you. It would ruin the surprise."

"It's not my surprise," he argued back and straightened his tie as they climbed the stone steps to the front entrance.

Fresh flower arrangements and twinkling lights covered the archway as they went through. The wide, double doors opened up into a grand circular hall with a reception desk and two entryways on either side, leading to the opposite wings of the museum.

Behind the desk was a proper and well-dressed man greeting the guests and taking coats. Eric led her past them. The ceiling was two stories high and graced with modern light fixtures that looked like silver waves running along the lines of the walls themselves. Blaine wobbled trying to look up at them. Everything looked amazing. "What do you think so far?" He asked.

"This is just the lobby?" She continued looking around.

"Yeah," he chuckled. "Loraine outdid herself."

"She did. I have to give her credit."

"Well, give the architect, the workers, and the city taxpayers more. Loraine just bossed people around in the right way."

Blaine laughed and nodded. "That's a skill too. Is that how you run projects? Bossing people around?"

Eric adjusted his tie and gently led her to the right, towards the first wing of exhibits. "I like to think I 'manage' them. Bossing makes it sound like I don't care how it gets done, as long as it's done."

"Isn't that how big projects like this one get done?"

"Projects are a team effort. People, I like to think, doing their best to create something larger than themselves. Something that's beautiful and lasting—work they can be proud of. That they had a hand in," he said.

Blaine looked up at him and smiled.

Her smiled back at her, his shoulders relaxing a bit.

"I know you love what you do," she said softly. "I'm sure sometimes it feels like an obligation. And I'm sure that's when you forget the joy."

"Do you ever forget the joy?" he asked before they approached the crowd of well-dressed guests filing their way into the exhibit hall.

"Sometimes," she shrugged. "I love what my mom had and what she loved. But sometimes I forget that there's a whole world out there of things to love and I shouldn't just be bound to what she built her life around."

Eric stopped and pulled them off to the side, into a secluded alcove, and put both hands on her bare arms. He stared down into her eyes, and Blaine looked up expectantly.

"What?"

"I just..." He stammered and looked at their feet, "I love—"

Before he could finish, a man called his name, and they both swung their heads around to see who it was.

"Who's that?" she whispered as Eric's hand slipped down to hold hers.

"Hello, Papá," he called back to the man with a nod.

Eric pulled her back into the hall behind him, swimming through the sea of people.

"You haven't even been inside and you're already skulking in the halls?" Eric's father said.

He was a handsome Latino man, with hard eyes and a serious brow. He was also intimidating. He carried the same build as Eric, but with graying hair at his temples.

He looked down at Blaine and his eyes softened. "Though one could not blame you for taking a moment."

Everything about John Morales's gaze said he was sizing Blaine up. Not in a physically objectifying way, but as if he was determining her character, by the color of her hair to the tips of her toes.

She held out her hand as seriously as possible. "Blaine. Blaine Reynolds. Back to—"

"Back to the conversation we were just having—yes—" Eric interrupted and squeezed her hand.

Blaine glared at him.

"This is my father, Blaine, John Morales."

"Reynolds?" John took Blaine's hand in his firm grip.

Before he could puzzle too long where he'd heard the name before, Eric cleared his throat.

"Ah, yes. Have you seen Mamá and Loraine?"

"Inside with everyone else. The speech and ribbon cutting are about to begin."

"Of course, thank you. I'm sure Loraine would make us both pay if we were late for it." Eric ducked his head, and it was odd for Blaine to see him so pious. His dad really did run a tight ship and Blaine felt sorry for him in that moment.

"Shall we?" Eric gestured to where the other people were going inside.

"We shall," John said.

Blaine felt his gaze on her as they continued into the stunning space that was built to house the majority of the modern art exhibitions that would visit the town. The current exhibit was blocked by a huge red ribbon in the front of the hall. The crowd gathered behind it.

John turned to Eric. "Excuse us, will you, Miss Reynolds? I will return him shortly."

John nudged Eric and his hand broke away from Blaine's as he was ushered up to the front with the rest of the family. Blaine closed her fingers reflexively, missing the safety of his hand in hers. His warm and protective height next to her. She looked around but didn't recognize many of the faces. A few from the newspaper that she suspected might be city council members, prominent business owners, other board members of Morales Construction, no doubt. Even in her heels, she couldn't see over the heads in the crowd. She tried to squeeze her way in closer to the front.

The ceremony began, and she was able to get close enough to listen to Loraine's speech. Despite her harsh manner, she was a beautiful speaker, and told about the museum's journey and what it meant to their family. Loraine wore a beautiful red gown that swept outward in a full skirt to the floor and had wide straps to accommodate her more endowed chest. Beside her was John, Eric, and a woman who Blaine assumed was his mother. Her soft gray dress with a flowing skirt and long sleeves contrasted with her dark, shoulder-length hair. She wore a proud smile as she watched her daughter talk.

Seeing the way her eyes lit up with happy tears at her daughter's accomplishments, the pride, the love, the support, made Blaine's eyes fill with tears. She'd never missed her own mom so much than in that moment. She suddenly felt very alone and abandoned to a world destined to destroy her. When she looked at Eric, he was studying her. Had he been staring at her all along? His brow narrowed, and he mouthed, "You okay?" She nodded and dabbed at her eyes quickly, ducking behind a taller man to collect herself.

The ribbon was cut with a large pair of golden scissors, and the crowd clapped politely before filing into the beautiful space to admire the artwork and architecture, and to visit with one another. Waiters buzzed through with champagne on trays, and Blaine snagged one, nearly finishing it from her nerves before Eric came back, two in his hands, and offered her one. She nodded, put the empty glass on a passing tray and took the refill.

"Are you steeling your nerve?" he smiled as she sipped the champagne.

"I'm trying to calm down."

"It will be fine. Ready?"

"No." She looked down to the gift in her hand and suddenly felt that it was stupid and cheesy. Something that didn't belong in a place like this. Almost like herself.

"Come on, *Cariña*, I won't leave your side." He squeezed her hand, and with more excitement than he'd shown before with his father, he pulled her behind him to where the crowd was clearing around the family from their well wishes and praise.

"Mamá," Eric said as they approached Loraine and his mother. "This is—"

"Blaine Reynolds?" Loraine practically shrieked.

Blaine felt the champagne flute slipping from her fingers but had the mind to grab it before making a bigger scene. Just as

Loraine's bright red pout could form more spiteful words, a voice drifted above the din. The kind of voice that was used to carrying above classes of yelling students.

"Hey Morales!" Lawrence yelled from the front of the exhibit over the crowd. He wore a sport coat that looked like it came from a thrift store he found on his way to the event. His green tie askew, blond hair in disarray, he maneuvered his way through the crowd with the ease of a man who knew his body well.

"Loraine, it looks like your boyfriend is here," Eric smiled wickedly, and Loraine looked at him with sisterly hate.

When Lawrence broke through the crowd and reached them, Eric held out his hand. "Hello, sir."

Lawrence took his hand to shake it, and his gaze fell down to where Blaine stood at Eric's side.

His eyebrows shot up. "Holy shit, Reynolds, is that you?"

"Uh, yep, last I checked." Blaine stammered. Her skin felt warm, and the effects of the champagne made her dizzy.

Lawrence shook his head and then took Eric's hand one more time. He pulled him in close and whispered in his ear, but Blaine could still hear.

"Morales, I'm tellin' you, if you hurt that girl, I swear on Bruce Lee's grave—"

Loraine cleared her throat and put her hands on her hips. Lawrence looked over at her, all thoughts of Eric lost.

"You clean up pretty good too, I guess," he said ,and a twinkle lit his eyes. He let go of Eric's hand and moved towards her; Loraine stepped back.

"That's some dress." Lawrence raised his eyebrows at her.

"What are you doing here?"

"Don't do that, you asked me to come here—"

"I didn't say . . ." She looked around to where people were starting to stare.

She took him by his cheap sports coat sleeve and pulled him off to a more secluded part of the museum. Eric, Blaine, and his mother watched them go with bemused smiles.

Eric turned back to his mother. "Mamá, this is Blaine. Blaine, this is my mother, Carmen."

Blaine's heart fluttered as she stepped forward. *Please, please don't let my dress fall down right now.* She had meant to hold out her hand to shake Carmen's, but both hands were tightly gripping the package and she held it out instead. Carmen looked down at it and smiled.

"Is this for me?"

"Yes." Blaine felt heat rush to her cheeks. "I know it's silly, but Eric mentioned something to me the other day about you, and I— well, I thought you might like this. It's nice to meet you." Her voice shook, and she studied the warm and patient eyes of Carmen.

The older woman smiled, the kind of smile a mother smiles when she sees a child in need of love.

"I'm sure I will love it. How kind of you." Carmen accepted the package and held it to her chest as if it were her kindergartener's first drawing about to hold a place of honor on the fridge.

"How did you two meet?" Carmen looked from her son to Blaine.

Before Blaine could respond, Eric cut in. "Blaine and I were in the same store at the same time, and well . . ." He took her hand. "She sort of made me forget everything else when she started talking to me."

Corny as it was, Blaine still fell into the sweetness of it. So did Carmen.

"Oh, *Dios.* That is how it happens, no?" She smiled at Blaine. "I'm so glad you spoke to him. He needs to stop and listen more." She pointed a finger at her son before a museum employee leaned over to whisper something in her ear. She nodded and rolled her eyes. "Will you please excuse me? I have to sort some things out in the back." With determined steps, Carmen took her leave. Blaine let out a whoosh of breath she hadn't realized she'd been holding.

"See? Not so bad. She likes you."

"She's probably just being polite. Don't all moms hate their son's choices in women?"

"No, Blaine." Eric sighed. "You have a different effect on people."

"What effect?"

"They immediately love you."

Blaine stared up at him. The crowd seemed to disappear. "They do? All of them?"

A ruckus erupted from the side of the room, beyond the crowd, and Lawrence's voice could be heard. Not like his true voice, but one that was sounded to Blaine as if he was covering deeper, more tender feelings. Like Lawrence had sounded at the bar. The soft side of a hard man, talking loudly to Loraine.

"Well, fine! If you didn't want me here, then why'd you asked me to come to your trumped-up dog and pony show?" He rushed out from the alcove where Loraine had pulled him away earlier. He looked red in the face, particularly around his lips. A daring, lipstick red.

"Fine, leave!" she yelled after him. Blaine saw them exchange a small smile, a conspiracy that was barely noticeable before Loraine stormed back towards Eric. "What an idiot," she fumed, even as Blaine and Eric noticed that her lips had been kissed, and her cheeks held a pretty pink blush.

Her anger seemed fake, and Blaine wondered if it all was just one giant act to dissuade her father from thinking she'd actually invited a man "below her" to the unveiling of her most important project.

Eric cleared his throat. "Did anything—happen? Do you need me to—"

Loraine stopped him with a pleading hand. "No. *Dios*, please." Her voice was small, and Blaine studied the sudden change in her features.

Loraine stared after the hulking man with a soft look. If Blaine was not an acceptable partner for Eric in John Morales's eyes, Lawrence would be positively nightmarish for his daughter. But sometimes, the heart doesn't listen to what the rules are. Blaine looked at Loraine with a new sense of sympathy.

Everyone wanted someone who understood them, appreciated them, who saw them. Someone who knocked their socks off and drove them a little bit crazy. Eric shrugged, and they watched as Lawrence gave one last, longing glance over his shoulder at Loraine, who looked softly back at him before turning away with her head high to go talk with someone more important.

Chapter Nineteen

"Well, shall we?" Eric asked and offered Blaine his elbow. She wove her hand in the crook of it, happy for the warmth and the sense of grounding he brought her as they moved through the exhibit hall. Beyond the artwork, which was a mixture of bold colors across canvases, a wall of segmented black-and-white photos of secret corners and alleys around town, and a hall of clay and mixed material sculptures, the building itself was a work of art, and Blaine tried to appreciate all the time and planning that must have gone into it. Eric pointed out specific details, the way a ceiling lofted, or the curve of a wall intended to make the hall seem like a giant wave. He also smiled to point out parts of the building that had brought them a lot of trouble, or had to be re-planned and torn down, only to be built up again.

"The architect wanted the ductwork to remain open here, but it was in violation of code."

He continued on about how he made it work without getting fined by the city, but Blaine watched the way he smiled and explained in calm tones the details of a world she knew so little about. He loved it. Especially the architecture and design of the building.

"Do you ever think about being an architect?" she said as they stood in front of one of the black-and-white photos, blown up to nearly the size of a door.

They focused on the image of an old window front of a downtown store, with old framing and peeling paint, and a gruff-looking cat staring at the photographer with a purely feline scowl. Eric didn't look at her, but studied the cat's face.

"Eric?"

"I—Architects don't make a lot of money and it's really hard to get started in this market."

She stared up at him without saying a word.

He finally looked over at her. "What?"

"I didn't ask if it made money. I asked if you ever thought of doing it? Sounds to me like you have a lot of respect for the process, maybe even a little excitement for it." She leaned in and whispered, "And I know what you sound like when you're excited."

He checked around for any prying eyes or listening ears. "Blaine, it doesn't—"

"Doesn't what? Matter? It does. It matters what you spend your day doing, Eric." Blaine let go of his arm and moved to the next painting.

"I like my job."

"I know you do. And you're good at it." She nodded and studied a painting, smeared in random lines with orange and yellow paint, culminating in thick oil paint ridges, canyons against the plain canvas. She quirked her head, thinking about it. How the texture pulled her eyes from the swoop of color and felt like a buildup of tension that crested in an unbalanced weight on the other side.

"So?" Eric asked.

"So, does it feed your soul?"

"What?" He chuckled and came to stand beside her. "What do you mean, feed my soul?"

"I mean," she leaned closer to him and touched her bare shoulder to his chest, pressing against him, so the heat of their bodies and her perfume mingled with his cologne. She wanted to nuzzle her nose into his chest, but she kept her reserve. "Does it *satisfy* you?" She enunciated the word.

Eric's hand went to her waist, pulled her against his body, and his head dipped low to the delicate space between her earlobe and neck.

"Satisfy me?"

"I'd love to," she said softly, and one of her hands curved up around his neck and into the thick hair at the base of his head.

He kissed her neck.

"I mean, does your work satisfy you?" she whispered, even as her breath caught in her throat. "Do you go home at night feeling fulfilled? Feeling like the work you did was enough. Do you sleep well at night and are you excited to go back to it the next day?"

"Come on, Blaine," he said, "Who has that? No one has that."

"You could. You deserve to," she said.

"Are you happy?" he asked and pulled away to look at her. "What is it—"

"Nice work on this, Morales." A guy in a gray suit pointed at Eric as he walked by.

"Hey, thanks, man." Eric smiled and put up a hand in thanks.

He turned his attention back to her. "I was asking, what is it you really want?"

"I'm mostly happy. But all the money in the world, the prestige, the fancy dresses, none of it can buy me back what I really want." Her gaze fell.

He pulled away to look at her.

Her eyes searched the room. They landed on his father and mother, who stood at the base of a large sculpture, holding hands and laughing. Then to his sister who stood nearby and seemed in a good mood, checking her phone, and texting, while others talked around her.

"I—" She felt small in his arms, suddenly selfish for asking for the thing she wanted most in that moment. To be loved. To have a family. To have her mother back. "I just want . . ."

"What? What is it?"

An older woman approached them. "Mr. Morales, we're so pleased with the work you and your family have done here. It's just the most beautiful building. Such a wonderful thing for the community." Eric paused and turned away from Blaine, hiding his frustration at the interruption.

"I will be sure to pass along the compliment to Loraine. Thank you, Ms. Stafford." He gave a slight bow, and the woman moved on.

"Blaine, what is it you want?" He turned back to her.

She looked into his eyes. Saw the brown depths searching hers as if no one else in the room existed at all. "I want you. I want to feel wanted, and . . . and to be held and . . ." she sniffed. "I'm sorry." She tried to pull away, worried that the sudden show of emotion would embarrass him in front of all of his friends and coworkers.

"Don't," he said and pulled her back by her wrists into his arms. "Don't feel like you can't cry. I know that you've lost a lot, Blaine. I know it's probably been very hard for you. I can't imagine what it was like for you." He paused to look towards where his parents were studying another piece of art. "What it would mean if I were to lose one of them." He caressed up her arm to her neck and gently held the curve of her jaw in his palm, making her teary eyes meet his. He kissed her tenderly.

"But I can't cry, because JT said my mascara would run and I'd look like a hot mess."

At this, Eric chuckled and kissed her again.

"You are pretty hot, but I wouldn't call you a mess." He put his forehead to hers. "Though I would like to mess up that lipstick of yours."

"Oh? It's called *Kissable*."

"It is. You are."

"You're making a scene," Loraine hissed as she passed by them, still staring at her phone and they jumped apart.

"Sorry," Blaine said, but Loraine was already moving on to schmooze with the next group of people.

Eric glared after his sister. "I'm not sure if I'd miss her."

Blaine put her hand up to his cheek and brought his gaze back to hers. "You would. You love her and she loves you. I sometimes wish I had a brother or sister. Maybe not your sister." She shrugged. "I'm sure you'd like a break from her once in a while."

"I wish she had more in her life than just work."

"Well," Blaine stopped and thought, her hip cocked as she looked back to where Lawrence had left earlier. "Maybe I can do something about that."

"You have connections, huh?"

"Well, I know where Lawrence works, and that he's lonely, and he really has a thing for badass women who put him in his place." She raised her eyebrows, and Eric couldn't stop the laughter that sprung from his throat as he took her hand and they moved on through the exhibit.

Eric and Blaine took their time, relaxing in each other's company and forgetting the crowd to study the art and feel what it brought with it. Some of it didn't bring more than an appreciation for the effort, but some pieces . . . a sculpture of a woman carrying a load on her back, nearly sunken to her knees. A painting of a horse stuck in quicksand. A photo of a little girl in angel's wings beside the shadows of two adults, heads bowed and dark . . . caused them both to pause.

"Is all art sad?" she whispered at the little girl's lament.

Eric squeezed her hand.

"Art is meant to make you feel. It doesn't have to be sad." He sighed and went on. "Like the moment in *The Breakfast Club*, when they have to hand in the essay, and it's all about how, even when life tries to box us in, we're a little bit of everything. And even though it was a movie, it was still art. It was a moment in the human experience that everyone who watched could feel. No matter who they were or how they grew up. Because we've all felt that kind of love, that self-acceptance, that rebellion, that freedom. Or we *want* to. We know what it means to be trapped, to be judged, to go without love. We all *fear* those things. Love, fear, joy," he paused, leaned over and whispered, "desire."

Blaine shivered.

"All these things connect us, over time, space, race, culture, country, belief. We all feel those basic human—"

Blaine took him by the lapels of his tuxedo and pulled him into her kiss before he could finish. Surprised but not dissuaded, his hands went around her waist and pulled her closer and his warm tongue tasted hers. Her hands threaded into his hair, and her heart melted into his words.

"Wow," he whispered, as they broke away from one another.

"Existential human understanding gets me kinda hot." She felt her cheeks get warm and wiped the sparkle from his chin.

He smiled and looked like he wanted to pull her into a hidden curation room and do unrefined things to her.

"I think we've been here long enough to say we've made a proper appearance." He quirked one of his beautiful, dark brows.

"Mmm . . . I haven't seen it all yet, though."

"I can bring you back another time."

She laughed. "This is your family's event. You can't just leave."

"But there's something else I'd rather be doing." He winked at her.

"You won't get any arguments from me." She smiled at him. "Just give me one minute for a quick trip to the ladies' room. You stay right here, and I will back in a flash."

"Ok, I won't go anywhere."

She made her way through the crowd to the other side of the room.

"Miss Reynolds." Came a deep male voice. "How are you enjoying the evening?"

Blaine stopped and looked over her shoulder. "Mr. Morales. Hello." She smiled and turned to face him, but inside her stomach was in knots. He had such a commanding presence, especially when she didn't have Eric by her side. "It's such a beautiful building and such a lovely event. Thank you for hosting."

"My pleasure. A lot of work goes into these projects. Sometimes with projects like these, things get in the way and make it more challenging to finish, but ultimately it works out, and it's nice to take the time to celebrate when it's all done."

"Yes, I imagine there are bumps in the process that make it difficult, but you have to work through them."

He gave her a slight smile. "So, you understand that even when something gets in the way, you must persevere. My son works very hard, and I'm glad to know that you understand the importance of his job and his efforts, especially now that you're dating."

"Wait, what exactly do you mean?" Blaine's head spun, and she felt John's seemingly polite words needle under her skin.

"I know you'd never do anything to jeopardize his work or his happiness." Before she could respond, he offered her a slight bow. "It's been a pleasure talking with you, Ms. Reynolds, but I must continue to make my rounds. Have a pleasant evening." He turned and walked away.

Blaine rushed to the ladies' room to catch her breath. She leaned on the sink. Was he talking about the brewery project? Was he telling her to stand down and not get in the way? Was she being selfish and hurting Eric by not relinquishing the store?

She pulled herself together and made her way back to Eric.

He frowned. "Are you okay?"

"Yes." She forced a smile. "My feet are starting to hurt. They aren't used to heels."

"Well, then, let's get you out of here." He took her hand.

As they walked, people stopped to talk to Eric, about the

museum, the business, what his next projects were, and what was next for Morales Construction. He didn't mention the Marshall Mall tear down, and she wasn't sure if that was because he didn't want to spoil the evening for her, or if he'd somehow managed a miracle that would save it. And after the conversation with his dad, should she even be hoping for this miracle?

Most people who stopped to talk to him didn't acknowledge her, especially the men from his office and subcontractors only there to sneak in more ways to earn the Morales family's business.

Occasionally, the person or couple would introduce themselves, and Blaine noticed that Eric seemed relieved to have her step up and talk about herself for a moment. In the space between meeting and greeting, he held her close to his side, like he wanted to rest his head in her softness and be done for the night.

The closer they got to the exit, the more relieved Blaine felt. Her heels were uncomfortable, she was getting tired of smiling, and she wanted to get away from anything work related.

Eric took her hand in his warm, large grasp and brought it to his lips. "What do you think, Cinderella, time to leave this ball?"

"Please," she sighed and leaned against him. They made their way to the door, but Loraine appeared out of their peripheral, a large book in hand.

"Thank God I caught you." She smiled so wide and so full that Blaine was honestly scared out of her mind by it.

"Uh, what?" she said.

"Before you two leave, I'd love to have Blaine sign the guest book."

"Guest book? But why?" Eric looked at his sister sideways and Blaine noticed.

"Everyone who's here is signing it. It's not a big deal. I just want to make sure we have a record of you being here for the museum. Is that okay?" she asked and held the book out, open to a marked spot just for her.

Blaine studied Loraine's face, thought about the soft spot she had for Lawrence, and what it must be like to be a woman in a construction business, having to work twice as hard, if not more, to make it in the same world. This was her project, and it was beautiful, and Blaine felt sorry for all the times she'd made fun of Loraine.

She smiled. "Of course. I'm happy to." She took the pen and signed exactly where Loraine pointed. Loraine swept the book away quickly.

"You did an amazing job, Loraine." Blaine said before Loraine could leave.

Loraine stopped and looked at her.

"This museum is so beautiful. You should be very proud. It was a lot of work, and I'm sure such a huge part of your life. I know the community is going to be enjoying it for a long time. That's a huge accomplishment."

Loraine held the book tightly to her chest. Her bottom lip trembled as she looked at her shoes.

She took a breath and stood tall again. "Thank you," she muttered, but her face fell as she walked away.

"She okay?" Blaine asked.

"I'm not sure. I think she's up to something. She seems guilty."

"Maybe she just feels bad because I gave her an honest compliment even after she's been such a hard ass to me." Blaine shrugged and watched her go.

Eric shook his head. "I hope that's all."

They made their way to the front door, and before they could escape, one more voice called Eric's name. Blaine groaned. Eric rolled his eyes, and they turned to see his father beckoning Eric back. Eric pulled Blaine behind him, but she tugged back against him.

"What?" he asked.

"I think he wants to speak to you alone." She nodded to where his dad looked at Eric with a worried brow. "I'll be outside. I can get the car if you want. That is, if you trust me with your baby?" she teased.

"Fine." Eric sighed and gave her hand a quick squeeze. "I'll be with you as quickly as I can."

Blaine went to get the car with the ticket that Eric handed her. She couldn't help but peer back up into the entryway to see if she could tell what was being discussed. The conversation she had with John earlier replayed in her mind, and she wondered if this had something to do with that. All she could tell was that John was disappointed about something, and that Eric was mad. He threw his hands up and said something like, "You don't know anything about it!"

"Don't raise your voice to me young man!" his father responded, loud enough to carry down the stairs, and Eric stormed out the door towards her, just as the valet pulled out in front with the car.

Blaine held up her hands as he approached. "Hey, are you okay?"

"Just get in, please." He yanked opened her door for her.

Worried about his sudden change of demeanor and what his father must have said to him, she did what he asked. He got in and they both rode in silence as he pulled away from the museum and onto the less-crowded street.

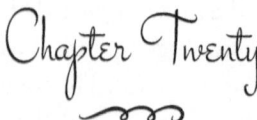

Chapter Twenty

It was late, and the orange glow of the city streets as they passed in waves overhead made Blaine feel dizzy. She opened the window for some fresh air and felt the cool breeze caress her cheeks. Glancing over, she saw that his fists clenched tight around the wheel and his shoulders hunched forward.

"Eric? Are you okay? What did he say to you?"

"I don't want to talk about it."

She paused for a moment, folded her hands in her lap, picked at a hangnail and took in a deep, steadying breath.

"That's the thing. I think you need to talk about it. I think if you don't, you're just going to either keep it inside until it eats away at you, slowly causing you to have a mental breakdown, or you're going to snap one day at the wrong person and someone will be hurt."

He didn't say anything, but his eyes shifted over to her briefly.

She went on. "I'm a safe space, Eric. You can say whatever you need to, tell me what you need to or want to. I don't have ties to your dad. I will always take your side."

The silence between them was sad, and she realized he was taking her back to her house. She wondered if he would stay, or if the pain of what his father had said had angered him too deeply.

"You know," she began. "I never knew my dad. He walked out on my mom before I was even born. She didn't feel like he was even worth the time for me to get to know. He must have thought I wasn't worth the time, either, because he never showed up. No birthdays, no holidays. Last I heard, he was playing some clubs in Vegas and gambling most of his life away. So . . ." Blaine choked down the emotions trying to escape.

Eric stopped at a light and looked over at her.

She looked up at him. "So, I don't know what it's like to have a dad who cares. Maybe it seems like your dad cares too much. But it's because he loves you. I can see it when he looks at you. I think some people are afraid to let go. Especially when they love and worry for their kids."

Eric stayed silent, as though all her words were trying to find a place in his busy brain to land. As though they had begun to cut through the static of the anger he had left the party with.

"Blaine, I'm sorry about your dad."

She shook her head. "I'm not. I had a wonderful mom who loved me, and took care of me, and showed me all the beauty in the world and then some. I'm sure there are things she'd wished I'd done differently. Dreams she had that she wished I would have pursued. But you have to believe me when I say that the best way to make your parents happy is by finding your happiness. Business or not, you are their son. They love you more. Even more than their company."

Eric's dark eyes filled with tears, and he sniffed. The light turned green. He didn't say anything, but hit the accelerator and sped the few remaining blocks to her house. He drove so fast that Blaine was concerned he'd be pulled over. He screeched to a halt in front of her house.

"Wow, we got here quick. I guess you're eager to get back to the party?"

"No." He unbuckled his seatbelt.

"No? You're right, that was a big night. You should go home and get some rest." She nodded and got out of her seat with some effort, only to find him there when she extracted herself from the small car. "Oh!" she said in surprise as he pulled her into his arms.

The cool night air surrounded them as he kissed her with an intense longing.

"I don't want to go back to my place, and I sure as hell don't want to go back to that party. I want to go home, Blaine," he gasped against her lips. "Your home, with your ridiculous guinea pig, and your shag carpet, and the poster of David Bowie on the back of your door. I want to be with you tonight, nowhere else." He pulled her closer and put his hand on her cheek. "I want to spend the night in your bed, in your arms, making love to you, until this world feels right again."

Blaine nearly melted to the ground, but he held her upright, and she shivered against the heat of his hands. She could only nod. She wanted the same things, the comfort and the release from the pressures and stress, and the feeling they could just be safe in one another's arms.

She took quick but wobbly steps to the door, with his hand in hers, and unlocked it. JT had long since left, and the house was quiet. Even Charles Dumar was contentedly passed out in his hay trough, snoring lightly. The first thing Blaine did was shed her shoes, kicking them off as he closed the door behind them. She took his hand and led him back to her bedroom.

There, she turned on the lamp beside the bed, giving her skin a soft, honeyed glow in the low light.

"You are so beautiful," he whispered. "You were stunning tonight, charming and wonderful."

She sighed. "Eric, you give me far too much credit. All I did was stand there in a dress. You, on the other hand, you wowed the whole room. People like you."

"People like you too." He smiled.

"I'm just . . ."

"What?"

"Ordinary."

Eric shook his head. "No, *Cariña*. You are anything but." He came to her and gently pulled the pins out of her hair, one by one, until it fell in soft waves over her shoulders. Then, with strong and capable fingers, he pulled the tiny zipper of her dress down her back. "You look amazing in this dress, but what I want now is underneath." He growled and gently bit into her neck.

She gasped, and her hands held onto his strong shoulders before pushing his suit coat down and stripping it off. She loosened his tie as his tongue traced a warm line down her neck, and her fingers fumbled with the buttons on his shirt.

Her whole body shook, aching to have his warmth and heat against her skin. As he pushed the weighted sequin dress down past her hips, she stepped out of it, and then he undid the rest of his buttons. He pulled off the stiff dress shirt, popping the undone cufflinks out, and tossed it to the floor before guiding her to the bed.

"Eric," she whispered as his hands wound around her rib cage to find the clasp on the strapless and padded bra.

While he struggled with that, she tried to shimmy out of the control-top garment but found it incredibly difficult while breathing heavily and wanting nothing more than to feel his skin against her.

She finally broke down in giggles and pushed him away. "Give me a minute to get out of all of this." She motioned at her undergarments.

"I can help . . ." He kissed her neck.

"I think the only thing that will help is the Jaws of Life right now. I don't want you to have to witness the struggle of extracting myself." Her cheeks felt hot, and he laughed along with her.

"I'll wait," he whispered and kissed her before she turned to leave.

He gently grabbed her backside, and she slapped his hand in surprise with a laugh. Alone in her bathroom, Blaine managed to get free of all the layers of confining spandex, but felt self-conscious at the idea of heading into the room wearing nothing at all, so she wrapped a towel around herself and came out.

She hadn't been the only one to get undressed, and her pulse jumped up when she saw Eric standing completely naked at the foot of her bed. He was combing through his hair with his fingers and looked at her with a smile.

"What's the towel for?" he asked.

"My modesty?" she squeaked.

"Unnecessary." He shook his head, crossed the room, and tugged the towel away before wrapping her up in his arms and carrying her to the bed. Blaine could have worried about a lot of things in that moment. She could have worried what his parents thought of her, or if they would help him save her shop. She could have thought about what the morning would bring, or if he was going to start following his dreams instead of his father's dream. She could have thought about what her mother would think about the whole thing, and if she would tell her to keep her heart and her store separate.

But she didn't think about any of those things. Only his hands on her skin, his mouth on hers, and the heated breaths they took together as they locked the rest of the world outside and lost themselves to the heat and need of being together.

Chapter Twenty-One

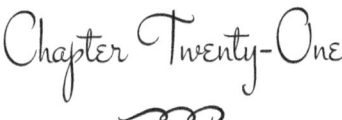

Blaine woke slowly to the steady rhythm of Eric's heartbeat below her cheek. She was hot. The man was like a furnace. She kicked a bare leg out of the sheets, but couldn't pull herself away from his delicious and relaxed body. He mumbled while he turned and spooned her tightly against him. Her whole world lit up. She snuggled back against him, and he made an animal-like grunt into her neck.

"*Cariña*, again? I need food." He chuckled, but she could tell, beneath the sheets, he was just as ready as she was.

"We could order in Abuelita's; they make really good breakfast burritos," she whispered seductively.

Eric groaned and undulated against her. "Chorizo, eggs, potato . . ." Every ingredient brought another hungry sound from his throat as he continued to kiss and bite her neck.

"Hot coffee," she gasped and turned in his arms to face him.

"We probably ought to eat first, sí?" He brushed the wild curls from off her forehead. His thumb traced the small circles below her eyes. "You didn't get much sleep."

"I was busy."

"Oh?"

"Mmm . . . had my hands full all night."

"You must be tired with all that work."

"Well, when you love your job, it never really feels like work." She snuggled in.

He cocked his head and studied her face, the pad of his thumb gently running over her bottom lip.

"Do you?"

"Do I what?" she whispered.

"Love your job?"

"You mean the store or last night's 'project'?" she giggled. He smiled, but it was a sad smile. She took a deep breath and stepped up to the fear. "Both. I love both."

"Do you . . ." The words stuck in his throat and his brow fell. "Blaine, I feel like I should tell you something."

The seriousness, the morose tone, the way he looked as though he might cry, made her wonder if it was about how he couldn't save her shop.

"Is it about the shop?" she asked and pulled away.

The coolness of the space between them seemed to frighten him. He shook his head and pulled her close. He settled her on top of his chest, straddling his bare hips. She sat up.

"No, it's not about the shop," he said. "It's that I think I'm falling in love with you, Blaine." He blurted out the words and then looked up at her.

Worried creases marred his beautiful brow, and she leaned down to kiss them, softly, slowly, until she made her way down his face, his cheeks, his jaw.

"Blaine, please tell me what you're thinking."

"I *know* I've already fallen," she whispered in his ear. "The minute you let me win at *Pong* just to spend more time with me, I knew I was in trouble. By the time you kissed powdered sugar off my nose, I was completely head over heels."

"Head over heels?"

"In love," she whispered and bit his collar bone.

With laughing and breathless kisses, they made love in the early morning sun, and tumbled back into bed until the growling of their stomachs forced them to get dressed and find something to eat. He had nothing but his tuxedo pants and dress shirt from the night before. Blaine laughed when he discovered, after the heated tearing off of his shirt, the cufflinks had been scattered somewhere in her bedroom. Not wanting to waste the time looking for them, he rolled his cuffs up his forearms and left the shirt untucked in a lazy, sexy way that made Blaine want to take him back to bed instead of to breakfast.

"Are you even remotely aware of how good looking you are?" she asked over the hood of his car as they leaned against it and ate their burritos from the foil wrappers, sauce dripping into the dirt parking lot beneath their feet.

He was being as careful as possible not to get it on his shirt, but failed at avoiding his pants. "What? No way."

"Come on." She looked him up and down. "Oh, yeah. You're hot, Mr. Morales."

"Well, how about you? You're gorgeous, and cute, and got that whole Madonna, 'Lucky Star' thing going for you." He winked and took a big bite.

"Flattery will get you everywhere," she said. "Want me to roll around on the hood of your car?"

"Please don't." He stopped mid bite.

She laughed and leaned over to kiss him, spicy sauce still on her lips. "Am I keeping you from big, important things today?"

He studied her lips and shook his head as he finished his burrito. "No, nothing too important—"

The Wicked Witch of the West cackled from his back pocket.

"Let me guess, your sister?" Blaine finished her burrito, crunching up the foil and wiping her hands on the tattered napkin they shared.

He pulled out his phone and silenced it. "How'd you know? Let's get out of here."

"Out of Abuelita's parking lot, or like, the country?"

"Let's run away." He looked over at her. "Let's get in the car and just drive."

"Wow, you really don't want to talk to your sister, do you?"

"I just want to get away from our lives, and these pressures."

"I want that too." Blaine moved over to stand between his knees as he leaned against the car. He smiled and kissed her when her hands threaded around his neck.

"Okay then."

"But we can't just run away from everything, Eric. Life doesn't work that way. We might get far away, but it won't stop things from happening."

He sighed, kissed her, and nodded. "You're right. But can we at least get out of town for the day?"

Blaine looked at him. She supposed she could take a day off from the shop. It wasn't like she was getting a lot of foot traffic, since most of the other businesses were moving out and the news had spread that the whole thing was about to get demolished for another beer haven. She shrugged.

"Why not? But just for today. Because you have Sunday lunch with your family tomorrow, and I'm supposed to be helping JT and Deb set up their new shop."

"Okay." He kissed her. His hands ran up her back, through her black mesh shirt and cami top, to her hair, tied in a bright neon scrunchie. "Get in then, Material Girl."

They sped out of town and up to the mountains on a long drive through the twisting roads and high granite walls that surrounded the river below them. It was quiet and calm, and neither said too much. It felt good to physically get away, but her mind didn't want to. She replayed the conversation with Eric's dad from the event last night. *Even when something gets in the way, you must persevere.* Was he saying that he was going to do everything necessary to move her shop out, or that Eric wasn't going to let anything get in the way?

Considering how quiet Eric was, Blaine suspected he had a lot on his mind too, and that it may or may not have to do with how he wanted to live his life going forward.

She knew that's what was on her mind.

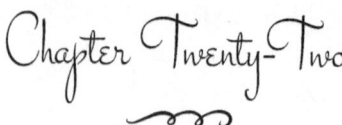

Chapter Twenty-Two

The trip to Estes Park for the afternoon was relaxing. He drove the mountain climb with precision, and the car hugged every curve. Blaine started to understand why he liked it so much. It was definitely a more comfortable ride than her Ford Escort.

They came around the corner, and the towering peaks of the Rocky Mountains created an incredible backdrop to the town. She hadn't been to Estes Park in years, and forgot the overwhelming beauty of it. Apparently, everyone in the state had escaped to the mountains to enjoy it, too. It used to be that Estes was only busy in the summer months or during elk rutting season, but now it didn't seem to matter what time of year it was.

"I remember when you could find parking right on the street." Blaine shook her head as they walked down the highway from a faraway spot he'd found to park.

"Shocking." He laughed. "I remember when there wasn't a line at the ice cream shop."

"Unheard of." Blaine smiled as they made their way toward downtown.

Eric held her hand in a familiar and reassuring way that made her feel warm and part of something. As if in an unspoken agreement, they didn't talk about the night before, the hard conversation with his father, or what would happen the next day. Right now, all that mattered was this moment.

They held hands and window shopped. They laughed as they people-watched and ate ice cream on a bench outside the bookstore. Across the street, a bronze statue of a girl dancing caught Eric's attention, and he told her a story of when they were kids and Loraine had wanted to be a dancer. Their father had told her that better work was to be done with her mind. When they'd gotten home from her last recital, their father canceled her dancing lessons and put her in the STEM program at a prestigious private school in Marshall. Eric soon followed.

"Wow, talk about grooming your kids for the life you want them to have," Blaine said over her melting scoop of bubble gum ice cream.

Eric licked the drips from his rocky road, and she watched his tongue with some envy for the ice cream.

He shrugged. "They did us a favor. They ensured we'd have careers." He stopped and looked at her with his eyes wide. "I didn't mean that your—"

"No—no need to try to salvage that one," she said and tried to brush it off. "Our parents had different priorities. That's all."

She held back that her mom had only one future wish for her daughter, and that was her happiness. Her mom always told her that money, career, success, and prestige were all things that could be easily lost, and would not always guarantee happiness. She didn't say those things to Eric. But she felt them deep in her chest. The ice cream turned in her stomach and she tossed the rest into the trash can beside her.

"You okay?" he asked.

She nodded and sat back against the bench next to him. "Yeah, it didn't taste as good as I remember. Plus, we have a winding road back to Marshall, and I'm sure you don't want me puking pink across your dashboard."

"I'd hold your hair back," he said.

"Protecting my hair over your interior? This must be true love."

"It is," he whispered and kissed her.

Chocolate and sweet, and sticky. Blaine kissed him back, hungrily, and for a moment, forgot that the world was outside this tiny mountain town, like a storm cloud waiting to descend. She felt like he had the night before. She just wanted to run away with him. And be free of the hard battles coming.

They finished their tour of the town and walked up the long road to the car when the sun started to set over the magnificent mountains.

"We should come back sometime. There are some cute cabins to rent in the area," he said over the hood before she got in. The future plans of his heart made her feel warm, almost hopeful.

"I'd like that a lot. Promise me we will," she said softly.

"I promise, *Cariña*. We'll come back and run away for longer next time."

When they pulled up in front of her house, she turned to him. "I know you have plans tomorrow, and if you want to sleep in your own bed, I wouldn't blame you for not wanting to come in—"

"Of course I want to come in, unless you don't want me to."

"Says the man who tried seducing me with his 'tongue and ice cream show'?" she laughed.

"You saw that?"

"The whole street saw it. Moms were covering their kids' eyes, while simultaneously storing that image of you in their fantasy banks."

"Shut up." He laughed and got out. "Would you mind if I took a shower, though?"

"I'd like that—but only if I can help."

"How about you can 'help' in the shower, if I can give you a private 'tongue and ice cream show'," he said in her ear as she unlocked the door.

Shivers ran up Blaine's spine, and her knees felt weak. She turned around, and his arms were set on either side of her head against the door, pinning her seductively against it.

"But I'm out of ice cream." She breathed softly and stared at his mouth.

His tongue wet his lips and he flashed her a perfect smile. "I'm sure I can find an acceptable substitute." He kissed her.

Blaine's hand fumbled with the door handle, and they tumbled into the house, a tangle of limbs, kisses, and laughter. Down the hall and into the bathroom, they stripped each other down and tossed their clothes unceremoniously into a pile in the corner of the room before starting the shower, and made good on all of their prearranged agreements.

Eric woke up sometime in the middle of the night, exhausted, every muscle in his body relaxed and warm. He looked over and saw Blaine, curled into a small ball on the other side of her queen bed, wrapped in most of the covers. The soft shadows of her unruly hair and the dip of her waist. The woman who had stolen his heart in only a few short weeks.

His abuela had always said that love worked in mysterious and powerful ways. Like a hurricane sweeps in, or an earthquake hits. It's rarely predictable, often unavoidable, and sometimes catastrophic. But Blaine was less like a force of nature, and more like a soft summer rain in the middle of a dry spell. He scooted closer, pulled her body close to him, and the tense ball of her midnight dreams relaxed under his warm hands. How could he ever destroy her shop now?

He couldn't.

He'd tell his father today. He'd find a new place, a new site. He'd work with the brewery to find an even better place. He'd talk to the previous tenants and see if they would like to move back in. They could find another buyer for the property. Maybe he'd even convince his father it was a property worth owning. The high hopes of these fanciful dreams seemed so clear and true in the dark. He never even questioned them when the dawn peered through her window sheers and landed on the bed where she still slept, curled trustingly into his arms. He would find a way. He had to.

He crawled out of bed quietly to let her sleep while he made coffee, and got lost in her kitchen in an effort to make her breakfast. She must not like to cook, given how little was on her shelves and the sad emptiness of her fridge. Though, being single himself, he knew how little time he wanted to spend on cooking for one at the end of the day. And looking at the sad, lone carrot in her crisper drawer, she could be struggling to pay bills. Eric's gut twisted as he closed the fridge door. Blaine had always said it wasn't about the money, but what if she was really struggling financially? What would happen if he couldn't convince his parents?

Couldn't wasn't part of the Morales family's vocabulary. He toasted up the bread she had left, and boiled the last four eggs, resolved to make sure he went grocery shopping sometime with her. It would be interesting to see what she would pick out. He'd seen a box of Cap'n Crunch in her cabinet and wondered if the universe knew they were soulmates from that alone. He washed the carrot and put it in Charles's pen to the pleased and happy grunts of the guinea pig. He was sure that was probably fine, right? Rodents ate carrots. He was almost sure.

When he came into her room, plate balanced with eggs, toast, jam, and a hot cup of coffee, she sat up with a startled intake of breath and nearly knocked the plate from his hand.

"Easy." He laughed and righted the eggs with a dexterity impressive for so early.

"What? Oh, God . . . sorry." She pushed her wayward hair

from her eyes. "You made me breakfast?" Blaine put her hand to her mouth and smiled at him.

"Well, it wasn't easy. You don't have a lot to work with in there."

She blushed. "Sunday is grocery shopping day." She shrugged as she sat on the foot of her bed and put the plate between them.

"Well, in that case you should know this is the last of your bread and eggs, and I gave your last carrot to the affable Mr. Dumar."

She smiled around her bite of toast and leaned forward with a light in her eyes.

"You fed my guinea pig?"

"I figured you may have forgotten last night."

"I did have other things on my mind." She leaned in and kissed him after his first sip of coffee. "Do you have to go?" Blaine handed him a slice of toast and cracked the egg against the side of the plate before peeling it.

"I do. Wish I didn't though."

"You don't want to miss the recap of the opening. Besides, who knows? Maybe Lawrence will be there to meet the parents." Blaine smiled.

"Ha! That would be a shock. For everyone. Loraine probably most of all." He handed her the cup of coffee. "Cream and no sugar, just like you like it."

"I love you," she said.

Eric's mouth turned up at one corner, and he leaned forward to kiss her cheek.

"I love you back, Blaine," he whispered, and wished it was enough to make everything outside of her bed right, despite the world that was working against them. "I should go," he said softly and kissed her jelly-sweet lips.

"Okay." She nodded and held the sheet close to her chest as he rose to collect his clothes.

"I'll give you a call tonight?"

"Of course, I'll need the play-by-play of Lawrence-Gate."

He hopped into his pants, put on his two-day-old shirt, now with ice cream stains, and leaned down to kiss her one last time.

"Get outta here," she teased and nudged his chin with her nose. "Before you make me want to keep you and get crumbs in my bed."

"No one wants that." He smiled, kissed her nose, and left before he could be tempted even more to stay.

Blaine watched him leave, heard him tell Charles goodbye, which melted her heart, and then the front door closed behind him. The sound of his engine starting up and driving away filled her with sadness, and she sat with it, her breakfast half-eaten between her knees. She should shower, get dressed, and try to look like she hadn't been in bed for two days before going to JT's new salon. She'd promised to help set some things up and give her honest opinion about the décor, and if she thought it would bring people in or scare them off.

Of course, JT probably wouldn't want to hear Blaine's preference for brighter colors and only 80s new wave hits being fed through the sound system. While she looked forward to seeing her friend and sharing the joy of their new place, all she really wanted to do was cuddle back into the pillow Eric had slept on and forget everything else. Thinking of JT's new place and the end of an era at Marshall Mall created a deep sinking feeling in her chest. She was the only one who hadn't moved on yet. She had put her hope in Eric and their arrangement. Was she being selfish by holding on to this hope and putting Eric in an uncomfortable position?

She wondered how he was really feeling. And what was really going to happen tomorrow at the official end of the bet. They hadn't talked about it last night, and it felt as though it were two different people who had made the original bet, about some other shop, in some other city that they weren't a part of. She wished that were true.

Worrying about it wasn't going to change what tomorrow brought. Blaine sighed and looked at the clock. She put the plate carefully on her bedside table and got up.

Eric drove away with such a distracted mind that he wasn't sure how he made it back to his apartment. He didn't remember any of the turns or traffic lights. He didn't remember anything, except his midnight revelation that he was going to save her shop and that he was supposed to talk to his dad about it today. In a matter of hours.

What in the hell had he been thinking?

The elevator took him to the top floor of the new and modern condo, and he distractedly opened the door to the quiet space. It felt unused and unloved. His fridge didn't make a soft humming noise, and there wasn't the gentle smell of hay from a guinea pig pen or the strange light of pink flowery curtains covering the windows. There weren't any posters on the walls, or pictures of 80s rock icons. There wasn't a haphazard pile of Keds and Chucks beside the door below coat hooks with an odd mix of denim and Members Only jackets. There just wasn't enough Blaine here, and he felt at a loss. On his way to the bedroom, he stopped to look out over the early morning city, bathed in a quiet purple-pink glow. He undressed, knowing the tux would probably be a lost deposit, given its stains and missing cufflinks, but he wanted to keep it anyway to help him remember two of the best days he had had in a long time. He put it in his hamper and slowly made his way to the shower, formulating a plan to convince his family that Back To The 80s and Blaine Reynolds were worth the chance.

Eric arrived at his parents' house early for Sunday brunch to talk with them alone before Loraine woke up. He needed to talk to his dad and mom without her interrupting. Tell him how he felt, tell him what Blaine had shown him. He wanted to reiterate his mother's own thoughts; that there had to be more to their lives than work, and Blaine had shown him so much. She'd shown him a world of love and light and brightness. And that was worth saving. He took deep breaths up to the door, and didn't knock as he came in.

"Hola?" he said.

His mother called back from the kitchen in an excited voice.

"Hola! Did you bring her?"

Eric didn't have to ask who she meant. His mother knew his heart better than he did, and he was sure she could see at the party how in love he already was. Maybe even before he knew it. He came into the kitchen.

"No, Mamá, not this time." He smiled and kissed her cheek while she stood in the kitchen in her Sunday clothes, covered with his abuela's apron.

She made a displeased click with her tongue. "You should have. I need to thank her."

"For what?" Eric said.

"For this." She took his hand and led him to the kitchen table where she had opened the gift. "I meant to wait for her to open it, but I just couldn't stand the suspense. So . . ." She clasped her hands together like an excited kid and spread them out over the shadow-boxed collection. The one he held in his hands only a few weeks ago. The Gloria Estefan t-shirt, signed ticket, and bangle, arranged within the protective case. A note sat next to it and Eric picked it up.

Ms. Morales, Eric told me Gloria Estefan was one of your favorites, and it just so happens I had this lying around in my shop. I hope it gives you so much joy. Thank you for inviting me to the opening of your beautiful museum. Thank you also for raising such an amazing young man.

Eric read it out loud in a whispered breath, as though in prayer. He smiled at the warmth of it. She hadn't made a profit from the photo. She knew he was interested, and she could have sold it to him the day he came to her shop for lunch, but Blaine knew it wasn't about the money. He looked at his mother, admiring the collection with such joy on her face. Blaine made happiness happen. And he couldn't imagine a world without Back To The 80s or Blaine Reynolds in it.

"Mamá, I didn't tell her to—"

"I know, *mijo*. I think she's just that sweet."

"She is." He kissed his mother's forehead.

"I'm going to go find a place for it."

"Mamá, where's Papá?"

"In his office. You know, always more work to be done," she said, exasperated, and still used to the normal they'd adopted over time.

Eric walked back to the office with a lump in his throat. He knocked softly and came in to see his father, his Sunday clothes getting wrinkled in the chair, tie loosened as he peered over his glasses to his screen.

"Is lunch ready?" he asked, mid work stride.

"No, not yet. Papá, I need to talk to you."

"Is it about the septic system of the old mall? I called the contractor last week, since you seem to be dragging your feet on it."

"No, it's not—"

"Is it the young lady? I know you seem to be pretty serious about her, Eric, but does she realize how much of a time commitment your job is? Especially with Snake River Brewery coming up so fast?"

"Papá, it's not about her. Well, I mean it's sort of about her, but it's more about her shop—"

"Her what?"

"I think what my little *hermano* is trying to say is that it's about her shop. In the mall." Loraine came in behind Eric with a sly smile on her face.

"What shop?"

"What are you even doing here, Loraine?" Eric shot his sister a glare. "I'm trying to talk to Papá in *private*."

"So talk to him. Tell him all about the little knick-knack shop she runs in the mall you're supposed to be tearing down *next week*. And how she still hasn't moved out." She looked less satisfied with the revelation, and more mad that he'd betrayed the family by falling in love with someone so inconvenient. Almost as if she wasn't happy about telling their dad either, but somehow felt obligated.

"Thank you Loraine, but I do know who she is and about her little shop." He looked over at his daughter, then at Eric. "But I didn't know she still hadn't moved out. Is this true, Eric?"

"Papá, please let me explain." Eric turned to his father, feeling desperate.

"She knows it's being torn down, right?" John looked sideways at him.

"Well, see, that's the thing—"

"They had a bet. He shook her hand, Papá, and bet her that she couldn't convince him it was worth saving." Loraine interrupted before he could explain.

"Loraine! What the hell?"

"Eric Hector! No blasphemy, especially on a Sunday." John reprimanded. "Did you give this girl your word?"

"It's more than that, Papá. I did bet her that she couldn't convince me the shop was worth saving. And there's no real way to measure that. But the bet doesn't really matter. She—her mother has the controlling say in the sale of the mall. She's supposed to have to sign it before the sale can go through. I did make a bet that she couldn't convince me. But I also wanted to help convince her to sign."

It was a half-truth made in desperation, trying to avoid his father's wrath. Suddenly, the ideas in his head from the night before and all the things he'd meant to tell his father fell away.

Dreams often die in the harsh light of reality, and Eric's stomach fell as he realized that Blaine's dream was no different.

"You don't even have to worry about the contract," Loraine said and pulled out a sheet of paper from her purse. "I meant to get this to you earlier, Papá."

"What in the he—"

"Eric."

"What is that?" he demanded of Loraine.

"Just a little insurance policy in case you started thinking with your 'wrong' brain and put the whole project in jeopardy." She nodded towards his groin.

"Loraine! Sunday." John reprimanded, nearly at his wits' end with the two bickering and irreverent children.

"What's that supposed to mean?" Eric asked her. "What's on the paper?"

"The solution to all of your problems." She smiled and handed it over to their father. He put his glasses back up on his nose and read through it.

"Looks like the contract won't be a problem," John said. "And you got this willingly? From her?" he asked his daughter, who arched one perfect brow with a shrug.

"Mostly. I mean, she did say she'd love to sign it."

Realization dawned on Eric. The guest book. That's why Loraine had been so insistent on Blaine signing it. She must have covered up the contract and had her sign on the line for it.

"You—" he sputtered. "You can't do that! It's illegal. There's no way she would have signed that willingly."

"Did you tell her she had rights to the sale of the mall, Eric?"

He hadn't. He wanted to, and even tried once, but then they wouldn't have gotten to see each other. She wouldn't have taken him to the movies, the concert, shown him what it was to be loved for who he was.

"I—" he said.

"Lunch is ready," his mom said as she popped into the office and then stopped. "What is it, what's happened? Who died?" she asked, spatula in hand.

"Blaine's dream." Eric's throat closed in, and the room got smaller. "Mamá, I'm sorry. I need to go." He stormed from the house to the sound of his father yelling at his back.

"You get back here, young man! You owe me an explanation!"

Eric slammed the front door and drove away. He couldn't go to her house. He couldn't go to his. He pointed his car south, towards Denver and got the hell out of town as fast as he could.

Chapter Twenty-Three

Monday morning was a blur. Most of the other tenants were busy trying to finalize their new arrangements. JT and Deb's salon was all but cleared out, so much so that they didn't even come in that day, and Blaine looked at the darkened and empty shop with a mix of sadness and worry as she pulled into the front of the mall. Was she being an idiot? She had to believe, after the month they'd shared, and especially after the weekend they'd spent together, that he would try his best to help keep her shop from being torn down. Eric was smart, she reasoned; he had to have something up his sleeve. He wasn't heartless. He loved her.

She hoped enough.

Lawrence was in the dojo early, and Blaine could hear him pummeling the only bag left when she got out of her car. He was a fighter, formerly an all-state champion, and she knew he'd faced a lot of hardships in his life. This would just be one more, and he'd probably roll with the punches and somehow come out on top. Like a scraggly tomcat with nine lives and then some. Still—she wished she could help him out too. For as gruff as he was, he'd never been unkind to her. She waved at him, and he paused in his punching to wave back with a head nod. Offhand, she wondered how his weekend went, and if he and Loraine really were a thing.

As she was unlocking the door to Back To The 80s, Stewart Peterson, the owner of the building, pulled up into the parking lot and honked to get her attention. The old Cadillac's horn sounded like a foghorn in the quiet morning, and it startled her.

"Hello Blaine." Stewart greeted her as he got out of his car. "How are things?"

"Well, they're—" she stopped short of saying "good," as they weren't really. "It's okay. I'm okay. I guess. How are you, Mr. Peterson?"

"I'm just fit as a fiddle. I'm glad that I caught you."

"What can I do for you? Come on inside." She unlocked the store and ushered him in. He took off his driving tam as he entered and looked around.

"I always did love this place. So did your mom."

"We all love it," Blaine said wistfully with a growing hope in her chest. "It's a shop worth having."

"I'm surprised you haven't packed any of it up."

"Well, I have unreasonable levels of hope." She shrugged.

He pursed his mouth and looked at her oddly.

"Blaine, speaking of that, I wanted to talk to you about your mom."

"My mom?"

"Right, and the contract. I'd nearly forgotten about our agreement until Ms. Morales brought it up during our negotiation meeting this morning."

"My, wait, what agreement? You had an agreement with my mom?"

"Oh yes, your mom and I had an agreement, many years ago, when she first moved in. It was just a little amendment to the contract between friends."

Blaine's hand paused over the light switch before flicking it on, and she turned to face him.

"What kind of amendment?"

"Well, you know. The one Loraine brought to you with the contract."

"I'm not sure what you're talking about. What kind of agreement did you have with my mom?" A strange sense of fear and confusion filled Blaine's chest, and she walked over to lean against a shelf in front of Mr. Peterson.

"Well, it doesn't really matter now as you've signed away your right as the executor of the amendment. I just came here to, well I wanted to tell you thank you for understanding."

"I didn't sign anything. What are you talking about, Mr. Peterson?" Blaine's voice rose. "What amendment?"

He looked at her as if she'd hit her head and forgotten what decade she was living in.

"Your mom and I had an agreement when she first moved in. She was afraid of someday not being able to afford the rent, and you were such a little kid at the time, that I—I wanted to help her feel more secure. So, I told her that I would write an amendment to her lease that if I ever sold the property, she would have to agree to the sale in order for it to go through. But that was nearly thirty years ago, and I had forgotten about it until we were going through with the sale and all that legal rigmarole that happens when lawyers get involved—"

"Wait, she had to agree to the sale?"

"Right."

"Of the whole mall?"

"Well, yes. And you, being her proxy . . ." he paused and held his hat as he bowed his head in a moment of silence, "now that she's passed, had to agree to it as well. I wanted to thank you for understanding, and for signing the paper so we could get the process going. Barbara and I are eager to retire somewhere warm before another winter here."

"But, I didn't. Mr. Peterson, I didn't sign anything." She felt like her head might explode while the world simultaneously fell around her.

Mr. Peterson looked confused, as if they'd crossed over into an alternate dimension. "But Ms. Morales called this morning and said she had the necessary paperwork, and that the sale would be going through today. I stopped by the Morales' office this morning and signed the final paperwork."

"Today?" Blaine's legs felt weak. Hadn't Eric just crawled out of her bed only yesterday morning, sweet and sleepy and drinking her coffee with no shirt on, smiling and kissing her goodbye? Hadn't he confessed how much he loved being with her and how she made him feel alive? When had she even had time to sign anything after they'd gotten home from the museum opening . . .

Blaine felt weak as the memory flooded back in.

Loraine. Loraine had asked her to sign the guest book. She was insistent upon it. Almost to a strange degree. That was the last thing she'd signed amid any Moraleses. She felt sick to her stomach and dizzy. Stewart steadied her with his arthritic hand.

"Easy, Blaine, are you okay? I thought you knew what it was all about. I don't think there's any way to take it back now."

Blaine didn't answer.

How could she have been such an idiot? Loraine and Eric had played her for a goddamn fool. One seduced her. The other snuck in to steal her store. She pushed Stewart's hand away and stumbled to the door of her shop.

"Can you please leave, Mr. Peterson? I—I have some things to . . ." Her voice trailed off as the tears began to fill her eyes and throat. The old man nodded, blue eyes watery and sad as he gently put his cap back on, tipped it to her, and walked out of her shop, probably for the last time.

Blaine let the door swing closed behind him but did not flip her sign over to open. Was it true? Maybe, she thought with the hopefulness of a heart too trusting, maybe Eric didn't know anything about it. She paced, chewed on a nail, and thought. How could he have said all those things while still knowing what his sister was planning to do? Had he seduced her because he knew she'd never sign it on her own? Only if he convinced her? Did the Morales family's business side run so deep and cruel that even love was a tool to bargain with?

She watched Mr. Peterson get in his boat of a car to drive away. The most likely story was probably true. Even if it hurt her to think about it. Eric knew. And he chose not to tell her.

"People can lie, Blaine. They often do, to get what they want," she said to herself while the tears welled up and broke over her thin resolve. She sank to the floor, clutching her oversized bag and her heart that had been so easily placed on her sleeve for Eric Morales.

She'd only ever been a roadblock to him. A speed bump in his fast track to partner. And he used everything in his arsenal, including playing into her big, dreamy sense of nostalgia and her romantic hunger, to take what he wanted. He preyed on her so artfully that the pain of his betrayal pierced her heart and seeped deep into her bones.

She sobbed, unable to control the volume of her grief, and shook against the shelf. She didn't even move when Lawrence burst through the door, coming around the aisle as if there was a threat to neutralize. He looked around, found the shop empty, and looked down at her.

"You okay, kid?"

She sniffed, wiped her nose on her sleeve, and shook her head, breaking into another fit of sobs that shook her whole body, and the cries became silent with lack of air.

"Ugh. I don't like it when girls cry. Especially you. What is it?" He looked uncomfortable and shuffled closer to her. "I mean, unless you need me to beat someone up?"

"It's me—It's all my fault."

"Well, I'm not beating you up." He smiled from one side of his mouth. "Today."

She didn't laugh.

"Get up, girl. Every fight, every time they hit you, you gotta get back up. So, who hit you? Where do I find them? And let me worry about where to bury the body." He kneeled down to help her stand up.

Blaine cried even harder at his words and the warmth he offered. She shook her head at the thought. Even with hating Eric as she did, could she really blame him? He hadn't been raised to know anything different.

"I—I signed away the rights to my shop. I didn't even know I had rights. I didn't know what I was signing. Loraine tricked me and said it was for the guest book, but she must have used it for the paperwork and—and now the mall is going down."

Lawrence looked at her as he took in all the new information and sighed.

"Well, it doesn't surprise me that she'd do something so shady and underhanded. That woman is an absolute shark." He paused and looked away for a moment, the corner of his mouth lifting to a smile, before shaking himself out of it. "But Blaine, this place was going down with or without your help. Some things just have their time, and when it's up, there's not much you can do to stop the end from coming."

"But I could have!"

"For how long? Until you had to afford a lawyer to fight them? You'd lose your shop anyway and end up broke in the process. There's nothing any of us could do, but you . . ." He pulled her in for a sweaty hug, his hands still in his fingerless MMA gloves and digging uncomfortably into her back, "you fought the hardest of all of us. You tried all you could, Blaine, and no one would ever blame you."

She choked into another fit of crying and gave him a squeeze before letting go.

"I'm sorry I got you wet," she snorted.

"I'm already sweaty. What's a little more salt?"

"Ew." She laughed and wiped her nose again. "I wish you could teach me how to punch Loraine."

"I'm not going to let you use your might for wrong, Blaine. 'Sides, that woman will get what's coming to her, sooner or later. And, well, I hate to say it, but she's just doing the only thing she knows how. I suspect she's spent most of her life trying to win her parents' love instead of just having it, free of charge." He paused. "Like any kid should."

"Wow, a fighter and a philosopher?"

"Just because I like to hit things doesn't mean I don't have a higher brain." He chuckled. "What she did was shitty. But I don't think it was personal."

Blaine nodded. She knew it wasn't. It was just business. And love had nothing to do with it. Still, she sniffed. If Eric really had loved her and chosen not to tell her about the contract, maybe even known what Loraine had been doing, then he didn't love her nearly as much as he did his job.

"You okay? Gonna be, okay, I mean?" Lawrence asked when she seemed to go far away into her thoughts.

"Yeah, I mean, no, I'm not. I don't know where I'm going to go or what I'll do with all of this stuff." She looked at her mother's collection, all the things she loved, all but destroyed by the only man she loved. A small seed planted in her brain and her tears dried. "I'll figure something out." She wiped her nose across the back of her hand and nodded. "Thanks Lawrence."

He nodded and gave her a nudge before he went back to his dojo. Just as she was flipping her sign, thinking about where she could possibly find enough boxes to transfer everything, thinking about the inevitable loss that was coming, her phone rang.

Eric's number and his smile, a picture she'd taken from the day in Estes Park, ice cream in hand, showed up on her screen. She tossed it back into her purse and started to go through her contacts, her customer list, her friends. Anyone she could think of who could offer her some advice on what to do. She had already looked at rental spaces. There were none she could afford that would accommodate everything. What would she do with it all? Sure, there were parties interested in parts of the collection, but that would take weeks to package up and send out. And she'd never be able to find a buyer for all of it.

Eric called again, twenty minutes later. She declined answering him and went back to work, trying to find a temporary spot to store her goods that would be protected enough and close enough so she could still try to manage the inventory and business from home. It was fruitless, and she couldn't bear the thought of having to talk to Eric on top of it all. The man who had been responsible for her downfall. Who had lied to her, misled her, used her. Her cheeks got warm, her forehead hot. Anger replaced grief, and she stamped her white Keds shoe on the floor with the burn of it. If she ever saw Eric Morales again, she'd give him a piece of her mind.

It would be so much easier than the piece of her heart she'd already given him. There would be no getting *that* back now. She sighed and looked at the shop, including the picture of her mom and her beside the register. Tears felt hot and came hard as her body shook.

"I'm sorry, Mom. I'm sorry I lost your shop. Boys can make you an idiot sometimes."

Memories filtered into the quiet space like sunbeams through dust motes, and Blaine fell back to the one time when she and her mom had been walking downtown, and the rain was coming down hard during a spring storm. They'd been hopping over the gutter, avoiding the cars, and Blaine had dropped her mother's scarf into the gutter. The rushing rainwater snatched it away, and it disappeared like a pink serpent down the drain.

Blaine was beside herself and crying in the deluge, when her mom kneeled down, dropped her umbrella, and took Blaine's tiny hand in her own.

"It's okay, sweet pea. It's all right," she'd said with the widest smile, her curly blonde hair plastered to her forehead. "If it was meant to be in our hands, it'd still be there. Sometimes you have to let things go." She had shrugged, smiled, and pulled Blaine up into her arms, and they danced and splashed in the puddles.

Eric's number flashed again on her screen.

Sometimes you just have to let things go. If they were meant to be, they'd still be yours.

She silenced her ringer, tucked her phone into her purse, and looked around at the pieces that had made up her mother's passion. The *Pac-Man* game, dark and unplugged. The music, tickets, t-shirts, and memorabilia. The old Rolodex her mother kept with collectors' numbers and information. The offer she'd recently considered from the Japanese businessman for Marvin's collection of Transformers.

Eric may have won the battle for the Marshall Mall, but if he won, then he was going to win it all. Let *him* bury the past. Maybe the shop wasn't meant to be hers after all.

Blaine dried her eyes and picked up her phone. She had calls to make, ends to tie up, and a lifetime of hopes and dreams to let go of.

Chapter Twenty-Four

Eric tossed his phone down on his desk after the third try. What was going on? Had she found out before he could tell her? He'd left her messages. "Please, just listen to me before you hear anything else." And "Don't worry, Blaine, we'll figure it out." But she hadn't picked up, hadn't responded to his texts, hadn't returned any of his calls. He'd even told the admin staff to forward every call directly to his phone. Nothing but the business of starting demolition and construction came in. His job was steam-rolling his efforts to make his personal life right again.

She must have found out. She might have even thought he'd somehow orchestrated the whole thing, winning her affection just to get her to sign the contract. His heart dropped to his feet, and he felt like he might throw up. He had to go over there. He needed to see her. He needed to try to explain. But as he rushed from his office, his father met him with a pile of paperwork needing to be signed and notarized today for the sale. There was no time. They wanted to start later that week with the demolition.

"I can't, Papá. It's—" he stopped short of mentioning Blaine. "I have something to do."

"Yes, you do. You need to get to these contracts, now, *mijo*."

"No Papá, I need to leave." Eric took in a deep, settling breath and straightened his spine. "I have to go see Blaine. I need to see her; I need to explain."

John's mouth fell into a grimace and he, too, seemed to get taller. "Eric, we talked about this. This deal was going to happen with or without that shoddy little clause. There's nothing that was going to stop it from—"

"I could have. I should have tried."

"Eric!" John's voice boomed through the office. Typing slowed, voices still. John leaned in. "Why don't you just call her?"

"She won't answer."

"Then she already knows and there's nothing left to explain, *mijo*."

"You don't understand!" Eric yelled. "All you do is work! All you do is work, and work, and earn money you never have time to spend and accolades that stopped meaning anything years ago. When was the last time you went dancing?" Eric yelled ferociously at his father, and all movement in the office stopped completely. Even Loraine stuck her head out of her office door with her phone pressed to her chest.

"Eric Hector Morales, you will watch the tone you are using," his father said through flared nostrils and contained anger.

"No! I'm tired. I'm tired of endless meetings, and answering emails every weekend, and never being able to leave my phone for fear I'll miss a call from you needing one more thing, even in the dead of the night. You and Mamá used to laugh, and smile, and have time to enjoy the things you worked for. Now, what? You barely even speak to her. I don't want to look back on my life in thirty years and realize that I spent more time working than living. More time at my job than with the love of my life."

Silence met him. John's heated stare stayed steady, and Eric wasn't sure if it was because he was building up a firestorm to unleash on him, or if it was because he was thinking through everything he'd said, and wondering if he'd exchanged his success for the love in his life.

John lowered his voice. "I get that this girl may seem important—"

"May *seem* important?" Eric started.

"But if you lose this contract, then we have entire departments that will feel the lost income. People will lose their jobs, Eric."

"*She's* losing her job! She's losing her whole business. Doesn't that mean anything to you?"

"She is not your responsibility. This company, this family! This is your responsibility!" his father yelled back.

Eric felt the pressure his father had laid on his shoulders. If he ran to her now, left the building, it was like telling all the employees that he cared more about his girlfriend than all of them and their families.

"I would like the chance to at least explain it to her. To be there for her," he said quietly. "She's going to be devastated. Heartbroken."

John took a deep breath in and let it out slowly.

Eric looked around at the sympathetic faces of the employees who loved and respected his father and their family. Even Loraine's eyes turned soft, no small feat for a woman so determined.

"Get back to work, everyone," John said calmly. The crowd complied, heads disappearing below cubicle walls, and office chairs scooted back into their own little workspaces.

"I understand, *mijo*," John said softer.

"I don't think you do. I think you've forgotten, Papá, what it is to have more than just the work. And I feel sorry for you because of that." Eric took the pile of paperwork from his father and fumed back to his office, slamming the door behind him, and not coming out again for the rest of the day.

Eric did his best to focus on the paperwork and getting this deal done. He tried not to think about Blaine, and what she must be going through, but that was a losing battle.

At the end of the day, a knock at the door interrupted his thoughts.

"Go away!" he shouted through the door.

"Come out of there!" Loraine shouted back. "You're acting like a spoiled little *niño*! You knew this could never have worked out . . ." She went on with less confidence. "You shouldn't have let her hope. It's really your fault."

Eric watched her shadow sink against his door, her back to him, facing the empty office, with no one to worry about . . . except her little brother. She sighed. Her voice turned soft and apologetic.

"I'm sorry, *hermanito*. I should have told you what I was going to do."

Eric's head shot up from his paperwork.

"You can't fix this, Loraine," he said in a low voice. "None of us can. But you got what you wanted, and I'm sure you'll never let me or Papá forget who really saved this project. Go home."

He listened to her sigh and stamp her foot, and through the frosted office windows, watched her shadow move down the hall. He heard the outer doors close, and Eric buried his head in his arms against the desk. It was too late for Blaine to be at the shop, but he would head there first. Maybe she was there packing.

Driving as quickly as possible, he crossed town and pulled into the parking lot, where burger wrappers tumbled across the empty space. It felt like a modern-day ghost town. All the lights were off, except for Talon Karate. He was sure, after Lawrence's threat at the museum opening, that he'd probably have no problem hitting him in retribution. Eric peered carefully over the dojo's half-frosted windows but didn't see anyone inside. Eric thanked God for that.

A man like that was probably likely to forget to turn off the lights. He didn't exactly shine with responsibility. Eric moved on down the length of the mall to Blaine's shop. Back To The 80s was uncharacteristically dark. No neon or bright colors. In fact, she'd drawn shades down over every window. He couldn't see in. On the corner of the last window was a small sign, red and white, the kind you could buy from Staples for a couple of dollars. It said "Closed" and written in marker below was "Indefinitely". He recognized her handwriting from the note she'd written to his mother. Slanted and loopy. Someone who still knew how to write cursive. Who didn't believe in letting go of things that made the world more beautiful, no matter how old they were.

He inhaled a sharp sob in his chest and thought of the lively and beautiful shop, and all the smiles, laughter, and memories people found because of Blaine and her mother keeping their favorite decade alive. Now it was dark and probably empty. Eric rushed back to his car and got in. He gripped the steering wheel, heart pounding and head swimming with helplessness.

He'd go to her house. He'd get on his knees and beg her to let him in and let him explain. They would find a place for her, a new place. Without even checking behind him, he backed up and sped out of the parking lot and up to the foothills where she lived.

He only hoped she would let him in.

Blaine had taken most of the day fielding calls while trying to build up the courage for what she needed to do. She'd called JT as soon as she'd gotten home, and they'd talked for most of the afternoon and into the evening, even as her call waiting chime would sound in her ear signaling that Eric was, once again, trying to get her attention.

She wasn't ready to talk to him. She only had one conversation in mind, and she wasn't having it over the phone. She went through her finances. She sent out emails, made arrangements, packaged up some of the more valuable collections, and took them to the UPS store. She cherry-picked certain things, like the photos of her mother and her, and boxed them up, loading them into her beat-up car, and tried to not make her poor eyes suffer any more bouts of crying.

She took the boxes home early in the evening and was almost afraid that he might catch her there. But knowing that the deal had gone through, she also assumed that he'd be too busy getting ready for the demolition and scheduling the new build to make time to talk to her in person. Plus, if he was feeling guilty, he may not have the guts to do it. She tucked the few boxes she'd brought home from the store into her closet and packed a bag. JT showed up a short time later with two family sized packages of Oreos and a bottle of wine.

"For the road," they said. "Well, the wine's not for the road. Open that when you get there. But the Oreos are fair game whenever."

Blaine tried not to sob as she pulled JT in for a fierce hug and they stayed, arms locked around Blaine, until she pulled away.

"Thanks for doing this," Blaine sniffed.

"Anything for my friend." JT nodded. "Charles and I will play video games, stay up late, and drink all your booze. Well, I'll do two of those things, he'll do the other."

"Thanks, JT." Blaine couldn't help but smile. She thanked her lucky stars that JT had come into her life when they did. She had never been in more need of a good friend.

"Hang in there, kid. When Wednesday comes, he's not going to know what decade hit him."

Blaine kissed their cheek and left. The first stars were just starting to shine over the distant glow of dusk. It was a quiet night, and Blaine stood beside her car for a moment, listening to the quiet rush of traffic that hadn't been there as a kid. Listening to all the ways the world kept changing, rearranging, and pushing her onward. She put her bag in the passenger's seat and drove away from town, taking any back road she could to avoid the traffic. She curved her slower, less agile car up the winding mountain road in search of the space she needed to recollect herself.

Not even a week ago, he'd said they'd do it together sometime. Find a quiet little cabin and just forget about the world. She knew now, that was never part of the future he had in mind. So, she was going to go by herself and hope that the quiet would help to mend the canyon-sized hole he'd torn in her heart.

When Eric arrived at her house, he pulled into her drive. On the outskirts of the main part of town, the little house was just as welcoming as ever. Her haphazardly tended flower beds were slightly overgrown and, like her, beautiful with just the right amount of chaos. He was so relieved to see her porch light on and the front windows lit up that he nearly cried. He parked the car and clambered out, nearly tripping up the steps. Pounding his shaking fist on the door brought a small ruckus from inside. He heard stumbling on the other side and his heart lit up waiting to see her.

JT opened the door and looked at him, unimpressed. "Ah, right on time, Señor Jerk-face."

His surprise at JT answering the door only lasted a moment. Blaine wouldn't just open the door for him if she'd been avoiding his calls all day. Of course, she would have planned for some interference. But he'd been waiting the last two days to talk to her, to try to make things right.

"Where is she?"

"Well, not here, jackass."

"What do you mean, she's not here?"

"Did I fucking stutter?" JT scowled.

"Hey. Easy." Eric scowled back, then looked away. JT was right to be angry and try to protect Blaine. He had betrayed her, even if it hadn't been willingly. "Look, I just need to know where she is so I can explain. So I can try to help."

"I think you did enough, don't you?"

"It wasn't me. I didn't even know what was happening. Loraine—"

"I have a hard time believing the left hand doesn't know what the right one's doing in that company. Were you ever actually planning to save her shop, Morales?" JT crossed their arms in front of their chest and glared. The piercing stare they gave him beneath their now crimson hair leveled any sense of self-righteousness Eric might have still been holding on to.

"I wanted to try. I was going to try."

"You know what they say about trying."

Eric looked up at them, confused.

"Trying ain't doing. Do or do not. There's no try."

"Didn't Yoda say that?"

"Look at the closet nerd showing his true colors."

Eric peered through the doorway, over JT's shoulder, in the event that they were lying and Blaine might come out. But nothing stirred except a guinea pig burrowing into the couch cushions next to a game controller. Apparently, he wasn't the only one who appreciated the old gaming systems, and of course Blaine would have one. They'd never spent much time outside the bedroom when he was over. His stomach sank. He may never have that chance. A renewed sense of desperation filled his chest.

"JT, I need to talk to her. I need—" his voice broke.

"It's too late. I've never seen her as heartbroken as she was today. Never. In one day, you, the man she loves, simultaneously betrayed her trust and took away the only world she's ever known."

"Jesus, JT. You can't imagine how bad I already feel. Do you have to make it worse?"

"Yes, Eric, I do. Because she believed you could be a better person. We all did." JT's voice wavered, and they stepped back into the house, getting ready to close the door.

"If—if you won't tell me where she is," he sniffed, and then quickly brushed the tears away from his eyes. "Can you at least tell her—" He choked on the words and all the things he needed to say. All the things he could not tell her.

JT narrowed their eyes on him. "Tell her what? That it was all just business?"

Eric seemed to fold in on himself, hands to his hips, bent over as if someone had hit him in the gut. He took a deep breath and tried to compose himself.

"Tell her I'm sorry."

"It wouldn't be enough." JT slammed the door and left him on the porch, alone in his misery. To add insult, they shut off the porch light. Eric stood in the dark, knowing he had no other option than to go home. Her car wasn't there, which meant she really had gone someplace else. She was gone and he couldn't follow her.

Chapter Twenty-Five

Morales Construction was nothing if not punctual. They had been so ready and determined when the final paperwork had come in that the necessary permitting was ready. It didn't hurt that a company that size had made good friends in high places along the way, who fast-tracked their projects. Back-scratching and wheel-greasing were just as much part of their business model as having airtight contracts and always meeting deadlines. The demolition of the Marshall Mall was scheduled to begin on Wednesday morning.

Eric hadn't been to the site since the night he'd tried to find Blaine. He was sure that she probably wouldn't be there that morning, either. Why would she want to watch her world being torn down? He hadn't been able to eat, sleep, or smile for days. He had called her and left message after message. She never responded. Tuesday night, in an effort to save his own heart, he stopped calling. Eric started to worry that he'd never see her again. What if she'd moved out of town? What if she'd moved across the country?

He got ready for work that morning, opting for a polo shirt with the company's logo on the right chest pocket, and jeans. He even put on his steeled-toed boots and got out his old hard hat from the top of his closet. He wasn't going to just be there to supervise. If he had a hand in the destruction of her life, he was going to be there to make sure nothing of hers was left behind, and that there was at least someone there with reverence for what the shop had once been. Someone to be with it in its final moments.

It was corny . . . and stupidly romantic. But maybe that's what she'd done to him.

The morning of the demolition, Blaine took more deep breaths than she could ever remember taking in her life. Every breath was a tiny step in letting go. She put on her jeans and her favorite slouchy sweatshirt that fell over one shoulder, put her curly hair up in a scrunchie, and over-shadowed her eyes with bright blue. Her shiny lip gloss, *Kissable*, was laid on thick as if to remind him of all the things he'd given up. She snuggled Charles Dumar, fed him an extra scoop of pellets, and slipped on her Converse before heading out the door. Her plan was to get there early.

She wasn't sure how she knew he would be there for the start of her shop's ending, but she had a feeling. This was, after all, his big chance. He probably didn't want to leave anything unsupervised. He had a corner office and the word "partner" at the end of his title at stake, after all. She was banking on him being a bit of a micromanager, and she was not disappointed. At exactly five minutes after six, his car pulled up, followed by a myriad of loud and large equipment. Giant bulldozers, backhoes, and trucks with large teeth, all belching out smoke and looking like they were hungry for destruction. Trucks hauled in trailers and dump trucks alongside them to cart away the debris.

Eric pulled up on the far side of the parking lot, and his eyes were immediately drawn to her shop. A neon sign glowed its letters brightly: *Back To The 80s*. Blaine watched from inside as his face stared at the sign with confusion. It probably seemed strange to him. Everything should have been turned off; power, sewer, gas. She watched him shuffle through his laptop bag and pull out his iPad before getting out. She could see the question on his face. How was there a sign lit up? Blaine looked down at the small generator keeping the sign alive and smiled. She took a deep breath and walked out her front door to meet him as he approached.

If she had been a mountain lion coming out of the door, he might have been more surprised. As it was, he stumbled back a step, and she saw how tired he looked. How sunken his handsome cheeks had become. Had he not been sleeping, either? She immediately berated her soft heart for even caring. He deserved whatever guilt he had.

"What are you doing in there? You need to clear out. You could have gotten hurt!" His tense voice was angry, and he slapped the iPad on the side of his strong thigh.

She studied him, looking so much better in jeans and boots than he ever did in a suit.

"Oh, you're worried about me getting hurt now?" She huffed a not funny laugh. "I just wanted to hand things over in person."

"The contracts have been signed, permits are done," he said and looked down. "You didn't have to—wait, what do you mean, things?"

Blaine crossed her arms over her chest, cocked a hip, and stared him down with her kissable lips pursed. "You know, after what you did, I started to think--"

"Loraine did it! I—"

"*Afterwards*," she interrupted. "I had to take a little time to myself and think about you. About us, about that stupid bet I was so naïve to make—"

"Blaine, *Cariña,* please—"

"Don't. Please don't call me that." She paused to sigh heavily. "God, you really know how to break a girl's heart in a million ways, don't you?"

He hung his head and held the tablet between both hands. Before he could respond, she went on.

"So, because I obviously lost, that means that nothing in my shop really means anything."

"That's not true. Blaine, you know I don't feel that way."

"Right, the *Pac-Man* game. You did win that fair and square; well, not really fair, as I was tricked into signing papers I had no knowledge of." She paused and looked up at him. "Underhanded to such a beautiful degree." She shook her head over her tears and settled into the jaded aftermath.

"Blaine, I don't want the game. I don't. I just want you."

"That's too bad, Eric, because you can't have me. But you can have the rest of it."

"What?"

"Like a *Price is Right* jackpot, Morales. You won the whole thing."

"What are you talking about?" His brow fell, and he looked at her, then back to the glowing sign.

"It's up to you what to do with it all. Since you hate getting off-schedule and costing Daddy too much time and money, I am sure the easiest thing to do will be to take it all down with the rest of the building."

"Blaine, I don't understand. Are you saying that everything is still in there?" He pointed angrily to the shop and its sad, almost noir sign glowing in the dark of the morning.

"Everything." She felt tears choke her throat. "You can have it all. None of it means anything, anyway." She hung her head and sniffed.

"No! You can't do this."

"I just did. Congratulations, Eric. You win." She shrugged, her sweatshirt slipping lower on her shoulder. She walked closer to him, stood on tiptoes, and kissed his cheek before walking away without looking back. Not even once, to the trucks, the plans, the demolition, and every dream she'd ever shared with her mom. Even the ones she'd shared with him. When she drove out of the parking lot, she glanced in her rearview mirror to see Eric still stood like a statue, staring at her retreating taillights.

It was hard for her to drive away. Harder than almost anything she'd done in the last few years. But she also knew that it was the right thing to do. If she couldn't convince him, maybe he was right. Maybe it was time for her to move on and let go of all the things that no longer served a purpose. It was time to stop hanging on to the past.

Blaine sniffed and let the tears fall all the way home, wiping them away on her sweatshirt sleeve and trying not to run into the high curbs along the downtown streets as she turned up to her home. When she got there, it was quiet. JT had left to get back to their new shop, and Charles was asleep in his small flannel hammock in the corner of his pen. Blaine flopped down on her couch in the quiet room and waited. For what, she wasn't sure. A sign? A phone call? A miracle.

Miracles didn't really happen. Otherwise, she'd still have a shop, and the man she loved would be following his own heart, not his family's preordained plans. At least when she had lost her mom, she had the store, a place where they'd built memories. Now all she had were five or six boxes and a few old photo albums.

Some people never even got that, she supposed. She got up and cracked open a bottle of wine left over from her trip to the mountains. She pulled the boxes from the closet, sat on her couch, and spent the rest of the day grieving her losses.

The brief warmth of her lips on his cheek after her heart-wrenching speech contrasted the cold way she'd walked away from him without even a backwards glance. Eric was frozen in place. God, he'd missed her. And now his last memory of Blaine could very well be the sight of her walking away from him, hating everything about him. The foreman came up behind him, clapped him on the shoulder, and roused him from his conflicted heart.

"Boss, you ready? Do we need to check on the electric again?" he asked and nodded at the sign.

"I, uh. I'll check on it. You guys, take a minute, get a cup of coffee. This won't take long," he said, but his voice sounded far away and raw. He marched to the store and walked in through the open front door. His heart stopped. Nothing had changed. She hadn't taken down a damn thing. She hadn't packed up anything. It was all there, still on shelves and in baskets, just as though she could open the shop at any second.

"Oh, Blaine," he sighed with his heart heavy and hurting. "No, *Cariña*, you can't be serious." Every record, every poster, every signed ticket and toy, was there, just as it had been the first day he'd walked in. And Eric was just as amazed at the enormity and eclectic nature of her collection. The only thing different was that she'd moved the arcade game to the front of the first aisle and put a big red bow on it. With a note.

Don't forget in your big, important business dealings to make some time to play.

He took the note and held it between his fingers, tracing over the words. It felt like he might break down and cry right there. But he didn't have time. Demolition was supposed to start in the next hour. She'd gotten the last hit in, and he couldn't believe she could have just walked away from it all.

He heard the foreman yell from outside.

"We good boss? Should we get started?"

Eric's heart felt like it was beating inside of his throat, and he looked back at the sign, running on a generator. He didn't know what other choice he had. He had to get started. He unplugged the sign and looked back at *Pac-Man*'s darkened screen.

The project had to stay on track, after all.

When Eric got home from work that night, a day that had lasted well into the evening, he was spent. Every muscle ached, every neuron buzzed from the noise, the dust, and the destruction stuck to his hair and the inside of his nose. The sweat made him sticky and rank beneath his clothes from the way he worked, in such pain, relentlessly alongside the construction workers to help erase the memory of the Marshall Mall. He was grieving. And now he had to go home and live with the same loss. But alone and without anything to keep his mind preoccupied. He could have stopped by the office to let his father know how things had gone. But he knew that John would be disappointed that his son had spent the day doing manual labor; work that was better left to someone without his advanced degrees.

Eric didn't care. He went to his fridge, looking even more bare than Blaine's had the morning he'd left. He found a six-pack on the bottom shelf, not even remembering when he'd bought it. Maybe last summer? He went to pull it up by the cardboard handle and it broke. Must have been at least last summer.

He carefully held it by its bottom and went into the living room, where he slumped onto his clean leather couch, dirt and dust billowing up around him. He cracked open the first bottle and dropped his head back after a healthy swig. His hands were raw from swinging a sledgehammer, his body bruised, and his heart a complete and utter wreck. He knew he couldn't go see her. Like JT had said. What good would apologizing do? He finished the beer, cold and quenching to at least his physical thirst. After the third, and still on an empty stomach, he collapsed sideways on the couch and listened to his quiet and uncomplicated life settling around him.

Tomorrow would be more of the same. The job. The work. The loneliness. Though he'd be expected to be back into the office and handling the schedules for the foundation work. But he didn't want to leave the flattened dirt lot that was once hers. All the memories of the things she'd loved and left behind. Him included.

Chapter Twenty-Six

He was at the bottom of the barrel of ideas. He'd tried calling Blaine every day, and stopped by her house, but got no answer at her door, not even a "go away." The last time he'd stopped by, she'd hung a sign on the door. "No Moraleses need apply".

He'd even hung around Abuelita's a few afternoons and mornings, hoping that she'd show up for a burrito or horchata. It caused him to be late and leave earlier than either his sister or his dad. It was starting to affect his work, his life, the project, and the way his family was interacting with him. Loraine, as always, had plenty to say on the matter. Just that morning, she'd ripped into him.

"Why are you being such an idiot? Where in the hell are you?" Loraine reprimanded.

"I'm here." He tugged at his dark and overgrown hair as he stared at the spreadsheet he had no intention of working on.

"No, you aren't. Where's your head?"

"It's—" He paused and shot daggers at her. "It's right here with the rest of me."

"Or it's wherever your groin is."

"What? Don't be disgusting."

"Well? Aren't you lamenting the loss of your side fling?"

"She wasn't some side fling, Loraine. I love her!" he yelled back and threw a stack of papers on the floor at her feet. When she stayed frozen and appalled at his outburst, he yelled, "Get outta here!"

She left, and he huffed down at the scattered contracts that would take him most of the afternoon to reorganize. As he hit his knees to gather them, a small pair of pumps stepped into his office and stopped next to him. His mother kneeled down to help.

"Mamá," he said softly, ashamed at how he'd talked to Loraine and for throwing things like a child in a tantrum.

"She deserved worse. That stunt she pulled? On that sweet girl? She's lucky Blaine didn't hire a lawyer. I wish I could make it up to that girl."

"Me too," Eric said softly. "I don't know what to do."

"Loraine was right, your head isn't in your work."

"I know, I'm sorry."

"It's with your heart."

Eric hung his head, hands limp on the paperwork, and felt the weight of her words in his heart. "What can I possibly do about that?"

His mother sighed, gathered up the remaining contracts, and knocked them against the floor to straighten them out before handing the pile back to him. Eric added it to his pile, got to his feet, and helped his mother up.

"The way I see it, there's only one thing to do."

"Let her go and get back to work?" He refused to look up at his mother.

She tipped his chin up and met his eyes with her own. Looking into the warm and unshakeable depths of them, so much like his grandmother's, he was mesmerized.

"No, *mijo*. Use your head to find a way to make things better for your heart. And hers."

"I can't. I don't know how. She hasn't even given me the chance to talk to her, to explain, to try."

"Then you have to find a way around her defenses."

"How? Without being a stalker?" Eric asked.

His mother smiled, and a glint lit her eyes.

"Every castle has a gatekeeper. Make friends with the gatekeeper, convince them that you are sincere, and they may help you find a way in." She shrugged, put the paperwork back in the folder, and set it neatly square on his desk.

"A gatekeeper?"

The gears in his brain turned over and around. The person who had been with her from the start. The one who brought them lunch, helped Blaine get ready for the opening, kept her space sacred when he'd come looking for her.

JT. He needed to convince JT that he was serious about salvaging things with Blaine. He couldn't just try. Trying wasn't doing. He was ready to do something.

"But you'd better have a good plan before you talk to them." His mother said before kissing his cheek and wiping away her lipstick.

He sat back in his chair, deflated. "I can't just have a good plan, I need a better plan," he said to no one, as his mother had already left.

He stared down at the spreadsheets, the contracts, the blueprints for the new brewery, just now getting its foundations poured, and the framing was scheduled to be finished in the next couple of weeks. He looked at the plans. The plans he'd helped draw up himself. The architecture he'd planned, fussed over, implemented. The work he'd loved doing, and the plans that had been the deciding factor which had won Morales Construction the contract from the beginning.

The brewery and the restaurant loved the design. The giant, lifelike river that ran through it, the cobblestone and timbers, the retail shop space that he'd made large enough for all the merchandise they might sell . . . and then some. Maybe Blaine was right, maybe if you loved what you did enough, you'd find a way to make money doing it. *Blaine*. The old familiar ache lit his heart, and he sunk into his chair, staring at the floor plans again. He stopped, cleared away the rest of the notes on his desk, and let his hands frame the two-dimensional space.

He dialed his father's number, but when the busy signal sounded, he hung up quickly and rose. He bolted through the office like a man possessed and knocked loudly on his father's door, insistent until John opened it with an angry scowl, his phone pressed to his chest.

"*Mijo*, this better be important."

"We need to talk."

Blaine was lost in the midst of another round of calls from concerned patrons and well-wishers who had tracked her down. She'd stopped advertising, stopped trading on eBay and Etsy. Lord knew she didn't need the money after her boon sale to a businessman in Tokyo that would keep her going for at least six months, and it wasn't like she had a shop to stock with new merchandise anymore. Although she was set financially, her emotional state was a different story. She spent most of her time watching her favorite old movies on repeat, usually falling asleep on the couch to them. Mostly, she was wondering what Eric was doing and if he was happy.

She hoped that he wasn't. She hoped he was miserable. She hoped he was in agony, missing her. Just like she was miserable and in agony, missing him. But the phone calls dwindled down. The emails, the texts, all the ways he'd tried to apologize were slowly drying up, and she knew it was in part her fault for not responding. She also knew she was under no obligation to accept any apology. No matter how big it was, it would never be enough to take back all that he'd done with one signature and the desire to earn his parents' love.

At least he had his precious project. She drove by a few times in the last week. Watched the barren ground become flooded with equipment and building materials. The concrete foundation, larger than the original mall itself, was clean and even over the hallowed ground that had once been her shop. It was like it never existed. She hadn't driven by since she saw the framing going up and realized it was going to be another two story, mountain themed with a modern flair, monstrosity.

She hadn't been giving much thought to what she would do now. Her whole life had been in that shop. She didn't know who she was outside of it. JT brought her two more bottles of wine the night she'd walked away, and they'd stayed up into the early hours talking and crying and finishing both bottles. JT had moved on. Moved into a new space, embraced the change they and Deb were making with some new clients in the new neighborhood. Maybe she should have done that, too. Just packed up and relocated. But something had broken inside her, the day she found out what Eric and the Morales family had done.

She stopped believing in the goodness of people. If she hadn't been so trusting in the first place, he never would have won her heart. She would have been able to see through all his charm and boyish sweetness, and that ass . . . Blaine let out a breath and got up off her couch. She dove beneath the kitchen sink to get her bucket of cleaning products. Nothing like a mad cleaning to set you somewhat right. She snapped on the vinyl gloves and put her favorite Madonna album in her cassette player, blaring it loud so it could be heard out on the street.

Charles Dumar headed for the farthest, darkest, most padded corner of his pen, and the world stayed out of Blaine's way while she swept, mopped, dusted, scrubbed, and shined her way through the heartbreak raging inside.

Chapter Twenty-Seven

The Mane Event Salon, now uptown, was more stylish than its previous Marshall Mall location. Then again, it wouldn't take much to be an improvement. Eric had visited their new website and scribbled down the hours and address. He knew that he needed to get on JT's good side if he was ever going to make things right with Blaine. And he *needed* to make things right with Blaine, because his heart couldn't live much longer without her. His life was a drab progression of meetings, budget proposals, and delays with the construction and labor shortages. It was all desk work and computer screens and angry contractors . . . nothing neon, nothing bright, no light laughter in dark theaters or the smell of sugar-and-cream skin. He had nothing to look forward to at the end of his day. So he needed this to work.

He parked across the street from the new salon, on the edge of the ever-expanding suburbia of Marshall. Wedged in between a wholesale granite supplier and a posh pet shop catering to the Colorado Front Range elite who demanded organic sea bass for their adopted tomcats, The Mane Event still had a temporary sign across the front, and the window was just now being painted. It looked like JT had found a local graffiti artist who was decorating the windows with loud and sharp lines of color, stepping back to assess the work as he went. Eric liked it.

He only hoped he wouldn't be thrown out the window and ruin all the kid's hard work.

When he stepped inside, the shop was buzzing with chatting clients and hairstylists. Blow dryers and clippers sang in varying tones. Every chair, seven in total, was full. Blaine hadn't mentioned they'd hired on more stylists, but then again, it had been weeks since they'd last talked. Over the din, he heard JT's voice from the back.

"Have a seat! We'll get to you next!" they yelled.

Eric knew JT hadn't seen him, or they wouldn't have been so welcoming. He sat complacently on the edge of one of the retro clear plastic chairs, with his leg bouncing neurotically. The chair was mismatched from all the others in the small waiting area, and it added to the eclectic atmosphere. Loud indie rock came from the overhead speakers. He sat for what felt like forever, but just as he was about to lose his nerve, JT came up to the front desk. Their face fell.

"No thanks, we don't serve assholes here," they said and turned to leave.

"Please." Eric pleaded, coming out of his chair and toward them. "Please JT, I need your help."

His voice caused them to turn around, a sly glare punctuated by their fiercely dark eyeliner. "I don't have time to chat with non-paying customers," they said.

Eric sighed. "I need your help. I need to see her, talk to her. I love her, JT."

"You getting a haircut or not? Because I'm not wasting my time on some heartless developer."

"I'm not—did you hear anything I said?"

"I heard something. I'm not sure how much of it I believe.

Next!" they yelled, getting up on the tiptoes of their black, chained combat boots to see if there was someone waiting behind Eric to take instead.

"Fine." He held out his hands. "I need a trim anyway. Thanks."

JT scowled and crossed their arms in front of their chest.

"Trim, okay. But you don't get a wash."

"Don't get a—"

"Way I figure, that gives you about ten minutes. So you better come up with something good and something fast to say to me."

Eric followed them to the farthest chair from the front of the shop. JT gestured to the chair impatiently and flicked out a clean cloak with a harsh snap as Eric slumped into the chair. JT adjusted the chair, but they didn't offer him the courtesy of doing it slowly, and when their foot hit the lever below the seat, he dropped to the lowest setting with a jolt.

Eric stared at JT's face in the mirror, looming over him with a twisted and angry mouth.

Eric held up his hands. "I love her. Please. You have to believe me. I'm miserable without her, JT."

The cruel expression on JT's face eased to a scowl. "That's a decent start—"

"And I'm an idiot and I screwed up royally."

"Keep going, hero." They grabbed the clippers.

"But to be fair, it was my sister Loraine that was responsible for the signature. I didn't have any idea she was—"

JT's hand rose and a sudden vibration shook through Eric's skull and the unmistakable buzz rang behind his right ear.

"Oops," JT said.

Eric pulled away and looked back at them, his hand going to the newly sensitive half-dollar sized bald spot.

"What the—"

"You knew about the contract and you didn't tell Blaine.

Loraine did what that woman is built to do. Win. You are not putting all the blame on her." JT swiveled him back around. "Now, are we gonna think about our own actions here, or do you want me to make the back of your head look like a damn wiffle ball?"

Eric dipped his head into his hands and sighed. "I'm an idiot, and I should have let her know about the contract sooner. I was afraid if she knew, she wouldn't go on any more dates with me, and I loved being with her so much. I thought I'd have more time to tell her and more time to help her figure out how to keep her shop."

JT didn't say anything. They combed the longer hair out on top and snipped carefully with their scissors. At least they'd put down the clippers. "And now, what?"

"Now I need your help. I think I know what I need to do."

"Well, shy of having a shop and decades-worth of her priceless 80s memorabilia back, I don't really see how that's going to be possible, Eric."

Eric stared at them in the mirror until his silence made them look up from their more dedicated work on his hair. JT scowled and threw their hands up.

"You destroyed all her stuff. She just let you have it, and you just bulldozed the whole damn building that morning."

"She did just leave it. All of her stuff, all of her hope—" he said softly.

"Cut out the sappy romantic act. You destroyed that entire place. Her memories and future included. All in the name of progress."

"Only I didn't."

"Uh—I beg to fucking differ." JT stopped and picked up the clippers again.

Eric ducked in the chair and covered the back of his head.

"I did level the building, and yes, the new brewery is being built, as we speak."

"So you don't think you somehow destroy all her hope?" JT's nimble fingers flicked on the clippers, and they whined menacingly close to his ear.

He ducked further into his hands and spoke quickly.

"I didn't let them destroy all her stuff."

JT switched off the clippers and leaned in. "What do you mean, exactly?"

"I mean, I walked in there, I saw all of her things and all of her memories, and I saw all of the times she'd made people happy, or found the things that brought them joy, and I couldn't just tear it all down like it didn't matter. Because it matters. It matters to her, and it matters to me." He looked up to see JT's face contort in a battle of not wanting to believe him and hating that they did.

"So you . . ."

"So, I had the guys bring in one of the loading trucks and they helped me move it all out. I drove it to a storage unit and spent most of the morning putting it there until I could figure out how to get it back to her."

JT cocked their head to the side. "You didn't sell it?"

"No. How am I ever going to win her back if I sell it? It belongs to her. And I'm not going to let her give up on what she loves." He looked into JT's eyes and the flicker of cynicism there. "Even if it's not me anymore. I mean, I'd rather she wanted to be with me."

JT sighed. They shook their head, made a few more snips, and brushed his neck off with a small broom.

"You're all done."

"But . . . that's it? Isn't there any way I can convince you?"

"Even if she did take you back, which I'm not really sure that's gonna happen, I've never seen her house so goddamn clean. And when that woman cleans, it means she's letting go of the trash."

Eric swallowed the lump of lost hope in his throat. JT sighed and looked toward the next waiting customer with a nod.

"Be with you in a minute," they shouted.

"JT please—"

"Even if you could convince her to meet with you, where in the hell is she gonna put all of it? She doesn't have a shop anymore, remember?" JT took off the cloak and shook it out before throwing it in the dirty laundry bin.

"I have a plan."

"Course you do. Moraleses always have a plan."

"This plan you might actually like."

JT sighed, scowled, and looked him in the eye. "Alright, Morales, I'll listen, but not right now. I've got work. Tonight, about 8, the little dive bar on the corner of Fifth and Main."

Eric's face lightened, and he nodded.

"Okay, I'll be there." His hand went back to the bald spot. He scowled at them.

"Don't be mad at me. You earned at least that much. And that'll be $50."

"Fifty? For a trim?"

"No, the trim was only $15, the rest is for me not shaving you bald."

"Seems like a fair price." Eric sighed and got out his wallet.

Blaine was pretty sure she was ready to pack up Charles Dumar and buy a minivan to tour the country with. Though her friends were here, and the people she knew, and the community she'd grown up in and loved her whole life. All the memories of her childhood, all the history of her mom, and the places she knew and loved were here. But Eric Morales was also here. She couldn't seem to go a day without falling into the misery of missing him. She drove by the worksite a couple of times a day, hoping to catch a glimpse of him on the ground, working alongside his team and crew and the subcontractors. Not to micromanage as he had once told her, but to be there, as part of the team. The idea of him in a t-shirt and jeans, getting dirty, and being at the heart of the creation he was a part of. And how quickly it was being built.

It seemed within a month the exterior was nearly finished. The brewery would still be able to take advantage of some of the summer tourist traffic at this rate. Eric would be proud of what he'd created, and, despite his insistent phone calls and visiting, which broke her heart a little more each time, and got harder and harder to resist answering, he would be able to have something positive from the whole experience.

Maybe he would come to terms with what he really loved doing and find a way to get his family to accept it. She wanted so much for him to be able to do what he loved doing.

At least that, in some part, would make her sacrifice worth all it had cost her. That he should find some happiness. She hated that she wanted him to be happy even after what he'd done. Wasn't that love? She sniffed and fell into probably her thousandth sob-fest of the week. Her mascara ran, and she wiped it away on her lace gloves. Charles, who had been sitting next to her on the couch while *The Goonies* played in the background, squeaked up at her, snuffling his long whiskered nose and sinking his deep brown eyes into hers.

It was all for food, she knew, but she liked to pretend that he was listening.

"Charlie, we need to do something with our lives. Everyone else is living their dreams. JT and Deb have the new salon. Even Sensei Williams has his new dojo. Eric . . ." She paused to inhale a shaky breath. "Eric has his project and his partnership. A brand-new brewery that'll be open before the summer is over. And what have I got?" she whispered and looked at the boxes in the corner of her living room. The too-clean house and near-empty cupboards. The clothes that fit looser for her heartache, and the pictures of her mom around the room.

"I have my memories," she said sadly. What she missed most

about the shop, besides being surrounded by the insane and quirky collection, was the way people who came in, sometimes from states away, would smile and laugh, giggle and remark. The way their eyes would go dreamy and soft, and she could almost see the memories playing behind them. Being six and getting their first My Little Pony. Being five when the first Nintendo gaming system came out, and having it shape their lives to be a gamer for life. To hold an ugly, red-headed Cabbage Patch Kid doll in their arms and get teary-eyed over the fact it was the only thing they'd once wanted in a life that now demanded so much. She missed helping other people find their happy memories. She missed that most of all.

He had leveled the world she'd used to connect with other people. Taken away their connection to the past.

He had destroyed it. To secure his own future.

The vision of her mother's scarf slipping down the drain in a river of dirty rainwater hit her fresh. She had let it go. She chose not to fight, in so much as an ant could fight the looming shoe of a giant.

She couldn't stay here. Not with the memories and the hurt weighing so heavily on her. At the current cost of living and the paltry pay for the menial jobs she was qualified for, she wouldn't make any big dreams happen. She was comfortable for now with her mom's inheritance, the house already paid for, and the collection she'd sent to Tokyo the day she'd left the shop . . . but comfortable wasn't content. Everyone needed work. She just didn't know what hers would be yet.

The path that made the most sense was to start a completely online business. She had the connections, the means, and the experience. But just like she knew Eric wasn't content (there he was in her thoughts again) with his family's construction business, she wouldn't be happy doing that. The joy of her job had been in the people.

Blaine sighed and tried to put her mind back on the screen

where the Truffle Shuffle was taking place. Life was easier when you could lose yourself to a world where happy endings came easily and within two hours. Pirates' treasures saved towns from big developers, and the good guy got the girl. She snuggled into her cushions and fell asleep before they'd even gotten to the Fratelli's.

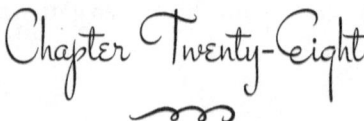

Chapter Twenty-Eight

After his meeting with JT, Eric felt better. He hadn't known they were including Deb and Sensei Williams in the meeting. But he had little choice in the matter, and thought it would be better to have more people on his side than less.

As Eric walked back to his car after the meeting, Lawrence grabbed his arm.

Eric stepped back. "Look, man, I don't want any trouble."

Lawrence rolled his eyes. "Relax, I just want to know how she's doing."

"Blaine? I told you, she won't talk to me." Eric held his hands up and looked at Lawrence like he must have been sleeping through the last hour of beers and planning.

"No. Not Blaine, Jesus. I'm talking about Loraine."

"What?"

"Your sister, genius."

"She's . . . fine? Aren't you guys seeing each other?"

Lawrence stopped to hang his head. "No. After I found out about what she did with Blaine and the contract, I got mad, and I told her what a shit thing that was to do. She hasn't really talked to me since. I mean, once in a while she'll send me a sad little text, like she's sorry, but when I respond that we should talk about it, she doesn't have any more to say. It's frustrating. I know she feels bad, I just don't think she thinks I'd forgive her. And I would. If she'd just talk to me."

"Sad? My sister? And she feels bad?" Eric said in disbelief.

"Yeah. Like, 'I miss you', and 'I wish I had done things differently'. And, well, I'm not going to get into the other ones," he stammered. "It's like she gets these weak moments and reaches out, but I'm out on the floor teaching and I don't have time to check my phone, so by the time I get back to her, she's put up her wall again, and I need to . . . that is, I'd *like* to know that she's okay. I want her to know that I forgive her."

"Why don't you stop by the office and see her sometime?"

Lawrence looked at him like he'd gone mad. "Are you insane? Do you even know your sister? She'd kick my ass out before I even stepped foot in her office. Especially in front of all those people. You saw how she was at the museum."

"Why is that, Lawrence? What did you do?"

"I haven't done anything she didn't ask me to. I think she likes me, but I don't fit into her world very well." This time Lawrence smirked, shuffled his feet, and looked back to Eric. "So, she's okay?"

"As good as my sister can be, but then again, she's never been open about her feelings to me." Eric watched the other man's face fall and felt a deepening sense of comradery. He sighed and looked around the parking lot as if he were about to spill a government secret to a foreign spy.

"She loves the ballet."

Lawrence looked up from his shuffling with a scowl. "So?"

"So, La Bayadère is at the Civic Center this weekend, and my family has a season box there, but we rarely go."

"And?"

"*Dios*, for a man supposedly aware of his surroundings, you're kinda thick. I will get you the tickets and make sure she's available, even if I have to take over her meetings. You show up at the office Friday night, tickets and flowers in hand, wearing something other than jeans, please, and I bet those walls will crumble."

"But are you sure she'll go with me?"

Eric looked at him, shook his head. Love worked in mysterious and chaotic ways, just like Abuela said.

"I've seen the way she looks at you, the way she talks about you. How crazy you make her, in all the right ways. She thinks she's above all the romantic bullshit, but no one's safe from their own heart all the time."

Lawrence shook his hand and nodded. "All right then. I'll get the tickets from you and see her on Friday."

As Lawrence drove away, Eric felt good about the match-making behind Loraine's back. Having had a taste of love, even though it ended up tearing out his heart, he'd never wish someone a life without it. If nothing else, Loraine would get to see a ballet and have a night off work with a man who cared about her. It was the least he could do for his sister. And maybe, just maybe, it would earn him some forgiveness and an ally for the next few weeks ahead.

When he got home, he sat on his couch with a roster that he'd made, and looked over the list in detail. He felt like he had more people on his side and maybe would stand a chance at getting her to listen. The plan was shaky at best, and he had no idea if it would even work. He called Blaine again, just to hear her voice on the message. When the beep sounded, he wondered if she was even listening to all his pathetic attempts at apologizing, or if she was simply deleting them. He paused.

"Blaine, I—" He swallowed. "Please don't give up on me. I'm going to make this right." He didn't know what else to say, so he sighed. "I wish you were on the couch with me right now, with a bowl of cereal and Charles scaring the shit out of me—" he stopped. "Miss you."

· · ·

Blaine listened to his message. She listened to them all, though she'd never admit it out loud. But this last one, he'd really landed too close to her heart. It made her laugh and cry, and made the ache in the center of her chest worse than it had been the last two months.

What did he mean he was going to make it right again? How could he possibly? She went to her cupboard to see what sad little meal she could throw together for herself, but there wasn't much there. She needed to go to the store, for Charles's sake, at least. She moved a few cans off to the side and saw the small boxes of cereal she'd bought for a road trip last fall. Cereal. After his message, the thought turned her stomach, and she closed the cupboard quickly.

Her phone rang again.

"Hey JT." She left her kitchen and tried to find some place in her house that didn't remind her of him. She hadn't been sleeping in her room, which was stupid and childish. He already destroyed her shop; he shouldn't get to destroy her sleep. But hearts were strange creatures that didn't listen to reason. And the couch was a place they hadn't ever landed.

"Hey." JT responded, as though they'd been holding their breath.

"Everything okay?"

"Sure. Just calling to check in and see if you've been to the grocery store lately, or if you were still moping, half-starved, in your pj's."

Blaine scowled into the phone and adjusted the waistband of her Care Bear pajamas. "I'm fine. I have plenty of food . . . and clothes."

"Don't lie to me, Reynolds. Last time I was there, you had two cans of green beans and some cereal. You're sleeping on your couch, and I'm not sure what in the hell Charles is doing for food."

"I'm feeding him." Blaine looked around. Even the twenty-pound bag of pellets was low, and the hay was nearly gone. "We're fine. Everything is just fine. What do you want?"

"Look, Blaine, we are all allowed to grieve. But there comes a time when you have to move on and eat something other than SpaghettiOs."

"What do you have against SpaghettiOs?"

"Everything. I have everything against them. Most doctors would agree. Listen, I need you to get yourself together, because you're going out with me."

"Going out? That sounds terrible."

JT laughed. "You haven't even heard what we're doing."

"If I have to leave the house, it's automatically terrible."

"What a grouch. I liked you better when you were getting laid."

Blaine pouted. "Yeah, me too."

"Sorry, listen. It's not for another month, so you have some time to get your shit together."

"A month? What could possibly be happening that far out? You never plan that far ahead. Why do I need to have my . . . stuff together by then, and where will we be going?"

"It doesn't matter where, and you need to have it together because by then I want you to be able to make some big decisions, and you need to be out of your pj's and well fed."

"I don't like how cagey you're being about this."

"Well, I didn't like how you just gave everything in your shop away, but I trusted that you knew what you were doing."

"You shouldn't have," Blaine whispered softly and felt the tears welling up. "You shouldn't have trusted me. I didn't know what I was doing."

"I think you did," JT responded softly. "I think you made the absolute right call. Tell me you'll go with me."

"Ugh—" Blaine tugged at her banana clip and sunk against the wall next to Charles's pen. She reached out and scratched his nose. He bit her, searching for food. Maybe JT was right. This wasn't her. She didn't like half living, waiting for life to come waltzing back through her door. Especially when she was actively locking herself away from it. "Okay."

"Yay! Attagirl. That's the old Goonies spirit."

"The what?"

"Pirates never say 'die'?"

Blaine sighed and rolled her eyes. "I appreciate how hard you're trying. And I love you to death. But please, don't ruin my childhood."

JT laughed and told her they'd bring her some groceries later on that afternoon.

"You can't live on Cap'n Crunch."

"Says who?" Blaine smiled.

"Says . . . well, pretty much every nutritionist. Go take a shower. I don't want to smell all that desperation when I get there."

"Jerk."

"I love you. It's gonna be okay, Blaine," JT said and the strangest sense that they knew it was true filled Blaine's heart. Either way, with or without Eric, with or without her mother's shop, things would be okay. Blaine hung up. She rummaged in the fridge, found a decent bell pepper and a wrinkled but not moldy cucumber and fed them to a ravenous Charles Dumar before heading to the shower.

Sitting under the spray, she thought hard about everything that JT had said, everything that had landed, heavy like a mountain on her shoulders the last few months; the scarf and the drain, the past and what lay ahead. This was, in a way, a chance to start things over. And while it was foreign and painful, it was not the end of the world. She scrubbed her hair and hummed a melodic rendition of Mr. Mister's "Broken Wings" as she scrubbed away the days' worth of tears and stewed in her own grief.

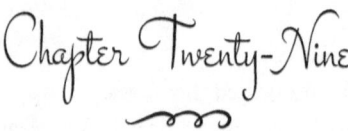

Chapter Twenty-Nine

Eric was in his office early the next morning making calls, sending out emails, and continuing to plan out the logistics. He had to get it perfect. The construction was now moving along nicely due to the good weather, and delays with materials were resolved. It was like fate was giving him a hand. Eric would take any help he could, divine or otherwise. It had already been three months, and that seemed too long. Any more time apart and he worried that, despite what JT had said about Blaine still living on Cap'n Crunch in her pj's, she might move on, and he would lose her for good.

Just as he was hanging up from a call with a local sign company that had readily accepted his order, Loraine knocked twice and came in, scowling as usual. She stood, not speaking, in front of his desk with her arms crossed and tapping a toe impatiently. He looked up at her from his notes.

"Sí?"

"Did you take the tickets?"

"What tickets?"

"The tickets to the ballet."

"I don't know what you're talking about." He looked away.

"I called the box office this morning to get them, and was told they'd already been collected." Her cheeks were pink but her lips trembled with hurt. "That's my favorite ballet. You know that."

"You'll have to talk to Papá, I don't know what happened to them."

"Never mind!" she yelled and turned to leave in a huff. Eric knew she wouldn't talk to their father about the tickets. He hoped she'd hang in a couple more days until Friday.

It felt like he was hoping a lot lately, riding so much of his future on leaps of faith and the true intentions of his heart. Blaine could still reject him. He had talked to the owner of the Snake River Brewery earlier that month about his idea. The man and his brother were huge 80s fans, and were so excited they practically begged him to go through with it.

The only obstacle left was Blaine. JT said that they'd talked to her and were working on getting her out of her slump. He hated thinking of her in a slump. How could someone so bright and buoyant not have bounced back, even a little, by now? She must have really loved him.

"God, I hope it's not past tense." Eric closed his eyes and prayed that the love was not gone yet.

Later that week, steeped in the extra work he'd taken on for his sister, Eric trudged through his lists. Every other employee had left. Only their father, him, and, of course Loraine remained in the building. While the rest of the company would assume they were all hard at work, it was probably closer to the truth that at least two of them were pouting. Loraine thought it was strange that Eric had taken on her spreadsheets and reports, but said she would start researching the new housing development on the north side of town with the extra "free" time. Even when she had a chance to take a break, that woman found an excuse to stay stressed. As he clicked through the reports, his eyes burning from the days of computer work and little rest, he heard his sister through the door and down the hall.

"What are you doing here?" Her sharp voice echoed through

the office hallway. Eric checked his watch. Williams was punctual, he'd give him that. Eric looked up from his desk and listened. The low tones of the man he'd been conspiring with filtered in.

"What? What does that mean?" Loraine's voice came through clearly.

Eric got up from his desk and walked to the door. He peeked through the crack and saw Lawrence Williams, in a tux, per Eric's suggestion, standing at her office door, roses and tickets in hand.

"I have tickets to the ballet. Box seats."

"How in the hell did you get those?"

"A friend suggested you might like to go."

Loraine's hard brown eyes found Eric's, even through the small space of his cracked door, and he slammed it shut. His heart raced like he was a kid getting caught stealing her favorite record.

"He did, did he?" she nearly yelled.

"Look, you can do one of two things." Lawrence's voice was commanding and seemed to cut through her protest with calm control. "You can tell me to scram and I'll even leave you the tickets. Or you can go with me. Either way, you get to see the ballet, because I'd never deny you something that made you happy. But I'd like it if I could go with you."

Silence fell heavily outside of the door.

Eric held his breath and listened for Loraine's response. But nothing came. He was worried she'd stabbed him with a letter opener, and cracked the door, expecting to see Lawrence's body lying face down and his blood soaking into the carpet. Quite the opposite. Loraine was in his arms, the flowers were scattered on the floor, and she was kissing him with a fiery purpose that made Eric blush. Lawrence held her tightly around the waist and met her passion in equal and enthusiastic ways. Eric stifled a laugh like a teenage boy and covered his mouth. He hid behind his door and felt giddy with happiness for both of them. The shuffling on the other side of his door stopped. Footsteps came closer, at a pace that made Eric freeze and put his weight into the door.

"You're an asshole, Eric Hector, and you'll pay for this." Loraine's voice came from the other side of the door, so close that it startled him. But then, quietly, she added, "thank you, *hermanito*."

Eric could feel the smile behind it. He listened to them leave, laughing and softly talking, headed out for a date. Two obstinate hearts that saw something in each other and finally stopped letting their stubbornness get in the way. He sighed. It felt like the end of one of Blaine's movies.

But it was far from the end. He had a lot of work to do in a short amount of time, and that meant there'd be no free time in his near future until he made sure everyone got a chance at a happily ever after.

Eric had underestimated how hard it would be to promote his project and not have the advertisements and promotions make their way to Blaine. JT said she'd go through her mail and steal any fliers that showed up. Deb said she'd disconnect the wire to her car radio. Apparently, in her youth, she'd lifted a few. Lawrence had been stealing her paper for weeks, to avoid her reading the full- and half-page ads for the brewery and its particular features. Lucky for all of them, Blaine wasn't one to spend her time on internet sites where the advertising of Snake River Brewery was ramping up for its grand opening. He hoped if she saw even the first letters of the name, she'd quickly close down the ad, or flip the page. Maybe her hurt would be good for keeping the surprise. Still, it was a constant source of anxiety to wonder if she was going to find out before everything was done.

Eric sighed, ran his hands through his now longer hair, and sat back in his chair to stretch. Only a couple more weeks and much of the anxiety would be gone. But, whether or not she took him back would make the difference on whether his life would be better or worse for all the effort.

Chapter Thirty

Blaine was at the quietest coffee shop she could find. Thunderheads had come in that morning and settled just past the mountains instead of blowing over. It blanketed the town in soft gray, making the pretty clear orbs speckle the window she leaned against. The droplets chased each other down the glass, over the letters that spelled "Cup of Joe".

She watched them distractedly, in her leg warmers and running shorts, a slouchy sweatshirt with coffee stains dribbled down the front, and worn-out Nike high tops tapping nervously against the metal rung of the table. She nibbled on a fingernail and looked around at the more fashionable college students poring over notes and engaged in great philosophical discussions, like which team's fans were drunker at the game last night. In their designer ripped jeans and crop tops, a 90s trend that Blaine had never really liked, they were the new generation that had probably never seen *Pretty in Pink*. They probably didn't even know who the Brat Pack was, or the A-Team, or that My Little Ponies used to actually look like horses. They didn't know that Reagan had once decreed that ketchup counted as a vegetable in public school lunch programs, or that Sally Ride became the first female US astronaut in space and Sandra Day O'Connor was nominated as the first female Supreme Court justice. They knew more about TikTok dances and starlet-driven trends that lasted for weeks, not years. They knew more about Elon Musk than they did about John Hughes. Blaine looked down at her Jane Fonda-like gear and sighed. Bottom line, she didn't feel put together at all. More than that, she felt like the world was moving on and leaving her behind.

Just like Eric had. She stared out of the window again and felt her eyes burn. She sniffed, wiped at her face with the sleeve of her shirt, and sighed. She needed to get back to living. Start moving forward.

She'd brought her antiquated laptop, which was one step up from needing to be plugged into a phone jack for internet service. It weighed the equivalent of a small elephant and could withstand being dropped from the fifth floor of any building. It was also slow enough that she had enough time to drink most of her coffee while waiting for the tab to open. The local community college's website loaded in bits and pieces, and when it was still, Blaine scrolled through the degrees offered.

History. Marketing. Business management. Construction.

She paused with her cursor over the word and thought about Eric. Where had he gone to school? Was he happy there, or had he longed to do something else? She wondered if he was enjoying the brewery project. If he was planning another already, moving on with the fast pace and the progression that was demanded by the march of time and his family's expectations.

She opened a new tab two minutes later, to a jobs page for Marshall and the Colorado Front Range. Two days ago, she'd tried looking in the local newspaper at JT's salon. Someone had been stealing her papers for the last few weeks. That's when JT informed her that people didn't advertise jobs in the paper anymore, unless it was a really "old fart" company, or it was some shady pyramid scheme. They took the paper away quickly and told

Blaine that if she wanted to find a new job, she needed to go online.

The romanticism of being able to circle a tiny box of newsprinted hope with a Sharpie was lost to the ability to instantaneously ship your information off with a few clicks to an employer who looked to fill a position. The fast-paced world had no place for long term.

At least those were the kinds of jobs that she could find at her skill level. Though she'd run a business for over a decade, and had worked in the shop since she was seven, the jobs out there weren't for people who could run their own business. They were for people who would be employees. And in that, she was entry level at best. In fact, she was entry level for most things in life. A person without the skill set necessary for a world now accustomed to instant responses, lack of face-to-face interaction, and fluid job movement. She was old-fashioned in a young body. Blaine sighed and leaned her chin on her open palm while she scrolled through the retail positions, counter clerks, and seasonal help.

She didn't need the work financially. She just needed something else to put her heart and brain into before she went bonkers.

The tinkling bell barely registered as she scrolled down the list and tucked one foot up in the chair, hugging her knee to her chest, and bit her lip. The sound of Eric Morales's voice caused her heart to stall and the whole world to stop spinning. She looked up from the minimum wage list, eyes wide as he strode up to the counter with another man. She'd know Eric's backside anywhere. Her heart pounded fitfully, like a dog at a fence begging for attention. Blaine shrunk down in the chair and looked around her for the closest hiding spot.

He let the other man order first, a long and complex list of half-caff and double almond creamer, one pump of mint syrup, one of chocolate, droning on to the barista whose glare grew with every added complexity. But Blaine had stopped listening and watched Eric, studying his profile as he turned his head to look at the bakery display. She wondered if he was still being his healthy self and mocking sugar. Maybe more so now that she wasn't around to tempt him. He certainly looked just as amazing as ever, and she liked his longer hair, even though there was some weird short patch in the back. She nearly cried.

When he got to the counter, it came as no surprise that he'd ordered a plain coffee, black, and no, he didn't need room for cream. What made her want to throw her laptop at him in a fit of unrequited love and rage was when he picked out a powdered donut from the case and nodded his thanks as he paid. His coworker looked at him with a questioning brow.

"Isn't that a little sweet? I thought you didn't put stuff like that in your body." The man scoffed. Eric shrugged.

"I like them. They remind me to enjoy life. They remind me of one of the best moments—" Eric stopped and shook his head. "I just like them."

His voice was rough and deep, and he looked down at his shoes before taking his coffee and his bag with one lonely donut from the barista. He turned to follow the other man out.

Blaine, having hung on his every word, hadn't thought to hide. She quickly grabbed the nearest fake plant, a fern on a corner shelf to her left, and placed it on the table in front of her, ducking behind it as best as she could. It obscured her face if she stayed low. She watched him walk out to his fancy car. Watched the other man get into the seat that she once sat in. She heard the engine fire up with its deep growl and watched as he drove away. She craned her neck until he'd disappeared.

It was bound to happen sometime, especially in this ever-growing town. She knew that she would see him out in public, eventually, even if they didn't really travel in the same circles. Truth was, she currently had no circle to travel in. At least he hadn't been with another woman, sharing donuts and laughing. And had he looked tired? Hadn't he looked a little too worn thin? She wanted to believe he was suffering, even just a little bit. His dark purple dress shirt was unbuttoned one button too low to be completely professional, a pair of gray Converse below the hem of his dress pants. Still rebellious but subdued. He was as handsome as ever, and she did hate him for that.

She moved the fern back to where it had been and finished the last cold dregs of her coffee. She took the yellow-lined notepad that she'd been copying potential leads onto in case her computer crashed, and looked at the list of possible jobs she might find some sort of joy in. A counter clerk at a nursery business. A pet store retail worker. A movie theater attendant. Nothing that seemed to bring out her inner sparkle. But then, she wasn't sure she had much of that left, anyway.

When Eric and one of his subcontractors had pulled up at Cup of Joe's for a coffee and breakfast on their way to Snake River Brewery, he'd seen a woman in the window that looked like Blaine. This was something he was getting used to. Flashes of curly hair. A face turned down with a hint of blue eye shadow. A pair of worn Converse walking by. But none of them were ever her. They were just flashes of what his brain was desperate to have. Ghosts of what he really wanted.

But walking up to the shop, seeing the familiar apparition of a curly, strawberry blonde head leaning into her hand, folded into the chair, like a kid trying to get comfortable in adult furniture, staring disheartened into the largest laptop he'd ever seen (did that thing run on a generator?) made him look twice. He paused outside, even in the midst of the light rain, to assure his brain it wasn't her. The woman wore bangles around her wrist, a scrunchie piling her hair on top of her head, leg warmers bunched up on her slender calves, her perfectly kissable mouth in a pout. Her eyes were sad and tired as she scrolled down the screen. It was Blaine Reynolds. He paused and wanted to tell Tom that they should pick a different shop, but he had no decent excuse. Tom motioned him in, out of the storm.

Grown men didn't run from their ex-lovers, did they? He was torn between wanting to leave and not suffer the heartache of being around her when he knew she still hated him, and wanting to be around her, even if she met him with an angry tirade. He followed Tom in, head down and heart beating. If she said something, he'd stop. If she recognized him, yelled his way, even shot him dirty looks, he'd stop and talk to her. But when he turned away with his coffee and the powdered sugar donut, his small way of saying he hadn't forgotten, that he was still thinking of her, she'd hidden behind a ridiculous fern she'd pulled onto the table in front of her. As though it was the perfect disguise.

He wanted to rush over, laughing. He wanted to pull the stupid plant away and take her into his arms. Explain everything. It helped him to know she was just as unsure and frightened to see him. Maybe she missed him. Maybe she couldn't trust herself around him. Maybe there was hope. Maybe, like JT had said, she wasn't over him just yet.

So he'd said a few things to Tom about the donut, dropping hints she might take, and left. He'd pretended not to notice the lip-biting girl, ducking behind a fake fern. It was actually lucky that she was at the coffee shop. Maybe now he would be in her thoughts. Given that she hadn't stood up and railed at him for destroying her life, he held out hope that maybe she didn't hate him as much as she should. He walked through the rain, not feeling it. His smile was uncontained, and Tom gave him strange looks as they got in.

"You okay? I haven't seen you smile in weeks."

"Yeah, I'm just having a better day than I thought I would." He drove away, glancing in the windows, but the falling rain made it impossible to see inside. He liked to believe she was watching him go, with even half the love in her heart as he held for her.

. . .

Blaine hadn't mentioned to JT that she had seen Eric in the coffee shop. She was still too embarrassed that she'd hid behind a fake fern. Wouldn't a grown woman have given him a good lashing? Or at least shot him a nasty glare? She didn't feel like a grown woman. She felt vulnerable and achy. Like all it would take was a little begging from him, and she might throw herself into his arms.

Blaine had been busy cleaning out the basement that week when JT stopped by with two iced coffees and a box of donuts.

"Isn't it past noon?" Blaine wiped the sweat off her forehead. Early afternoon and it was already hot, but she wanted to go through the boxes and furniture that her mom had stored away. There wasn't a lot to get excited about, but she did find a few collector's items from the heyday of daytime game shows. An original *Wheel of Fortune* board game in the wrapping, *Family Feud,* and *The $10,000 Pyramid*. She entertained ideas of starting up her online store again, but without the inventory she used to have, there wasn't much of a point.

"Donuts don't have a time limit. You can't tell a grown ass adult when they can eat donuts."

"You certainly can't," Blaine said. "What are you doing here?"

"I just wanted to check in and see how the job hunt went. Did you find anything?"

"No. I mean, not much to get excited about. I think with classes over, most of the remedial stuff I'm 'qualified' for is getting taken by the college kids."

"You're not remedial."

"I never," Blaine paused, and wiped away her running mascara, "I never finished my degree." She went to get a glass of water from the sink.

"I know your mom always wanted big things for you, Blaine," JT said softly.

"She did. And I had them, once. I loved that shop. I loved the people and the vibe and everything. Then I fell in love with the wrong big thing," she said, but this time there were no tears in her eyes. "And now I don't have any of it."

"So, what are you going to do?"

"Start over, I guess? I don't know."

"Okay, well, you don't have to figure it out today. Have a donut. Are you still up for Friday?"

"Friday?"

"Yeah, remember? You said you would go to that thing?"

"What is this thing?"

"The best surprise . . . sheesh, why do I have to keep reminding you?"

"My brain's been distracted lately," Blaine said, not exactly lying since she'd been preoccupied with thoughts of her near miss with Eric. JT didn't say anything, but there was a strange, knowing look on their face that made Blaine look again.

"What?"

"Nothing. I gotta get to work. Keep the rest of the donuts. See ya Friday." JT snagged a chocolate with rainbow sprinkles on their way out.

"Uh, okay, bye?" Blaine yelled at the closing door. It was strange for them to rush off so quickly. Then again, it was strange that they'd avoid being direct about anything at all, but especially where they were taking her on this mysterious outing.

Blaine sighed, sniffed her sweaty armpit, and decided it was past time for a shower. She put her coffee in the fridge and fed Charles half a plain donut before stripping down and jumping under the warm spray. She scrubbed hard, trying to wash away all the uncertainty stacking up in her life.

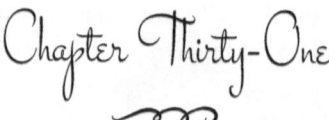

Chapter Thirty-One

"Why am I wearing this again?" Blaine looked at her reflection with a scowl. It had been weeks since she agreed to go along with JT's plans. Now she was definitely having second thoughts and wondering what her friend was up to.

JT shrugged. "Because you trust me."

"I most certainly do not."

"I thought you would love it. Look at it. It's totally your style."

"If my style is Molly Ringwald a la *The Breakfast Club*." She paused, staring at herself, lip between her teeth. "I don't want to wear this."

Thoughts of the movie brought back one of the last discussions she'd had with Eric, and all the pain that came along with it. *We're all a little bit everything*, he had said. But the one thing he wasn't, was hers.

"What? You can't back out now. Come on. I thrifted all week to find this." JT protested as they adjusted the V-neck blouse, a warm pink that complemented Blaine's complexion, even if she was paler lately. The look was completed by a brown skirt that went to her knees, and a leather belt.

"I just don't want to. It feels too—"

"Too what? Vintage? Retro? Don't pretend like you don't like it," JT scoffed.

Blaine sighed and felt like she'd never change JT's mind, so she might as well not make it any more painful. Besides, she really did like it.

"Where are we going, anyway? Not the cover band, right? I told you I don't want to see The Rubix Cubes ever again. I know you don't believe it, but I'm trying to put the 80s behind me."

"But why? You love them. They are the era you were meant to be in."

"I *loved* them. But they don't belong to me anymore," she said softly and moved to unzip the skirt. "I don't know what I'm meant for."

JT stilled her hand with theirs. "Look, okay, I get that this is taking a leap of faith just to go. But I'm your best friend. I'm not going to lead you astray. And I say you need to do this thing tonight. This might be a life changer."

Blaine studied the seriousness of their eyes, even below the now bright, neon pink mohawk that had been spiked up to its full five inches with God knew how much product. Blaine sighed. It was one night. What was just one night? Especially if it meant something to her friend, who'd been with her all through her heartbreak.

"Okay. Fine. But do I have to wear the boots?"

"Yes, of course. Oh, and here . . ." JT paused to take two diamond studs out of one of the many holes lining their ear. "You definitely have to wear these if we're being authentic." She placed them in Blaine's palm. Blaine smiled sadly and put them on.

"You're lucky I love you." She let out an exasperated breath, as if this was the hardest possible thing she'd ever done.

"Love you back." JT smiled at Blaine over her shoulder in the mirror. "You're gonna knock hi—their socks off."

"What?"

"Nothing. I mean, in general, where we're going. You're gonna knock the people's socks off where we're going. You're gorgeous. Let's go." They hurried out of the bathroom and started to collect their Cyndi Lauper jacket and combat boots.

"Do I need a jacket?" Blaine self-consciously adjusted the low-cut shirt.

"Nope. You'll be warm." JT handed Blaine her purse and made a direct line for the door. Blaine gave herself one last look in the mirror. Pink shimmery lips, but not *Kissable*. She'd thrown that away weeks ago. She'd tried to throw or give away everything that had reminded her of him. Yet here she stood, looking like she'd been pulled back into the 80s once again. She just hoped he wasn't anywhere near where they were going.

Eric paced nervously in the lobby of the office. He didn't know what he expected to happen tonight, but he was gearing himself up for the worst. He adjusted the dark gray slacks, the slouchy black combat boots, and the rolled up red bandana tied around one boot. The white Henley was maybe the nicest part of the outfit, but it was covered by the red flannel shirt with cut-off sleeves. Leather, fingerless gloves and a denim jacket rounded it out. He ruffled his hair, and it fell almost to his collar in the back. He hadn't cut it since he'd started planning this whole thing. Plus, after the whole haircut incident with JT, he was a little clipper-shy.

His father stepped out of his office and nearly hit the floor with his gaping mouth.

"What is this? What are you wearing?"

Eric turned to him, cleared his throat, and looked down at the ensemble. He knew she would recognize it. But his father, for sure, would not.

"Uh, this is what I'm wearing tonight."

"I hope you mean *until* the opening."

"I mean *for* the opening."

"Are you out of your mind, *mijo*? You can't possibly represent the company at the opening of your first major project looking like a rock concert reject."

Eric's mouth screwed up into a frown. "I'm wearing this tonight. It doesn't matter what I wear. The Snake River Brewery will open just the same, and no one will even care what I look like."

"What's going on here? First, I get a call on Monday asking me about the proper fixtures needed for the side store, which I never remember us discussing, then I hear your sister took an afternoon off—" he paused with the horror. "An. Afternoon. Off, Eric."

"So?"

"She said she was meeting someone to help out with a side project. We don't have side projects in this company."

"Well, that might have just been—"

"Then you're telling me that this is what you're wearing to the opening? The sleeves to your shirt have been cut off, and what the hell is wrong with your hair?" John's voice rose so loudly that Carmen came into the hall from the front offices to see what the fuss was about. She looked at her son, mouth wide, and eyes as big as saucers.

"Eric, *mijo*, what are you doing?"

"I'm going to the opening."

"Like that? You look like—" Carmen paused, she tilted her head, her eyes softened. "Oh! *Mijo*—is this the night?"

"Sí, mamá," he said, voice choking.

"What night? What are you talking about? Why isn't anyone telling me anything?"

"Juan Hector Morales, do not yell." Carmen reprimanded. "You need to start trusting your children to make the right decisions for themselves." Her commanding tone was so out of place that they both straightened their spines and hung their heads.

"*Cariña*," John whispered. "But he looks like an idiot."

Carmen looked at her son, reached up to kiss his cheek, and gave him a gentle pat on the chin. "He looks perfect. There will be other openings and other opportunities for suits. Tonight, he needs to dress the part."

"The part of what? A hobo?"

"Of a man trying to win back the woman he loves." Eric blushed, and his father looked at him.

"Is this about the 80s shopkeeper?"

"Yes."

"How much of it?"

"All of it. The clothes, the side project, the special allowances made in the building. All of it."

John closed his mouth and for a moment, Eric wasn't sure if he was about to explode or faint. His father's dark eyes got misty, and he looked at his wife. He shook his head and ran his fingers through his still thick but graying hair.

"*Dios,* I see hopeless romanticism runs in the family. Bueno. Go. I'll see you there. But if this doesn't work, you are changing into a suit."

Eric's smile spread so wide it was almost painful. "Sí, Papá."

He kissed both his father and his mother on their cheeks and gathered his things to go. His heart raced as he took the stairs two at a time and rushed to his car.

JT's bright yellow Nissan Cube tucked into the turns as they sped through the crowded streets on this warm Friday night. Blaine held on to the passenger armrest to keep from toppling over at every erratic change of direction. JT's car always smelled a little bit like patchouli and Hot Pockets. Twizzler wrappers, hair magazines, CDs with cracked cases, and a good level of trail dirt from their frequent hikes littered the floor. Every time Blaine let them drive somewhere, it felt like being in high school again. And every time, she was slightly worried that they'd end up in a fender bender.

After the third time they'd passed the same store, Blaine came out of her withdrawn haze and looked at JT. Were they stalling? Or did they not know where they were going, either?

"Uh, what are we doing? Did you just doll me up like an 80s princess to go drag Main? Shouldn't we be getting to the thing?"

JT checked their phone again. "I'm just making sure I have the address right."

Though they appeared to be texting someone, they put the phone down quickly when they saw Blaine looking over.

"You are being cagey as shit."

"Whoa! When did you start cursing?"

"What is going on?"

"You'll see soon enough." They laughed and sped down the road without taking the same turn they'd stalled with for the last five minutes. "I don't suppose you'll close your eyes for the last two miles?" JT asked.

"Why in the hell would I do that?"

"Because it's a surprise."

"No."

"Come on. You used to like to have fun."

Blaine sighed. Wasn't she supposed to be trying to move on? Wasn't she supposed to be trying to have fun again? Plus, it would make JT happy, and they might let her go home early from whatever this was if she played nice.

"Fine, but then I get to go home early."

JT shrugged and kept their eyes on the road. "If you really *want* to go home early after we get there, I guess I can take you."

"Deal." Blaine crossed her arms in front of her chest and huffed out a sigh as she closed her eyes, trying not to get sick with the wild motion of the car. Blaine sat back and took a few deep breaths. When she tried to find a peaceful place to put her mind, the first thing that came to mind was lying in his arms, his fingers gently caressing up and down her back as she listened to his heartbeat. How he'd told her about his grandmother. How he told her he was scared to have a family because the job would steal away the time with children. How he loved her. Blaine felt tears burning behind her closed eyelids and quickly shifted her thoughts.

Anything, she thought, just think of anything but him.

A vision of Charles Dumar in a shower cap and towel, carrying a tiny scrub brush to the shower made her question her sanity. That was certainly anything but Eric. She lurched forward so suddenly that she barely had time to put her hands out and keep her forehead from hitting the front dash.

"What the—"

"We're here. Keep your eyes closed. I'll come around and get you."

"What? Why are you being so weird?" Blaine started to say, but JT had already slammed their door. A rush of warm night air flooded in, and Blaine stayed still until she felt JT's hands on her arms, tugging her to her feet. "Can I please open them now?"

"Soon." JT led her a few wobbly steps forward. They adjusted Blaine's shoulders to face a different direction, and sighed as though they were about to jump off a cliff. "Okay."

Blaine opened her eyes, even while scowling. She was disoriented and at first didn't recognize where they were at all. The front of some building. In a new parking lot with small new trees and bushes planted on all the islands. The building itself was monstrous, but somehow . . . pretty. The pillars on either side of the large wooden doors were made of huge river rock, and large beams above them made a steepled A-frame that looked like the outside of a giant cabin.

Blaine's eyes caught on the black sign with white, rustic writing and her whole body froze. Snake River Brewery. Blaine looked around frantically, left to right. Nothing about the parking lot where her shop once stood looked the same. Nothing about the space seemed familiar. It was as if her mother's shop, her shop, had never existed.

"JT, what have you done?" Tears threatened, and she backed away, heart sick. Her thoughts were interrupted by loud music.

Blaine's gaze fell to a man standing in the doorway of the brewery. The song "Don't You (Forget About Me)" blasted through the parking lot as he came closer to her, wearing a red flannel and white Henley, gray pants and combat boots, complete with the red bandana. She looked down at her own clothes, the perfect match; the rebel and the rule follower, only the roles felt reversed. She looked back at Eric; his hair had grown to a rebellious level for an office job, and she longed to run her fingers through it. She drank in the sight of him, like she was dying of thirst. But the sign of the brewery glowing brightly above his head made her clench her fists at her sides and her eyes narrowed.

"This isn't funny, JT. Why would you do this?"

But Eric kept walking towards her, the words *don't you, forget about me* ringing out in the background. Blaine turned to leave, but JT blocked her way to the car.

"Just hear him out, okay? Then, if you're not even the slightest bit interested, I'll take you home."

Blaine shook her head at the betrayal and tried not to listen to the small voice of reason that said if JT was willing to give him a chance, maybe there was something worth listening to. After all, JT was less forgiving than she'd ever been. She sighed and turned back to Eric.

"You have five minutes."

"Five? That's not—"

"Four and fifty-five seconds." Blaine interrupted, a mix of emotions surging through her.

"Okay." Eric looked like he was torn between wanting to kiss her and knowing five minutes wasn't long enough for both an explanation and the kind of kiss she deserved. He reached for her hand, but she backed away.

He took a deep breath. "I'm sorry about the contract. I tried to tell you about it once, but didn't try very hard, and that's no excuse. I thought there'd be time to let you decide, but my sister is . . . well, my sister. That was my mistake, and I own it. I want to make it up to you. I love you. I haven't been the same since you've left my life and I hate who I am without you—"

JT cleared their throat. "We've only got 4 minutes left, Romeo, and she needs you to *show* her, not *tell* her."

"Right, okay." He nodded and held out his hand again for Blaine's. She wrapped her hands around her middle, protectively, and glared.

"Please, come with me?"

"Fine," she grumbled. "But don't expect anything at all to change."

He only nodded, a worried crease in the center of his brow that she hated because it was cute and concerned and she wanted to kiss it flat again. She held her ribs tighter.

He turned and led them into the new building. As they entered the large double doors, Blaine was impressed by the tall and lit foyer of the brewery, the open rafters and stonework, the sound of rushing water somewhere. The front desk sat between two dividing paths, each with rich stone flooring leading on. One went towards the restaurant and tasting room, the other was for the brewery tours and the shipping and warehouse. The girl behind the reception desk, young with deep brown eyes and straight black hair, smiled when she saw Eric come in, and offered the same warmth to Blaine.

"She made it. You two look great. Are you ready to start the brewery tour?"

Eric cleared his throat. "Thanks, Clarise, but we only have—"

"Three minutes," Blaine interjected.

Clarise's eyes went wide. "Okay, well, then, just the big reveal." She nodded towards the restaurant side, and Blaine looked to the space filled with large beetle-kill pine wood tables, and a large river rock fireplace in the center of the room. It was beautiful and cozy, and somewhere she'd probably come to at least once a week.

"Not very busy. Sure hope it doesn't fail spectacularly in the first month." She glared at him. "It would be awful to work so hard on something only to have it not work out."

Eric took a deep breath, like he was holding back a comment. "We're not technically open yet. The big launch is later tonight. You're the first person here. The first person I wanted to see it."

Blaine tried to not let that melt her heart. He was sharing it with her first. His project. The one he'd designed, planned, organized, and built. She couldn't keep the hatred in her heart. She looked down.

"Okay, so? Is this it then?"

"Not quite." He nodded towards the restaurant, and they walked around the tables, chairs, serving stations, and mountain themed décor. A small, rocky river ran along the edge of the main walkway and created a relaxing ambiance. Elegant antler chandeliers hung from the two-story ceiling, and quiet music played over the impressive sound system. Fighting the urge to be impressed, she stuck up her pert nose at the lot of it.

"I don't know what we're doing here, Eric. I've seen how beer is made. I mean, I live in Colorado; it's probably the first field trip any class gets to go on here," she said, somehow feeling nervous the closer to the end of the tables they got. Where in the hell was he taking her?

"I don't have time to show you that. We're headed straight to what's important."

He kept walking. The pathway opened up and curved around towards the other side of the building, probably connecting to where the brewery tours would let out. There was another set of double doors to the outside as they turned the corner. Blaine imagined it was so that people could enter straight to this side from the south parking lot.

Above the doors was a stunning wall of A-frame windows that faced the foothills, lending a beautiful view that she never got to see from her shop, since the mall shops had been situated facing the road, not the mountains. She sighed. How stupidly talented was he? She hated and loved him for it. She turned around. The curved wall facing the windows had two separate shops. One, closest to the tour's end, was the brewery's gift shop and tasting room. The other, equally sized, caught her attention with its bright neon and colorful sign.

Her heart stopped beating. Her mouth parted with words that would not come, from air that refused to leave her lungs.

"Eric," was all she could manage.

It was her shop, her whole shop. All the things she'd left behind that day, left to him to be destroyed. All of it, neatly placed, organized on new shelves. Her music collection, her displays, her large arcade games and posters. Even her *Back To The 80s* sign, or one that had been made new just like hers, hung above the large open doorway. Her knees felt weak.

"Eric," she whispered, "How did you do this?"

She stumbled forward.

Eric reached out and tried to take her elbow to steady her, but she pulled away. "Is this . . . my shop?"

"Yes. Well, most of it. There were a few things I couldn't find. I assumed you took those. But yeah, it's everything you left that day." His voice died away.

"Everything?"

"Yes. Even me," he said.

Still confused, she walked towards the shop.

"There's no rent due, not ever. You own the space."

"Me?" She looked back at him, trying to process what she was seeing. Blaine's hands shook as she pointed toward the store. "I own this space?"

He came and stood next to her. "I made a deal with Snake River. Thankfully, they're huge fans of the decade, and Morales Construction was more than happy to avoid a lawsuit from its shady acquisition of your shop by offering you the space for as long as you want it."

Blaine inched closer to the doorway. Her breath felt like fire in her lungs until she remembered to let it out in a whoosh.

"Why did you do this? All of this, Eric? It must have cost a fortune. And your time? And all the work—" She paused as a lump rose in her throat. "Why?"

"Because I love you. Because I loved your shop. Because it didn't deserve to be torn down. Because the world needs it." The words tumbled out, and he took a deep breath to finish. "And I need you."

Blaine looked at every memory on the shelves, sweeping over the shop and the pictures that had brought her hours of entertainment from her mother's stories and recollections. Even the demonic Cabbage Patch Kid sat next to her retro Sanyo cash register. She stared up at the sign, the DeLorean coming out of the wall, and the neon letters bright over their heads. Eric stood next to her, hands shaking.

"Blaine, please say something," Eric said.

She shook her head, her eyes falling to every picture, toy, game, cereal box, and album. It was all here, but the thing she grieved losing most was him. She turned to Eric, tears in her eyes.

He looked down at her. "I'm sorry."

"Stop saying that." She shook her head to wipe away her tears.

"But I am."

"Stop being sorry."

"I'll never stop."

"But why?" she said and let the next round of tears fall over her cheeks.

"Because I hurt you, broke your trust, and lost months' worth of kisses I could have been giving you. I'm sorry for any day I don't get to kiss you, Blaine. Any day I don't get to talk to you or laugh with you, or berate you for your lack of food, or your stupid, loveable guinea pig. Any day I'm not shaking my head at the brilliant light of you, wondering how I got so lucky—that's a wasted day.

And I'm sorry." Eric stepped closer, dried her tears on the sleeves of his shirt, and cupped her face with his hands.

She looked up at him. "I'm sorry too."

"For what?" he said. "You have nothing to be sorry for."

"For not listening, for being so stubborn. For not returning your calls."

Eric shook his head and rolled his eyes skyward. "*Dios, Cariña.* I deserved all of it."

"He's right, he did," JT said, and they both turned. "Sorry, did I interrupt the moment? I'm just gonna go over . . . there." They pointed towards the left.

Blaine turned back to Eric; her shaking hands held his strong shoulders.

"So, what do you say we get you back into your shop?" Eric said.

Blaine pulled him gently closer. "No."

"What?" Eric pulled back.

"You still owe me months' worth of kisses before I accept it." She quirked her eyebrow up and smiled at him. "I figure if we start now, we should be close to done in a few days."

Eric's beautiful mouth broke into a smile, and he picked her up in his arms. She giggled in delight, and he kissed her with such warm sweetness that her body melted into his. He set her on her feet gently, his strong hands trailing long lines across her body. Blaine felt weak in the knees and held on to him as their kisses intensified.

Someone cleared their throat loudly a few times before the sound of it broke through their fevered kissing and Eric reluctantly pulled away. His hair was a mess, his lips red and his eyes the deep, dark shade that made her whole body shiver. She kept her hand on his shoulder even as he kept a hand possessively around her waist.

They turned to see Loraine and the inexplicable sight of Lawrence Williams standing next to her, with their hands intertwined.

"Loraine," Eric said, his voice still husky.

Loraine looked at Blaine with remorse and humility. "Blaine, I'm sorry. I'm sorry for what I did. I was afraid Eric was going to lose his project—that Morales Construction was going to lose the project—but I was wrong. It was so much worse for him to lose you. And I'm sorry."

Blaine couldn't hold any anger for Loraine. Not knowing all she did about the little girl who never really got the childhood she deserved.

"It's okay. I understand," Blaine said softly and nodded. "What are you doing here, Sensei?"

"I wasn't going to miss being here for my favorite little fighter. What do you say? You gonna forgive this jerk? Or do I get to mess up his pretty face?"

Blaine turned back to Eric with a sly smile. "Well . . ." she paused and tilted her head. "There is a shortage of pretty faces in the world. It would be a pity to mess his up. Maybe we give him a second chance." She laughed when Eric swooped her up in his arms and spun her around in front of her store.

Chapter Thirty-Two

On Friday nights, Blaine's shop closed early and Morales Construction Inc. shut down at six, and even John Morales was no longer allowed to have late night hours on Fridays. Because Fridays were for dancing. They were the nights that began at a local venue with live bands and good music, dinner at a nearby restaurant, and laughing over stories about Blaine's mother and Eric's family. Carmen and John, Eric and Blaine, and eventually even Loraine and a less-willing Lawrence, gathered over music and food, and built the kinds of memories that Blaine had always wanted as a kid. Fathers, mothers, sisters, and brothers, a world made warm and complete. And at the heart of it all, her heart, was Eric.

After they'd all exhausted themselves by dancing and deep belly laughing, Eric drove them back to her house. His condo had sold in a few short days with the hot housing market, but Blaine's house had plenty of space for his new office, where he was slowly building his architectural business. Charles Dumar welcomed a new playmate (after all, Eric needed his *own* guinea pig. Blaine insisted after Eric started stealing all her cuddle time with Charles). They affectionately called him Ducky Dale, and Eric built an enclosed run for them that traveled up walls and over doorways. A house that had been so lonely for so long slowly became the warm and happy home that Blaine had always wanted.

While they each had their own dreams to chase, they shared all the space between. Their mornings. Their nights. Their takeout burritos and Sunday morning 80s movie marathons with, of course, cereal on the couch. Their weekend getaways into the mountains and late-night discussions over which hair band was indeed the Best Hair Band of the 1980s. Blaine maintained that Def Leppard was the only one worth mentioning, while Eric resolutely stuck by Bon Jovi. Early that next summer, a year after their first fated meeting at the Marshall Mall, he came by on his lunch break to her shop and flashed tickets in front of her nose as she dusted the *Star Wars* window display, complete with a miniature Han Solo frozen in carbonite.

"What's that?" she said, but he pulled the tickets away before she could read the band name.

"A concert at Red Rocks. This Friday." He wrapped his arms around her waist for a hug and she dropped her duster.

"That's dancing night," Blaine said, and tried to get free while people passed by and smiled at their affectionate play. She escaped and grabbed her duster, pointing it at him like a sword. Eric held his hands up in surrender, with the sexy smile she loved.

"Yeah, but it's a concert. We can dance at the concert."

"What about your parents? What about Loraine? You know since she found out she was pregnant, she's worried we won't include her anymore."

"They're coming too." He was being oddly tense.

"Who's got the money to buy six tickets to a concert at Red Rocks, Moneybags? I mean, the shop is doing well, but I refuse to sell your *Pac-Man* game to finance that kind of thing."

"I have it handled, and we won't have to sell the game. Please, just say you'll go."

Blaine looked at him sideways and crossed her arms. "Who's playing?"

"It's a surprise. Please, just say yes?"

"Uh, okay?" Blaine took a breath to argue, but he kissed her and stole any other thought away. She dropped the duster for good, held on to his shirt, and tried to convince him to come to the back room with her, but he pulled away with a chuckle.

"I'm already late. You're going to get me fired."

"Your mother wouldn't fire you." Blaine laughed.

"Friday?"

"Yes, Friday. But there'd better be dancing at this thing."

"You can bet your mixed tapes on it." He winked and left the shop. Blaine watched him go with a smile she couldn't suppress. What was that man up to now?

The drive didn't take as long as Blaine expected, or perhaps it seemed shorter with Eric and her discussing the finer points of trying to incorporate more neon into his next project. His laugh made her heart feel full. She loved how he listened to her ideas and plans and everyday joys at work, where most of her patrons had found her and the business was doing better than ever before, with more memorabilia coming in and out of the store weekly.

They walked up the long hill after parking farther down and met with his parents, Loraine, and Lawrence inside the venue. They were only a few rows up and Blaine wondered how he'd gotten tickets so close. She still wasn't sure who was playing, but he'd approved of her outfit that night as they'd changed to get ready. Torn acid-washed jeans, a black t-shirt, ripped along the neckline to make neat rows of fabric, sneakers, some of the biggest hair she'd been able to rock in a long time, and her blue eye shadow above thick lashes. She hoped they weren't there to see John Mayer.

He'd held his hands over her eyes as they passed the merchandise booths, and his mother had distracted her enough with talks about the concerts she'd attended in her youth that she hadn't been able to sense the band from t-shirts or other conversations.

"Can you at least tell me the opener?" she said as the crowd started to shuffle in.

Eric shook his head. "No opener. Just a couple of old guys touring together."

"What? That's lame. You're a terrible liar."

"I kept a pretty good secret from you for a couple of months."

"Well, we weren't talking then, so you had it easy."

"I didn't have it easy at all." His eyes turned sad.

"Me neither."

"Let's not do that again, huh?"

"Deal." She nodded before kissing him. When she ran her hands up his thigh, her fingers traced over a hard lump in his pocket. At first, she blushed and lifted an eyebrow, deepening the kiss. Before she could look down, the band took the stage and broke into a loud and raucous chorus of "Any Way You Want It". Blaine jumped up and down, but her breath was stuck in her throat from surprise, so it took her a minute to join in the collective scream that rolled through the crowd. After she'd regained air in her lungs, she hugged Eric tightly around the waist and reached up on tiptoes to kiss him.

They danced and sang along with the crowd and enjoyed the music of Journey alongside his parents and Loraine. Though Lawrence looked unimpressed, probably wishing it was Mötley Crüe, he still swayed with his protective hands around Loraine's growing belly and kissed her neck. "Faithfully" began to play, and Blaine smiled at the soon-to-be parents. She wondered if that was the path she and Eric would go. It didn't scare her, and she couldn't imagine another person she'd rather share the adventure with. When she looked at Eric, he was holding something carefully in both hands. His eyes lowered as he took deep breaths.

"You okay?" she yelled over the crowd.

"I hope so." His eyes swam with emotion, looking deep into

hers. When she looked down to his hands, he opened them. The small round box that had been in his front pocket was now open, and a ring sat expectantly, nestled in the black velvet. The band itself was inlaid with pink sapphires, and the round-cut diamond sparkled beneath the flashing lights of the show.

"Blaine?" It was the only word he got out before she squealed, hands to mouth, and froze before him.

"What is that?"

"It's a—well, it's a ring, Blaine."

"For what?"

"For as long as you want me?" he said, one eyebrow raised.

"Eric," Blaine felt tears sting her eyes, and the crowd and noise and lights seemed to melt into the background of her heartbeats and the soft look of love in his eyes.

"Is that a 'yes', or a 'I'll think about it' or . . ."

She nodded, then pulled him in for a kiss. Eric wrapped his arms around her and held her tight.

"You sure—"

"Of course I am, you ridiculous man. Even though I know you're only doing it to get to my arcade games."

"Well, I mean, that is a pretty sweet part of the deal." He pulled back to smile at her.

"If you bring me breakfast in bed, I'll let you play my video games."

"Sounds like the perfect partnership."

They kissed beneath the lights and to the screams of the crowd. Carmen and John laughed and clapped and joined their son and new daughter in a hug as the melodic voice of Journey's new lead singer sent perfect notes up into the stars above the mountain stadium.

Sometimes new things could make the old better, Blaine thought as Eric slipped the sparkling bright band on her finger. You didn't have to lose the past to look forward to the future.

Rate and Review

We hope you enjoyed *Back to the 80s by* S. E. Reichert and Kerrie Flanagan. Please take a moment to rate and review this title, as ever review helps our authors.

Rate and Review: Back to the 80s

Meet The Authors

Sarah Reichert (S.E. Reichert) grew up in Wyoming, where everything was at least one decade behind. So the 80s were the era she remembers most fondly. She is a writer, novelist, poet and blogger. She is the author of the Southtown Harbor Series and is a member of the Writing Heights Writers Association, WyoPoets, and Wyoming Writers. Her other works have been featured in various poetry and short story journals. Her novella, "Saturn Rising" was recently produced as a five-part audiocast from Ngano Press Studios. She has three novels coming out in 2023 with 5 Prince Publishing, set in her home state. Reichert lives in Fort Collins with her family. In her non-writing hours, she is a mother to two teenage girls, a wrangler of cats, a hiker of mountains, and a snuggler of dogs.

Kerrie Flanagan is a child of the 80s who obsessed over Journey, spent way too much time curling her hair each day, loved hanging out at the mall and remembers the launch of MTV. Now as an adult, she realizes the 80s were the best decade. When not reminiscing about Hair Bands and John Hughes movies, she is a freelance writer with hundreds of published articles and essays and is an award-winning author of 20+ books, including the book, 100 Haiku for the 80s Generation and 3 sci-fi and fantasy series with a coauthor under the pen name, C.G. Harris. She has been a professional writer for over two decades, a writing instructor, and a writing consultant.

Other Titles from

5 PRINCE PUBLISHING

www.5princebooks.com

Composing Laney *S.E. Reichert*
Vampires of Atlantis *Courtney Davis*
Liz's Roadtrip *Bernadette Marie*
Back to the 80s *S.E. Reichert & Kerrie Flanagan*
Granting Katelyn *S.E. Reichert*
Ghosts of Alda *Russell Archey*
The Serpent and the Firefly *Courtney Davis*
Raising Elle *S.E.Reichert*
Rom Com Movie Club No.3 *Bernadette Marie*
Rom Com Movie Club No.2 *Bernadette Marie*
Rom Com Movie Club No.1 *Bernadette Marie*
A Crossbow Christmas *Ann Swann*
Hot For Teacher *Felicia Carparelli*